TENNESSEE NIGHT

By Stephen Leather

Children are killing themselves across the State of Tennessee. Is it a horrible coincidence, or are dark forces at work? When Jack Nightingale learns that there is a mysterious list of children who are at risk, he takes the case, spurred on by the fact that he knows one of the names and that makes it personal.

His investigation brings him up against a demon from Hell who is being used on a mission of revenge. But if he is to save the children, and his own soul, he'll need help from an old adversary.

Jack Nightingale appears in the full-length novels *Nightfall, Midnight, Nightmare, Nightshade, Lastnight, San Francisco Night* and *New York Night*. He has his own website at www.jacknightingale.com

CONTENTS

CHAPTER 1 7

CHAPTER 2 9

CHAPTER 3 13

CHAPTER 4 17

CHAPTER 5 19

CHAPTER 6 21

CHAPTER 7 33

CHAPTER 8 35

CHAPTER 9 45

CHAPTER 10 47

CHAPTER 11 51

CHAPTER 12 58

CHAPTER 13 61

CHAPTER 14 67

CHAPTER 15 69

CHAPTER 16 73

CHAPTER 17 75

CHAPTER 18 81

CHAPTER 19 83

CHAPTER 20 85

CHAPTER 21 93

CHAPTER 22	95
CHAPTER 23	99
CHAPTER 24	101
CHAPTER 25	105
CHAPTER 26	109
CHAPTER 27	111
CHAPTER 28	113
CHAPTER 29	117
CHAPTER 30	123
CHAPTER 31	135
CHAPTER 32	139
CHAPTER 33	151
CHAPTER 34	155
CHAPTER 35	157
CHAPTER 36	165
CHAPTER 37	167
CHAPTER 38	169
CHAPTER 39	173
CHAPTER 40	177
CHAPTER 41	179
CHAPTER 42	189
CHAPTER 43	191
CHAPTER 44	193
CHAPTER 45	195
CHAPTER 46	201
CHAPTER 47	203
CHAPTER 48	205
CHAPTER 49	209
CHAPTER 50	217
CHAPTER 51	225

CHAPTER 52	227
CHAPTER 53	231
CHAPTER 54	233
CHAPTER 55	237
CHAPTER 56	243
CHAPTER 57	245
CHAPTER 58	249
CHAPTER 59	251
CHAPTER 60	253
CHAPTER 61	257
CHAPTER 62	265
CHAPTER 63	271
CHAPTER 64	275
CHAPTER 65	277
CHAPTER 66	281
CHAPTER 67	283
CHAPTER 68	287
CHAPTER 69	291
CHAPTER 70	295
CHAPTER 71	297
CHAPTER 72	299
CHAPTER 73	305
CHAPTER 74	313
CHAPTER 75	315

CHAPTER 1

Dudák stood in the middle of the small cavern, eyes fixed on the far wall, though there was no light by which to see anything. Dudák was naked now, since the clothes that had once been a trademark had rotted away with the passing of the centuries. Time had meaning for clothes, but none for Dudák. Nor did hunger, thirst, heat or cold, stiffness of muscle or sinew, tiredness or boredom.

Dudák merely stood and waited.

If necessary, the wait could continue until the mountain itself split open, crashed into the valley below and Dudák could walk from the remains and into the light again to resume the quest. Those millennia would have as little meaning as a nano-second in the great scheme of the universe. It had been ordained that Dudák was to be entombed here for a time, and at another time released. The time between was of no consequence.

But the wait was not to be millennia.

A mere 734 years, in the time that passed in the world outside. Nothing at all for those like Dudák.

The first sign of the coming liberation was a tiny shaft of light that came from the direction of the long-blocked mouth of the cavern, and shone past Dudák, casting a faint shadow of a head onto the wall at which centuries had been passed in motionless staring. The shaft of light grew wider and stronger, the shadow now becoming more clearly defined, and encompassing the body as well as the head. As the last of the giant stones and rubble blocking the cave mouth melted into slag, the whole cavern was filled with sunlight.

Still Dudák remained motionless, staring at the far wall in silence, even as the footsteps moved towards him and stopped a foot or so behind him.

The voice which broke the silence was quiet, almost affectionate in its tone, yet completely authoritative.

'Dudák, there is work for you. The sort of work you enjoy.'

For the first time in centuries, Dudák moved, the head lowering in acknowledgment, and then the long-unheard voice answered. 'There will be...food for me?'

A gentle laugh came from behind. A laugh with no humour to it, but a cruel anticipation of what was to come.

'Oh yes, Dudák. I can promise you that you will be very well fed. Very well indeed.'

Dudák turned round to face the newcomer, looked into the long-awaited and well-remembered face and gave a mirthless smile.

'Thank you. I would certainly welcome a feast. What must I do?'

'You must do what you do best, Dudák, What else?'

Again Dudák smiled and nodded. 'It will be my pleasure to serve you. Where must I go?'

'Far away, to a new country. And also, I think, a new shell. This one has served its purpose.'

Again the smile and the nod. 'Indeed. I have needed great effort to maintain its integrity, far beyond its normal span. A fresh one would be welcome.'

'Come with me and listen to what is to happen.'

The light disappeared from the cave.

It was empty of living creatures.

Just the rows of small, bleached skeletons staring sightlessly on for eternity.

And a new, larger one.

CHAPTER 2

The new shell lay naked, slumped on the floor of the hotel bathroom, its limbs splayed at random, and its head leaning over the side of the toilet bowl. There were some traces of vomit in the bowl, but none on the clothing, the bathroom trip had been a pointless diversion, the pain in the stomach had been reflected from the heart and could not be vomited up.

The previous owner of the shell had left it behind less than a minute ago, when the combination of acute respiratory distress syndrome in the lungs and intravascular coagulation in the blood vessels of the heart had shut down breathing and heartbeat. The death was due to bad luck, as much as anything else. The ecstasy pill had been unusually pure, with a high concentration of MDMA, and, combined with too much alcohol, and a low tolerance level, the effects had been rapid. Of course, the previous owner had been aware of the need to drink plenty of water to counteract the effects of dehydration from the hot night-club and energetic dancing, but again inexperience had told, and too much fluid had been taken which worsened the lung problem. The friends who had noticed the lurching and falling over on the dance floor should have called an ambulance at once, but they were none too capable themselves, so it was decided that the victim should just be taken back to the hotel room and left on the bed to sleep it off. Nobody was left to check. The mistakes proved fatal, though the friends would never know that.

The air in the adjoining bedroom shimmered, then time and space seemed to fold in on themselves, and two figures stood there. One would have seemed reasonably normal, or at least recognisable to any human observer, but the second would have sent them screaming in fear. It bore no relation to any animal on Earth, but might have sprung from the fertile imagination of the special effects designer on a fifties science fiction film. The huge gaping mouth would have caught the attention first, opening and closing as if by reflex action. The limbs were covered in scales of a colour that seemed to flicker through blue, green and yellow. The actual number and type of the limbs also seemed to vary, never settling long enough to be counted, as if the creature were in a constant state of flux, never able to form itself fully in this environment. The head grew and shrank in size almost with every breath, and there was nothing on it which resembled human eyes ears or nose, just a mass of writhing skin and scales. But always the mouth stayed a constant size, opening and closing to reveal the saliva-coated fangs.

The soft voice spoke, still with its commanding tone. 'I think this will do nicely,' it said. 'Very recently vacated, no prospect of return, but no time for deterioration to have set in. Strong, and with many years left to it.'

Dudák could not form spoken words in its natural state, but its thoughts made themselves heard just the same. 'Was this a follower of yours, one who gave its shell willingly for a greater purpose?'

'No, not one of mine, though the possibility had occurred to me. Too unpredictable, I fear, but I'd been watching, so I was ready when it happened. It was inevitable, these foolish creatures think they're immortal at times. They are so fragile, yet they take so little care. You should lose no time.'

This time, Dudák expressed no thoughts, but a loud splashing sound came from its mouth, as it drew itself up to its full height, which was little more than five feet. More splashing was heard, steadily settling into a pattern, as the creature started to melt from the bottom upwards, with its ever-fluctuating and shimmering body slowly turning into a pool of silver liquid, which lay motionless on the floor for a minute or so.

One end of the pool slowly grew narrower, becoming a stream an inch wide. It flowed across the bedroom floor towards the shell on the floor of the bathroom. It flowed over the dead body, until it covered it all, from feet to hair, then the silver glowed brightly, and was gone.

The new shell began to throb gently, as Dudák took control of it, forcing blood at pressure through the heart valves to clear the blockages, bringing its temperature down to normal, and repairing the inflammation in the cells of the lungs. The shell took a ragged breath, gave a gasp, and then the breathing settled into a regular pattern, at first loud and rasping, then quickly becoming normal and inaudible at any distance.

Dudák stood up, stretched the limbs, then turned to look in the full-length mirror on the wall. A nod of the head indicated approval. 'It will suffice, in fact it is quite satisfactory. Some differences to which I will need to become accustomed, but it should present no problem.'

There was a peal of unpleasant laughter in response. 'Oh yes, it's certainly very different, but it's exactly what's needed. Now, rest it for a while, Dudák. Tomorrow you have a journey to make, a long journey. And then you will have work to do, for me.'

Dudák smiled at the reflection. 'And I may feed soon? I wish to feed. I need to feed.'

'Oh yes,' came the reply. 'Certainly you may feed. That will be the most important part of your task.'

The air shimmered again, and Dudák was alone. Dudák needed no rest, but the new shell would need time to recuperate fully after its experiences. Dudák made it walk to the bed, and had it lay down to rest for the night. It would also be a chance to absorb the memories, experiences and personality traits that its previous owner had left behind so suddenly.

CHAPTER 3

Olivia was a good girl, her parents knew they could trust her, but that was what sealed her fate. Six to seven each evening was homework time and she spent the full hour at it, five nights a week. If the teachers hadn't set enough to keep her busy for a full hour, she was supposed to fill in the rest of the time reading, but that was no chore. She loved to read, and she took her Kindle with her pretty much everywhere. Her mother had introduced her to Nancy Drew a month or so back, and Olivia had spent a good part of her allowance on the girl detective's adventures ever since. She found the world of the sixties fascinating, no mobile phones, no home computers, no internet and so many people walking everywhere.

At seven o'clock Olivia glanced at her bedside radio alarm and shut the Kindle down. She was allowed a half-hour with the computer. In the early days, Mom and Dad had popped in to check regularly on what she was doing with her new toy, but these days they knew the parental controls would stop her accessing anything unpleasant. Not that she'd be likely to go looking for such things. Olivia was a good girl, as her Mom told the coroner afterward.

Tonight Olivia didn't bother with her full half-hour, just sat smiling at the keyboard for around twenty minutes, until she finally logged off and pressed SHUT DOWN on the laptop. She knew Mom and Dad wouldn't be up to say goodnight for another twenty-five minutes, by which time they'd expect to find her washed, in her pyjamas and sitting up in bed waiting for her story. Maybe ten was a little old for a bedtime story, but it had always been a special time for the three of them, and Mom and Dad took it in turns to read, this time from a proper book. They'd just started the second Harry Potter story, and Olivia was loving the series.

The computer had finished shutting down and Olivia closed the lid, straightened up her desk, gave a little sigh, and walked over to her toy cupboard. Her mouth was set, her soft brown eyes a little sad as she moved a few things aside to find what she was looking for. Her skipping rope. Not the one with the handles that she used by herself, but the longer one that she often took to school to play with her friends. They would chant one of the old rhymes with two girls turning it round while another four or five jumped in time in the middle. She found it, and untangled it on the bed.

The noose was easy enough to tie. She'd been a Junior Girl Scout for nearly two years and already had her Wilderness badge. It was wide enough to slip over her head easily, and strong enough not to come undone with the weight of her slim young body. She tested it once more, then picked the rope up, opened her bedroom door and walked out onto the landing.

She hummed a little tune to herself as she fastened the free end of the rope over the balustrade with a good strong reef knot. Right over left, left over right, just the way her troop leader had taught her. She didn't want to risk a granny knot, which might slip and ruin everything. She pulled on the rope as hard as she could, but it didn't give an inch.

Sukie wandered up the stairs, her dark grey fur matching the carpet to perfection, mewed playfully and rolled over on her back showing her white stomach and expecting her usual rub. Olivia didn't even spare a glance for her much-loved pet, and the cat mewed again in puzzlement. Olivia lifted herself onto the rail, balanced there a moment with her arms and head on one side and her legs on the other, then shifted her weight forward and plunged down headfirst.

The skipping rope was just the right length and the drop and sudden stop snapped the fourth cervical vertebra, even as the noose tightened and crushed her trachea. Olivia felt nothing beyond one agonising crack, and then her body hung from the bannister, eight feet from the floor, swinging slowly and spinning until her weight reached equilibrium.

It was five minutes later that her mother opened the sitting room door, the Harry Potter book in her hand, walked across the hall, stopped open-mouthed at what she saw, and started screaming.

Dudák stood in the street and looked up at the lights shining in the window of the first floor of the house, heard the woman's voice screaming even at this distance, and slowly returned the rhythm of respiration to normal. The red flush on the neck faded away, and the eyes rolled back down so that the shining green pupils were visible again. Dudák smiled and slowly walked away from the Taylor house and was half a mile away before the first police car arrived.

CHAPTER 4

Jack Nightingale was well used to being summoned across America by Joshua Wainwright at a minute's notice, but he rarely enjoyed the experience. The young Texan billionaire generally left the travel arrangements to his assistant Valerie, whose concern for Nightingale's comfort usually extended to finding him a seat in economy between the two fattest people on the plane. He headed for the Delta check-in desk at JFK with a resigned look on his face, which changed to a smile as he saw the attractive blonde in a mini-skirt waiting for him.

'Amanda? This is a pleasant surprise,' he said.

'Jack, change of plan,' she said, the South African accent a little less noticeable now after more time in the US. 'Mr Wainwright has sent the Gulfstream for you. This way.'

This made no sense at all to Nightingale. The Delta flight to Miami would only have taken three hours, and he doubted that Wainwright's private jet would shave much off that time. What could be so important? He said nothing, assuming the man himself would give him his answers in a few minutes.

Amanda led him to an unmarked door, punched a number into the door lock and it swung open, closing behind them. They were outside now, in a restricted area, and there was a black Mercedes limousine waiting for them, the engine running. Nightingale threw his bag on the back seat, followed it in and hardly had time to close his door before the car was moving.

Four minutes later, the car stopped in front of Wainwright's gleaming white Gulfstream jet. Amanda stepped out and waved him up the front steps, following close behind him. The next surprise came as he turned right at the top of the steps. There was no sign of the affable billionaire, the white leather seats were all empty. He turned to Amanda and raised an eyebrow.

'Mr Wainwright isn't with us this afternoon,' she said. 'Please take a seat, we'll be leaving directly.'

Nightingale took off his raincoat. Amanda took it from him as he chose one of the huge seats next to a window, sat down and buckled up. Amanda pressed some buttons to fold up the steps and close the forward door, then walked to the back of the plane with his coat. Nightingale heard a click as she strapped herself into her crew seat. The plane pushed back almost immediately, then started to taxi out to the runway. Inside two minutes, it was racing down the runway, and Nightingale felt the familiar lift in his stomach as the wheels left the ground.

As the plane reached its cruising altitude, Amanda went over to his seat. 'Feel free to move around and you may smoke if you wish,' she said. 'Flight time today is around three hours fifty minutes. Can I get you anything to drink, Jack?'

Nightingale had no idea what might be waiting for him, so he settled on a cup of coffee. 'Amanda, wouldn't it have been faster for me to go by scheduled flight? It's only three hours to Miami by Delta. Why the big fuss?'

'We're not headed to Miami,' she said. 'Our destination is Brownsville.'

Nightingale pulled out his pack of Marlboro and lit one. This made no sense, Wainwright's SMS message had definitely said Miami. And it probably wasn't a coincidence that it was the place where Joshua Wainwright had been born and raised. He knew Amanda would have no answers for him, so he had no option but to wait and see. He closed his eyes and tried to drift off to sleep. If past experience of working for Wainwright was anything to go by, sleep might be in short supply in the days ahead.

CHAPTER 5

Sergeant Bonnie Parker was not far shy of forty, though she'd managed to keep her coffee-coloured skin pretty unlined, and her shoulder length brown hair free of any trace of grey, though only she and her hairdresser knew how natural that was. She hit the gym whenever her schedule allowed and had managed to stay in pretty good shape, so far. Her husband had always told her that he'd first been attracted to her by her smile, but there was no trace of it today. She was wishing that someone else had caught this case, as it was looking like a real stinker. She'd been ten years on Homicide and never come across anything like this. Even assuming there had been a crime committed, the scene had been hopelessly compromised. Not that she could find it in herself to blame anyone. Parker had two school-age kids herself, and if she'd found either of them hanging from a bannister she'd have raced to cut them down too, probably tried CPR as well, even though it had been useless, and she would surely have called the paramedics before the police.

The chances were she wasn't really going to be needed on this case. She didn't smell homicide here. The only other people in the house when the kid had died had been the parents, and they both seemed completely distraught. The mother was sitting in an armchair, her head in her hands and her body racked by sobs. The father had needed to be pried away from his daughter's body so the ME could complete the formalities of pronouncing her dead. He was standing over by the window now, gazing in every direction except towards the body.

The two uniformed cops who'd answered the 911 call were still hanging around, having taken brief statements from the parents and passed on the facts of the case to Parker. The kid had been ten, upstairs doing her homework and enjoying a little computer time. A good kid, trusted and trustworthy according to the parents. No, she hadn't seemed any different lately, no trouble at school, no indication she might be being bullied, she was her normal happy self.

Ten years on Homicide and Parker thought she'd seen it all, parents killing their kids, wives their husbands, brothers their sisters. And vice-versa. She'd seen death in every brutal form imaginable, and some she'd never cared to imagine. She'd seen all kinds of suicides, from teenagers right up to men and women in their nineties. But in all that time, she'd never known a ten-year-old girl to hang herself.

The ME, a tall black woman in a dark pant-suit walked over to her. 'I'm done for the moment, Bonnie' she said. 'Death by hanging, cervical vertebrae broken, also her windpipe crushed, but the fractures killed her, though that's not official until I write up the autopsy.'

Parker nodded. 'Any other marks on the body?' she asked.

'Not that I could see, I wasn't about to strip her naked in front of the parents. No bruising to arms or legs. I think she may have a broken rib, but chances are that was post-mortem. The paramedics say the father was trying CPR pretty aggressively.'

'Wasting his time?'

'Of course, but what would you expect? Situation like that you'd try anything.'

'Anything to suggest it isn't what it looks like?'

'Come on, Bonnie, you know better than that. I give the medical verdict, I'm no detective. We'll be looking for rope fibres under her nails, on her clothes. My guess is it's exactly what it looks like.'

'Not much to see here, I guess. Will you take her now?'

'If that's okay. This is the part where you take proper statements from the parents?'

'Yeah. Has to be done. Never gets any easier.'

'Sooner you than me,' said the coroner. 'You might want to take them into the sitting room, while we move the body.'

'I can try.'

CHAPTER 6

The Gulfstream landed at Brownsville around ten minutes ahead of Amanda's prediction, and the plane had barely stopped taxiing before Amanda had the door open and the steps lowered. 'Your car's waiting, Jack,' she said, and Nightingale unbuckled his belt, picked up his bag and raincoat and headed for the exit.

This time the limousine was a long white Mercedes but the tall black driver in the dark grey chauffeur's uniform seemed like the twin of the one in New York. He asked Nightingale if he wanted to put his bag in the trunk, but it was small enough to travel with him. Besides, there were one or two things inside that Nightingale preferred to keep close. The car swung out of the private terminal headed for downtown Brownsville. It wasn't Nightingale's first trip to the city of Wainwright's birth and he knew it was the county seat of Cameron County, named after a Major Jacob Jennings Brown who had died during a Mexican attack on what had then been Fort Texas.

The limousine drove onto a gated estate where every house occupied a lot the size of a football field, then pulled up in front of Wainwright's mansion. The chauffeur opened the rear door and as Nightingale stepped out the front door of the house opened. Valerie was as tall and elegant as ever, dressed in a white skirt suit which was a striking contrast to her ebony skin. She favoured him with a tight smile, though her brow kept its frown. Nightingale was puzzled. What could be worrying her? Normally she made the Sphinx look demonstrative. 'Good evening, Jack. Welcome to Brownsville. Mr Wainwright is waiting for you.'

Nightingale nodded a greeting, but she'd already turned away and was walking down the wood panelled entrance hall with its curved staircase, towards an oak door, which stood open. She walked through without knocking and Nightingale followed. The room was large, though not ostentatiously so, and dominated by leather sofas and chairs in Wainwright's preferred colour choice of cream. The man himself was sitting in the middle of one of the sofas, and looked up as Nightingale entered. Unusually there was no broad grin.

'Glad you're here, Jack. Take a seat.'

Nightingale looked at him closely. He was a little less casually dressed than normal, with a light grey sport jacket, white shirt and a plain red tie, though the knot hung around his second button, and the shirt collar was open, revealing a thick gold neck chain. He wasn't wearing his trademark baseball cap and he clearly hadn't shaved that day. He was smoking one of his usual foot long Cuban cigars, but seemed to be puffing on it more frequently than normal, and the muscle at the left corner of his mouth twitched occasionally. Nightingale sat in the chair opposite and lit a cigarette. 'I thought I was going to Miami,' he said.

Wainwright shook his head. 'Something else has come up now, and you're the man I need for it. You want a drink?' He pressed a remote control which was lying on the coffee table in front of him, and a stunning tall blonde woman came in through the far door almost immediately.

'Large Glenfiddich for me, please, Maria. Jack?'

'Will I be driving?'

'Not till tomorrow, I guess.'

'A Corona would be great, then. Thanks.'

'In the bottle?' asked Wainwright. 'With a slice of lime.'

Nightingale grinned. 'You know me so well.'

Maria was back inside a minute with the drinks, and the two men nodded their thanks. She took away Wainwright's empty glass, and Nightingale wondered how many the young man had got through today. Probably made no difference, Nightingale had never known him to show any effects from his intake of single malt. Wainwright waited until Maria shut the door behind her, then reached into the red cardboard file that lay on the coffee table in front of him, pulled out a single sheet of stiff-looking yellowish paper, put it down on the table again and pointed at it. 'Take a look,' he said.

Nightingale put his bottle down and reached the paper, but stopped suddenly when his fingers were still an inch or two away. A puzzled look came over his face.

'You feel it?' asked Wainwright. 'You're getting much more sensitive about these things.'

'I feel something,' said Nightingale, closing his eyes in concentration. 'Not quite sure...cold, hate, evil. What is this thing, Joshua?'

'Take a look. Far as I know, it's not dangerous, but I got the same vibrations from it you did. It has power, and it's not designed for good.'

Nightingale shuddered, and opened his eyes, trying to banish the uneasy feelings. He pulled his hand back, but leaned further forward in his chair to take a good look. It wasn't paper after all, but thicker and stiffer, the edges less regular. Parchment maybe, or vellum. Or some kind of skin, hopefully animal. There was writing on it, the words picked out in a deep red. The colour of dried blood, thought Nightingale, with another shudder.

Wainwright sat still on the sofa as he smoked his cigar, his eyes fixed on Nightingale. Finally Nightingale stretched out his hand and pulled the sheet towards him, turning it around so he could read it. The vibrations had gone now, and he read the words in front of him. It was a list of names. Names that meant nothing to him at all. The first three had wavy black lines drawn through them, but the names could still be read easily enough. Nightingale read them aloud, keeping count on his fingers as he did so.

'Susan Johnson, Martin Brown, Madison Moore, Olivia Taylor, Timmy Williams, David Robinson, Charmaine Wendover, Julia Smith, Kaitlyn Jones, Emma Miller, Carmen Garcia, Naomi Fisher. Twelve names, the first three crossed off.'

Wainwright nodded.

'So who are they, and what does it mean?' asked Nightingale.

'As for what it means, damned if I know, I just know it can't be good. I found that list on my nightstand three days ago. Not here, another place I own.'

'In Brownsville?'

'No,' said Wainwright, and left it at that.

'So who was in the house with you?' asked Nightingale.

'Maria, Carl, who's one of my drivers, Valerie and Mary Chan the cook. All of them have been with me years, none of them know anything about it or how it came to be there.'

'So they say.'

'Yeah, so they say, and I'm inclined to believe them. None of them know anything about the...other side of my life.'

Which meant none of them knew Wainwright was a well-experienced adept of the left-hand path, a practitioner of the Occult, a powerful Satanist. 'So how could it have got there?' asked Nightingale.

'My guess is that whoever wrote it made it appear there. It's called apparation, when an object is moved through the Astral plane by sheer force of will.'

'Apparition? Like a ghost?'

Wainwright shook his head. 'Apparation. With an "a". From the Latin apparatus. To appear magically.'

'That's possible?'

'Yes, very much so. But out of my league at the moment.'

Nightingale took a sip of his Corona. If it was out of Wainwright's league, then this was heavy stuff. 'So what does it mean?' asked Nightingale. 'Who are these people on the list?'

'Until this morning, I'd never heard of any of them, and there seemed no point in Googling them. Most of the names don't seem that uncommon, I'd have ended up with thousands of hits, and no information on how to link them.'

'So what changed this morning?'

'Well, first you need to know that when the parchment arrived, there were just nine names on it. All of them strangers to me. Two days ago, when I looked at it again, there were ten names, but the first one had that line struck through it. There was a new one at the bottom to take its place.'

'The line and the new name just appeared?'

Wainwright nodded and put his cigar down onto a large crystal ashtray. 'And the parchment hadn't been out of my sight since it arrived.'

'So the crossed out name, do you think...'

Wainwright held up a hand to stop him. 'Same thing happened yesterday, the second name, Martin Brown, was struck through, and there was an eleventh name at the bottom, Carmen Garcia. So I did some checking. A girl called Susan Amanda Johnson died at about the time her name was crossed off. Eleven years old. And this is where it gets weird – she died in Brownsville, Tennessee.'

Nightingale frowned. 'Brownsville? Where we are now?'

'Different Brownsville. Population ten thousand or so. To the west of the State. Brownsville Tennessee and Brownsville Texas were both named after general Jacob Jennings Brown.'

'I was never great at history or geography,' said Nightingale. 'But this can't be a coincidence, can it?'

'It's as if someone is trying to send me a message, Jack.'

'How did the girl die?'

'She fell out of her bedroom window. Her parents think it was an accident. Homicide detectives had attended, but found no suspicious circumstances. The girl had been alone in her room at the time, and appeared to have climbed onto her computer desk to open the window, before falling.'

Nightingale winced at the image.

'My people checked for any deaths of Martin Browns and sure enough they found one. Another kid. Also in Tennessee. This time in Memphis. Martin was ten years old. He was in the bath and his parents had become concerned by the length of time he'd taken and his father had finally broken down the locked door in a panic. Martin had sliced vertically several times down both wrists with his father's razor, and was dead when the paramedics arrived. Again, the police had found no signs of anyone else being involved in the death. But this one was clearly no accident.'

'So you think someone is causing this to happen?'

'Has to be, Jack. And it gets worse.' Wainwright closed his eyes, opened them again and looked at the ceiling. His cigar was burning unnoticed in the ashtray in front of him. He exhaled deeply. Nightingale was surprised, he'd never known the young billionaire to be anything but direct, yet here he was seemingly taking forever to say what was on his mind. Finally Wainwright clenched his jaw, gave a curt nod and spoke. 'Same thing this morning, name number three,

Madison Moore was crossed out, and there was a new name written at the bottom. Number twelve. Naomi Fisher.'

Wainwright stopped speaking and closed his eyes again.

'And?' said Nightingale.

Wainwright sighed. 'Naomi Fisher's ten years old, Jack. And she's also my niece.'

Both men were silent, and Nightingale used the pause to light another cigarette. Wainwright remembered his cigar, picked it up, looked at the glowing end and took a deep drag.

'There's probably quite a few Naomi Fishers in America,' said Nightingale but he could hear the uncertainty in his voice.

'Probably. How many of them have an uncle who gets sent a cursed list of names with her on it? I'm betting it's not a coincidence. This is personal, Jack. I'm sure of it.'

Nightingale nodded. Coincidences did happen but more often than not things happened for a reason. 'I never knew you had a niece.'

'Why would you?' He shrugged. 'She's my sister's daughter. My younger sister Sarah lives in Tennessee.'

'Hillbilly country.'

Wainwright grinned. 'To be fair, a large chunk of the State is inhabited by gap-toothed yokels high on moonshine. But it also has Nashville, the home of country music, and Memphis, home of the late, great Elvis Presley. That's where my sister lives. Memphis. She's married to a Baptist minister.'

Nightingale's tolerance for shocks was pretty high, but this one was too much for him. His eyebrows shot skywards. 'A Minister? Your sister is married to a man of God?'

'There's no need to be so surprised, Jack. I go to a lot of trouble to make sure that no one knows who – what – I am. As far as anyone in my family knows, I got where I am through property deals and a lot of good luck.'

'So when they were married, you went to the wedding?'

'You mean did I go to the church? Sure. I'm not a demon, Jack, I'm not going to run screaming out of a church at the sight of a crucifix. I must say I was very happy not to be asked to be Naomi's godfather, that could have been difficult. But it was never going to happen. Maybe Matthew picked up some vibes from me.'

'Matthew is your brother-in-law?'

'Yeah, the Reverend Matthew Fisher. He's a good guy, his heart's in the right place.'

'Have you checked on the girl?'

'What would you think? I was on the phone as soon as I saw her name. Naomi's fine, doing great at school, star of the soccer team, happy and healthy. I hope I was casual enough that Sarah didn't pick up on anything being wrong.'

'And Madison Moore?'

'She died at about the time her name was crossed off. Also in Tennessee. Knoxville. To the east of the State. Swallowed a bottle of drain killer. Just sat down in the kitchen, unscrewed the top and drank it down.'

Nightingale shuddered.

'So three names crossed off, three kids dead, at least two of them suicide and Susan Johnson could well have killed herself. That list wasn't sent to me for bedtime reading, Jack. Someone's out to get me, and maybe because I'm kinda hard to reach they've decided to hit my family.'

'Who'd do that? You have enemies, people out to get you?'

'A few months ago, I'd have said no. I'm a good way down the left-hand path, but I've kept a pretty low profile. My business dealings are done through offshore companies, no personal grudges that I know of, and I was no threat to anyone. Until that business in San Francisco.'

'San Francisco?' asked Nightingale.

'Yeah. I kind of stuck my neck out on that one, my name got known, and there are a lot of people connected with that who might not wish me well.'

'But you seemed pretty sure none of them would be around to do much harm. You told me most of them would die in prison.'

'Yeah, well I figured without American law, and maybe the pull they had, in a lot of areas. I spread a lot of money around, pulled plenty of strings, but it seemed they had money and strings too. Their influence went a long way up, and I mean a long way. Even higher than mine. Their cases dragging on, arguments about whether the cops even had probable cause to break in, the whole thing's a mess.'

'But we caught the whole bunch of them, red-handed.'

'You may remember that you personally didn't stick around long enough to give a witness statement. Which makes it hard to bring charges. So far not one of them's come near to doing any jail time, or even been brought to court. Maybe they never will be.'

'Well I wasn't there, but that policewoman Amy Chen knew the full story.'

'Well, that's another thing. I checked, and nobody seems to have seen or heard from her for a few months. Not showed up for work, and without her to give evidence, there's hardly any case at all.'

Nightingale's eye's widened. 'So you think...'

'What do you think, Jack? I doubt she's gone to Disneyworld and forgotten to tell the SFPD. Meantime a lot of very powerful adepts are walking round on bail, pissed at me, and probably you.'

'But most of them were minor-league, except for their leader, and she's dead.'

Wainwright sighed. 'Maybe.'

'There's no maybe, Joshua. Amy Chen shot Abaddon. Shot her dead. Two bullets to the chest.'

Abaddon was a woman by the name of Margaret Romanos, the leader of a Satanic coven who had been causing mayhem in San Francisco until Wainwright had put Nightingale on the case. But she was dead, Nightingale was certain of that. Though he was equally certain that in the world he lived in, the dead didn't always stay dead.

'I'm sure you did, but here's the funny thing, her body never showed up at the morgue.'

'What?'

'That's right. As you might expect there was all kinds of confusion going on there, and it seems nobody can remember who took the body away, Maybe that was incompetence on somebody's part, but you know Abaddon had contacts all the way up in the SFPD. Anyway, no ambulance was ever traced, and nobody knows what happened to Abaddon's body.'

'Do you think she could still be alive?'

Nightingale shuddered at the thought of the woman who'd been responsible for more than a dozen obscene ritual murders in San Francisco, as part of her attempt to free the demon Bimoleth and potentially bring about the End of Days. Nightingale himself, the SFPD policewoman Amy Chen, and two young children had narrowly escaped being the final victims of her powerful coven of highly-placed Satanists.

'I have no idea,' said Wainwright, 'all I know is there's no body, and she had some pretty powerful friends, inside and outside the coven, human and ...maybe not so human. Who knows what they might have done?'

'You mean raise her from the dead?'

'You've probably read about it being done. Guy called Lazarus, chapter eleven of John's Gospel, if you're into that kind of thing. That's assuming she even was dead in the first place.'

'Come on, Joshua, you can't believe that. She looked pretty dead to me.'

Wainwright shrugged his shoulders. 'She was a very powerful adept, Jack. Once someone gets to one of the top three levels, there's almost no limit to the power they can channel.'

'Maybe, but immortality is never up for grabs, no matter what level you reach, and who you make a pact with. You and I both know that.'

'Okay, it's pretty far out there, I'll admit,' said Wainwright. 'At the moment I'm just guessing, and the only guess I have is that it's someone from the San Francisco mess making this happen. And whatever is happening, Naomi is in the firing line.'

'You want me to protect her?'

'I don't know what I want yet, Jack. I can hardly send you up there without explaining to Sarah and Matthew, and they're not going to understand. And then I don't know what it is she needs protection against. I'm working blind here.'

Nightingale blew smoke up at the ceiling. 'If they just wanted to get at you, they could have killed Naomi without any kind of a warning. The list was sent because they want you to do something about it. Maybe expose yourself, so they can get at you more easily. I'm guessing that whatever the plan is, they'll be making it clearer soon.'

'You think it's some kind of serial killer thing? You must have seen a few when you were a cop?'

'Actually none. Outside of books and movies, serial killers don't really exist. You get the odd twisted guy who kills kids, maybe prostitutes, but as for the evil genius sending cryptic clues to his next ritual murder, forget about it. Whoever's doing this is probably using the other names just to prolong your agony.'

'So far he's doing a great job.' He looked down at the parchment and his eyes widened and his jaw dropped.

Nightingale followed Wainwright's gaze and he too stared at the parchment. As they watched, a black line appeared, moving slowly from left to right until it had crossed through the name of Olivia Taylor. Neither man spoke, as red letters began slowly to appear at the foot of the list, until a thirteenth name burned there.

Sophie Underwood.

Nightingale stared in horror at the two words at the bottom of the parchment and Wainwright picked up on it straight away. 'That name means something to you,' he said.

Nightingale nodded, as the memories of the day that had changed his life forever came flooding back. Finally he found some words. 'Yes, my last ever job as a police negotiator. Little blonde girl, nine years old. She'll be a teenager now. She'd been raped and abused by her father, her mother looked the other way and the kid finally decided she couldn't take any more of it. She took her doll, went and sat on the balcony of her thirteenth floor flat. I was sent to try to talk her down.'

'I remember you telling me. And did you talk her down?'

Nightingale paused. It was a simple enough question, but it was a difficult one to answer. On the day, the little girl had indeed jumped to her death. But Nightingale had done a deal with a devil, and that deal had given Sophie a second chance at life. But there was no way he could tell Wainwright or anyone what he had done. 'No, I didn't,' he said. 'She jumped, and I managed to catch her. She lives with her mother now.'

Wainwright stared at him, and the soft brown eyes suddenly hardened, as if they were trying to look inside Nightingale and burn the truth out from him. 'You know, Jack, if I were a betting man, I'd put money on there being a whole lot more to that story. It's kind of tied up with there being a whole lot more to you than I managed to figure out yet. Like how you seem to know stuff you've never been through, how sometimes you have a direct line to powers I can't begin to understand, yet you still seem to know almost nothing about the left-hand path.'

'Allegedly,' said Nightingale. He wasn't ready to let Wainwright in on his full history, and doubted he ever would be, not that he was even sure himself how much of it had ever really happened. Sophie Underwood and her evil bastard father were real enough, though.

Wainwright was talking again. 'So this Underwood kid means a lot to you?'

Nightingale gave that one some thought, and lit another cigarette before answering. 'I don't know how to explain it.. My life changed that day, and it never would have if I'd been called to another situation. I'd probably still be a cop in London now. But after Sophie, I knew I could never go back to the Job. For a while she was the first thing I used to think of every morning, and the last thing every night. So yes, I guess she does mean something.'

'Whoever sent that parchment must think so. And must know something about your past. Any ideas who that could be?'

Nightingale had one idea, possibly two, but he wasn't ready to share either of them with Wainwright until he knew a lot more about this situation.

'Not at the moment,' he said. 'But the Underwood case is a matter of public record, as was my part in it. Wouldn't be hard to find out.'

'Not for anyone who knew you were still alive, which is meant to be nobody in Britain.'

Nightingale nodded. He'd thought he'd covered his tracks pretty well, but not, it seemed, from anyone who really wanted to find him.

'So where's Sophie Underwood now?' asked Wainwright.

'Like I said, with her mum. But I'm not sure exactly where. I'd guess she's still in the UK.'

'And Naomi's in Memphis. Makes it hard to know where to start.'

'I can't go back to London anyway. There are people who want me dead, and people who'd charge me with murder,' he sighed. 'What do you want me to do, Joshua?'

Wainwright had no immediate answer to that, but sat smoking quietly. He picked up the parchment again, and stared at it. 'We need a lead on the rest of those names, Jack, try to see what they have in common. See what the threat is, and I'm damned sure there is a threat. Whoever sent this parchment is powerful, and they didn't do it for kicks.'

'I'm sure you're...'

Wainwright's mobile phone beeped to let him know he had received a message. He picked up his phone and frowned at the screen and his face went ashen.

'What's wrong?' asked Nightingale.

'Message from a police contact,' he said. Memphis PD and paramedics called to apparent suicide by hanging in the Hickory Ridge district. Victim deceased, African-American female, named as Olivia Taylor, aged ten.

Nightingale stubbed out his cigarette. 'Looks like I'm headed to Memphis.'

'Jack, I want you to make sure no harm comes to my niece. I guess you want to keep this kid Sophie safe, preferably without a trip to London. So if this is centered around Memphis, it means stopping it there.'

'And the other people on that list?'

Wainwright gave a grim smile. 'Well, I never heard of any of them, and people die all the time.'

Nightingale took a long drag on his cigarette before replying. 'We're missing the point though, aren't we? This isn't about Naomi and Sophie. They're just a means to an end.'

'What end?'

'Whoever sent that list wants you to know they're after Naomi, and they've put Sophie on the list as another sign. They want to hurt you, and they know you'll send me in to try to stop whatever this is.'

'True enough, so what?'

'So it's not about the people on that list, it's about me. They want me to go after them, they want me out in the open.'

'Why?'

'I'm guessing I'm not due a medal. They know I'm coming, they know where I'll be, and my guess is they want me dead. Or worse.'

'So let's get started,' said Wainwright. He took a quick glance at the gold Patek Philippe watch on his left wrist. 'It's 8pm, you'll be needing some sleep, but we can get you there by morning. Valerie will organise everything, go talk to her, second door on the left. Tell her I said top priority. Meanwhile I'm out of here, there are things I need to do that I can do better elsewhere. Stay in touch, Jack. Don't let me down on this one.'

It was obviously a dismissal, so Nightingale nodded at him, got up and headed along the corridor to find Valerie.

CHAPTER 7

Bonnie Parker was getting nowhere with the Taylors, and she was pretty sure by now that there was nowhere to get. The mother, Janice, was holding up better than her husband, who hadn't managed to get his head out of his hands often enough to contribute more than monosyllabic answers to the detective's questions.

'Everything just seemed completely normal,' said the woman, going over the same ground yet again. 'Olivia went up to do her homework, she probably spent her half-hour on the computer and then when we went up to read to her we found her...just...just...'

'Makes no sense,' said Mr Taylor. 'No sense at all.'

Parker looked at them in turn. Rich and privileged, but good parents by all appearances. She was in corporate finance, but had said she was always home to walk Olivia to and from the school bus stop. Her husband worked in administration at the Gibson factory, and he made a point to be home by six to do his share of the parenting.

Parker tried again. 'And you're both sure she had no problems at school?'

'Nothing we'd ever heard of,' said Mrs Taylor. 'Her grades were fine, she seemed to have plenty of friends, she never mentioned any problems with other kids. She was happy, always happy. Her teachers were always pleased with her.'

'I just can't believe it,' said her husband.

'And she never mentioned any arguments, unpleasantness on the internet?' asked Parker.

'Never. She was too young for the social media sites, and they were blocked on her computer anyway. She could email her friends, chat to them and she played a couple of games, but never for very long. She preferred sports, playing with the cat, practising piano.'

'What games did she play?' asked Parker.

The parents looked at each other, and this time it was Mr Taylor who answered. 'Minecraft, I think. And there was one about horses. Oh, and Farmville.'

'Did she spend money on them?'

The woman shook her head. 'No, she couldn't have. We're not the kind of people who leave our credit card numbers around and then never check the bills. Olivia wasn't that interested anyway.'

Parker thought again. Her own kids played Minecraft and Farmville, and they were both harmless. No chance of cyber-bullying making anyone's life a misery and driving them to desperation. It was sites like Facebook and Twitter where bullies thrived and most sensible parents kept their children well away from them. 'I'm sorry I've had to ask these questions at such a difficult time, but we have to look into any sudden death. We'll probably send an officer to ask a few questions at the school, and it's up to the coroner to make the decision, but from what I've seen it's not a homicide matter, it seems Olivia took her own life. All I can say is I'm sorry for your loss.'

'Sorry?' snapped the father. 'What good is that? My daughter's dead, and I want to know why.'

His wife put her hand on his arm, pressed gently, and he was quiet. 'Thank you, Ms Parker,' she said. 'We appreciate what you've done. As I'm sure you'd expect, we're looking for answers now. I'm sure you'll let us know if you find anything.'

Parker nodded and got up to leave. She had the awful feeling that Olivia's parents were never going to find their answers, and nor was she.

CHAPTER 8

At ten o'clock the following morning, Nightingale landed in the Gulfstream at the general aviation terminal of Memphis International Airport. Every other plane in sight seemed to bear a FedEx logo, and Nightingale assumed the delivery company must have some operational hub here. One of Wainwright's fleet of limousines drove him, and his bag, to the terminal. He picked up the keys to his car from the VIP queue at the Hertz desk and drove out of the airport in a white Ford Escape. The SatNav guided him to the Peabody Hotel without any problem, where he let the valet take care of the parking.

The Peabody was a brown cube, right in the middle of Downtown Memphis, and Nightingale put his bag on the sidewalk and looked up at it, trying to count the floors. He made it thirteen, and hoped that Valerie had put him somewhere near the ground. He walked into the lobby and stopped again, looking round to take it all in. It was a much bigger space then he had been expecting, stretching the entire length and breadth of the building. The lobby also seemed to function as a lounge, bar, and general meeting area, and was very busy, with most of the tables occupied, waiters and waitresses striding around with trays, and, much to his surprise, quite a few people, including children, sitting on the floor, either side of a red carpet, which led from the side door to the octagonal fountain in the centre of the room. The fountain was topped with an enormous spray of flowers, and stood directly underneath a great crystal chandelier, which looked as if it had been there since the hotel was built.

The second floor was more of a mezzanine, with balconies overlooking the lobby, and there were people up there too, looking down expectantly. Nightingale wondered if there was someone famous due to arrive, though he had no idea who might rate their own personal red carpet. He glanced at his watch, which showed dead on eleven.

The side door opened, and a tall young man in a red jacket with gold epaulettes and piping, and black pants walked in. He was holding a long black cane, topped with gold. He held the door open, and five ducks waddled through, along the carpet, up the steps and into the fountain, where they started to swim contentedly, while their audience applauded politely. Despite his name, Nightingale was no ornithologist, but he recognised the one bright male with his white collar and oily-green head and his harem of plain brown hens.

'Nice work if you can get it, son,' he muttered to himself, and walked over to the check-in desk.

Michael was the receptionist who took Nightingale's name and found his reservation.

'Yes, Mr Nightingale, we have you in 1215,' he said, and Nightingale's heart sank.

'You don't have anything a little nearer the ground, do you?' he asked.

Michael leaned over and ran his fingers over his computer keyboard, but his frown was discouraging. 'I'm sorry, Mr Nightingale, nothing else available at the moment, we're very full. Couple of conventions in town.'

'Can't be helped,' said Nightingale, then asked hopefully. 'Is that a smoking room?'

'I'm sorry, sir, the Peabody no longer has smoking rooms.'

'Can I smoke on the balcony?'

'Sorry, sir, I wouldn't advise you to try that. The Peabody has no balconies.'

'I thought it was the English who were always apologising.'

'I'm sorry?'

'Doesn't matter,' said Nightingale. 'English humour.'

Nightingale took his key, handed five dollars to the waiting bellhop, but told him he'd carry his own bag, then headed off to find the stairs.

'Elevators over there, sir,' said the bellhop, trying to help, but Nightingale shook his head.

'I'll take the stairs,' said Nightingale. 'I'm not a big fan of elevators.'

'But that's the twelfth floor, sir.'

'Isn't it just,' said Nightingale, walking away, while the bellhop shrugged his shoulders behind him.

Nightingale cheered himself up for the first few flights, by reminding himself that America started counting floors with number one at street level, so he really only had eleven flights of stairs to climb, but that psychological boost wore off quickly, as he trudged on upwards. He took off his raincoat on the fifth floor, and was breathing too heavily for comfort by the time he reached his room. He unlocked the door and looked around and decided it made a pleasant change from the generic chain hotel bedrooms he was used to. The armchairs looked old and comfortable, though they showed no wear, and the bed headboard, nightstands, closets, table, desk and drawer units were all dark wood and looked reassuringly solid. Real furniture, as opposed to veneered chipboard. The walls were painted grey, the ceiling white, and the carpet was a subdued pattern of browns. The only jarring note was the black wide-screen television on top of a chest of drawers.

He badly wanted a cigarette after his exertions but walking down twelve floors to street level didn't appeal at all. For a moment he thought of breaking the rules, but the red light of the smoke detector, and the nozzle of the sprinkler system dissuaded him.

The flight up from Brownsville had given him plenty of thinking time, but he hadn't firmed up any ideas yet. He was pretty sure the whole idea of the list was to flush him into the open, and wrong foot Wainwright. He still couldn't think of anyone with a grudge against both of them, except the surviving members of the Apostles in San Francisco, several of whom were walking around on bail at the moment, and probably keen on revenge. Though without their leader none of them wielded real Occult power, according to Wainwright. Or maybe Wainwright wasn't really a target, just another means to an end, and Nightingale himself was the one they really wanted. Whoever 'they' might be.

Or whatever.

Nightingale shuddered at that thought. Human beings were quite nasty enough for his tastes, he had no wish to be dealing with any other kind of creatures.

Nightingale was pretty sure that whoever was calling the shots would make something happen soon, but in the meantime the obvious place to start was with Joshua's sister and her family. A call from Wainwright had arranged the visit, and they were expecting him that afternoon.

The original parchment was still with Wainwright but Nightingale had a copy. He took it out and stared at it, hoping for inspiration, but none came.

He picked up the hotel services menu and learned that the Peabody Duck walk happened every day at 11am and again at 5pm. The custom dated back to the 1930s and out of respect duck was never served in the Peabody's restaurants. Apparently the ducks lived in a two hundred thousand dollar Duck Palace on the hotel roof, when they weren't swimming in the fountain. Nightingale did some quick calculations, and decided that the duck's new house had cost more than his old flat in Bayswater. He also learned what was available on the room service menu, and called down for a club sandwich and coffee. He unpacked his clothes while he was waiting for his order to arrive, but left some of the more unusual items in his bag, which he stored in the bottom of the closet.

A discreet knock announced the arrival of Lucille with his order, and he signed the bill, letting her have another five dollars in addition to the twenty percent service charge and four dollar delivery charge already added. It was all Wainwright's money, and who knew when he might want a favour from someone in the hotel.

As he ate his sandwich, he pondered again where to go from here. There was no cover story he could think of that would get him in to see Olivia Taylor's parents, and the idea of a supernatural list would have them calling the police before he got a foot in the door. Concentrating on Naomi Fisher, Wainwright's niece seemed his only option, but even there he was pretty much hamstrung. Wainwright had been insistent that he shouldn't mention any threat to the parents, and especially not the existence of the list, or any connection with the Occult.

'Still,' thought Nightingale as he sipped his coffee. 'Nobody ever said life was easy.'

Nightingale had checked the distance from the Peabody to the Fisher home on Google Maps, but had no idea what the Memphis traffic might be like at that time of day. Assuming it would be horrendous, he allowed an extra hour for the trip, but the GPS got him there twenty minutes before his appointment, so he decided to take a look around Fisher's neighbourhood. He parked in the empty lot in front of the Galilee Baptist Church, which was Reverend Matthew Fisher's place of business, as shown by his name, written in gold lettering on the bottom of the notice board along with the times of services.

Nightingale stood next to the car and smoked a cigarette as he gazed up at the church. It was a two-storey brick building with half a dozen tall arched windows set along the sides, the frames painted white. The entrance was set under a white stone pediment, held up by four white stone columns. The grey slate roof was in good repair, and the whole building looked freshly cleaned. Nightingale had noticed that American churches generally seemed to be in better condition than their British equivalents. Probably due to having bigger congregations. Or richer ones.

Attached to the rear of the church was a brick tower, a storey higher than the rest of the building, with a spire covered in the same grey slates. On the side nearest him, there was a stained glass window that ran almost the whole width of the tower, and was the height of the second storey. It showed Christ, inevitably a young white man with light brown hair and beard, standing in a pure-white robe, surrounded by an aura of light, a halo around his head. All around him were what Nightingale thought of as junior angels, chubby-faced kids with small halos and wings.

As often happened when he looked at churches, Nightingale pondered the paradox of Christian churches being pretty much everywhere throughout the Western world, while Satan worshipers made every effort to keep their places of worship hidden. And yet, Nightingale knew several different ways of communicating with members of Satan's demonic horde, and had used them many times in the past years, and met others who had done so. But he had no idea at all how to contact God, Jesus or an angel. Had never read any instructions on how to do so, and had never met anyone sane who claimed they had managed it.

He stood on his cigarette butt, and looked up at the figure of Jesus on the stained glass window. 'I mean,' he said, 'come on. If you're really up there, why do you make it so hard for the good guys, and so easy for the opposition? It's almost as if you want them to win.'

As ever, God and Jesus gave him no sign of listening, so he headed off down the street.

The Reverend Matthew Fisher lived about a hundred yards or so from the church. Nightingale thought that his house didn't look much like a vicarage, or if Americans even used that term. It was a double-fronted, two-storey detached house, with a well-kept patch of lawn and flower beds in front of it. The house was clad in sandy-coloured wood planking, which stretched right up to the grey slates of the roof, where two semi-circular windows looked out like half-closed eyes. Presumably to give light to an attic. Five stone steps led up to a plain red wooden front door.

Nightingale walked up the steps, rang the bell, and the door opened almost immediately. 'You must be Mr Nightingale, come on in.' Sarah Fisher looked to be in her mid-thirties, which, since he'd said she was his younger sister, meant that Nightingale would need to revise his guess about the perpetually youthful Joshua Wainwright's real age. She shared her brother's dark skin and warm brown eyes. She was a head shorter than her brother, and was dressed casually in a pale green shirt and blue jeans, which showed off the fact she kept herself in pretty good shape. She led Nightingale down the hall and into the family sitting room, comfortably furnished with a long green sofa and chairs, which blended well with the cream walls. There was a long glass and brass coffee table in front of the sofa, and a large television opposite, with an X-box connected. A black cat was curled up asleep on one of the chairs. Nightingale couldn't see any ashtrays, or smell any trace of smoke, so he assumed that Sarah didn't share her brother's taste for tobacco and kept his Marlboro in his pocket.

'So, what can I get you, Mr Nightingale?' she asked. 'Tea? Or is that too stereotypically English? Coffee?'

'No, I'm fine thanks,' said Nightingale. ' And make it Jack, please. Nice house you have here.'

'Thanks, it does the job. We were lucky to find one so close to the church. My husband will be back pretty soon, he had to go out for a while to visit one of his lady friends.'

Nightingale failed to hide his surprise, then noticed the wide grin.

'Hah, not really,' she laughed. 'Ellen Wade's nearly ninety and can't get to the church any more, so my husband takes the communion wafer round to her every week. He'll be back soon. And Naomi will be back from school in twenty minutes.'

She pointed at a photo in the middle of the shelf-unit to the right, and Nightingale saw a bright-eyed girl with a gap-toothed smile. Her skin was lighter than her mother's, but they shared enough facial features to make the relationship obvious. Naomi's hair was short and curly, but her mother wore hers shoulder length and straight. 'Pretty girl,' he said.

'She hates that photo. She's just reaching the age where she's started to think more about her appearance. She'll be taking selfies soon.'

'She uploads photos of herself onto Facebook and stuff?'

'Oh no, we're pretty strict about that, she's not allowed social media accounts yet. In fact we're so cruel she doesn't even have a mobile phone, though she's working pretty hard to break us down.' She smiled. 'Things were a lot simpler when I was a kid, We just wanted the latest Barbie outfit.'

'Yeah, I had quite a collection,' said Nightingale. He smiled. 'Joke.'

'Yes, Joshua warned me about that English sense of humour. How's he doing, we don't see much of him these days?'

'Nor do I really,' said Nightingale. 'He's usually airborne, making some deal or another. You know what he's like.' He smiled but he was pretty sure that Sarah Fisher had absolutely no idea what her brother was really like. Or the effort he was going to in order to protect his niece.

'How do you come to know him?' she asked.

The question was innocent enough, but Nightingale noticed that she was studying him closely while she waited for his reply. 'Books,' he said. 'We share an interest in collecting, and I've helped him track down a few items. We're not in competition, of course, I couldn't afford to think about some of the prices he pays.'

'That why you're in Memphis? Book buying?'

'Pretty much. On the trail of something unusual, and he suggested I drop by to say hello. To be honest, I think he feels guilty about not spending more time with you. You know how busy he is.'

'Glad to have you here,' she said. She leaned towards him and lowered her voice conspiratorially. 'Though...maybe it'd be best not to talk too much about Joshua's book collection when my husband get's home. Doesn't bother me, but Matthew doesn't really approve. As you might expect.'

Nightingale nodded. 'I won't mention it,' he said, smiling again but wondering how much Sarah Fisher actually knew about her brother's Satanic book collection.

The front door-lock rattled, opened and closed and a deep male voice rang out. 'Hi, honey. I'm home.'

Sarah rolled her eyes. 'Matthew, not every time. We have a guest.'

Nightingale stood up to shake hands with the tall man in the dark suit and clerical collar who strode into the room. His sandy hair and pale skin showed the origins of Naomi's lighter colouring, and his ready smile mirrored his wife's.

'Matthew Fisher,' he said, releasing Nightingale's hand from his strong grip. 'Good to know you, Jack. Any friend of Joshua's is always welcome. We don't get to meet many of them. And we don't see the man himself very much either. He's always so darn busy.'

'I know he wishes he could spend more time with you guys,' said Nightingale. 'I think that's why he was so keen that I dropped by.'

'I'm not sure I really count as a friend,' said Nightingale. 'We just have a few mutual interests.'

'And what would they be?' asked Matthew.

Before Nightingale could answer they heard the front door open again. 'That'll be Naomi,' said Sarah. 'Hi, sweetie.'

'Hi mom, hi dad,' came the answer, and Naomi walked in, a year or so older than in the photograph. Her adult teeth had grown in to fill the gap in her smile, and her hair was longer and straighter, maybe following her mother's lead. She was nearly as tall as Sarah now, though very obviously still a child. She stopped as she saw Nightingale, put her head on one side, then glanced a question at her mother.

'Naomi, this is Mr Nightingale,' said her mother. 'He's popped by to visit for a while. He's a friend of your Uncle Joshua.'

Was it Nightingale's imagination, or did the girl give a little frown at the mention of Wainwright's name?

'Pleased to meet you, Mr Nightingale,' she said, solemnly holding out her hand for him to shake. She looked at her mother again. 'Is Uncle Joshua here too?' she asked.

'No,' said Sarah. 'Not this time.'

The girl didn't seem too disappointed, but turned and headed towards the kitchen.

'Lovely girl,' said Nightingale.

'We think so,' said her father. 'We've been lucky, she's thoughtful, works hard, always happy, and never gets sick.' He reached over and tapped a side table. 'Touch wood. Her guardian angel does a good job.'

'You believe in guardian angels?' asked Nightingale.

'Of course. Why not?'

'Why not indeed? Joshua says she's ten now?'

'Good that he remembers, though he's almost out-of-date, she'll be eleven on Saturday.'

'Big party?'

'Not this year, she's just doing the cinema with a few friends, then back here for cake and Coke. Seems only yesterday she was in diapers. I tell you, Mr Nightingale, having kids makes you realise just how quickly time passes.'

Nightingale smiled but he was running out of reasons to stay. It had seemed a good idea to see the family, but it hadn't got him anywhere. He'd picked up no vibrations of evil, or impending doom, the Fishers seemed an ordinary happy family with a lovely, well-brought-up daughter. So all was well with the Fisher world, so far as he could see.

Except, according to Wainwright's theory, the ten-year-old daughter been marked down for imminent death.

CHAPTER 9

Timmy Williams heard the sound of the car in the drive, then the door opening downstairs and knew that his mother had come home. He turned off his iPad, walked out of his room, across the hall and downstairs to meet her. Mrs Williams gave her son a perfunctory hug, then steered him out of the door and into the rear seat of the car, which was waiting in the drive, the motor still running. Mrs Williams backed out of the drive, turned up the street then headed uptown.

She glanced in her mirror from time to time, but Timmy was just staring straight ahead. He looked a little young for twelve, but she knew that boys often had their growth spurt later than girls of the same age. He was wearing Adidas bottoms and sneakers and his favourite Memphis Grizzlies sweater. He never enjoyed visiting the dentist, but he wasn't usually as quiet as this. 'You okay, honey?' she asked cheerfully. 'Nothing to worry about today, just a little check-up, and you never need any work. All that brushing and flossing is paying off. Filling free for ten years now. And those adult teeth are coming through nicely. No retainers for you.'

The boy still said nothing, just nodded and carried on looking straight ahead.

Five minutes later, Mrs Williams pulled into the parking lot opposite the dentist, opened the back door to let her son out, and the two of them walked up the street to the crossing. Anyone watching would have seen an attractive blonde woman in her thirties wearing a stone-coloured raincoat over a grey business suit and low heeled shoes, leading her kid along by the hand. Not that anyone paid them any particular attention at all, except for Dudák, who kept pace with them on the opposite side of the street, sparing them just an occasional glance.

The red 'Don't Walk' signal was on when they reached the crossing, with heavy rush-hour traffic flowing pretty freely. She looked down to smile at Timmy, who didn't hesitate at all on the curb, but stepped straight into the street and under the wheels of a beer truck that was rolling past. It was all over before his mother had chance to move or scream.

The truck was doing no more than twenty miles an hour, but that was more than enough. The driver had no time at all to react and his huge vehicle crushed the life out of the little boy instantly. He hit the brake as soon as he felt the impact, the truck screeched to a halt, with a grey SUV running straight into the back of it. The SUV driver leaped out, the angry curses dying on his lips as he saw the mangled body of the young boy. The truck driver gaped in horror for a few moments, then threw up on the side of his cab.

The woman still stood motionless on the curb, staring at what was left of her son, her mind unable to comprehend that her whole world had been destroyed in the space of a few seconds.

She was still frozen when the police and paramedics arrived.

Dudák stood leaning against the crossing sign on the other side of the road, while people milled around opposite, traffic backed up, horns were sounded and the whole junction ground to a halt. Nobody took the slightest notice, and by the time the police started taking witness statements, Dudák was long gone, fed and satisfied.

CHAPTER 10

Nightingale drove back in the direction of the Peabody, stopping at Pizza Hut for an early dinner. An hour later, he was suitably fed, but no further forward in figuring out any of what was happening. He'd just left his car with the valet, when his mobile phone rang. It was Wainwright. 'Jack? You saw my sister? Everything okay?'

'More than okay as far as I can tell, the definition of a happy family. Naomi's lovely, seems a hundred per cent happy, not a care in the world.'

'Shit.'

'That's a bad thing?'

'No, but it doesn't get us anywhere. If there's a threat to her, it doesn't look like she or her parents are aware of it. Look, it gets worse.'

'Tell me.'

'The fifth name crossed itself off an hour ago. Timmy Williams.'

'Any information?'

'Not yet. But when Timmy Williams's name crossed off, nobody else showed up on the end of the list. Looks like it's complete at thirteen names.'

'Thirteen?'

'Yeah, just like in a coven. Like the coven you busted to Hell up in San Francisco.'

'You think that's a lead?'

'To be honest I have no idea. I'd have thought only their leader, Abaddon, was powerful enough to pull this off, but she's dead. Thirteen is a powerful Satanic number anyway, so maybe there's no connection. Can you think of anyone else with a grudge against you, or me?'

Nightingale could have mentioned quite a few names, but he wasn't ready to share everything with Wainwright yet. 'Not unless Bimoleth's managed to get himself free and wants to settle accounts.'

There was silence at the other end for a few moments. 'You know, Jack, that's not even close to being funny. But if he was loose, the whole world would probably know about it. We need to find something soon, Jack. I got that list four days ago...'

'Yeah, and four of the names on it are dead. Five if Timmy Williams is already dead. I did the maths.'

'Me too. Whoever sent it is telling me that my niece has only a week or so to live. Anyway, Valerie has emailed you everything we managed to find on Olivia Taylor. I hope that'll help.' He ended the call.

Once back in his room, Nightingale used his phone to check his emails. Valerie's was the only unread item in the inbox, which was no surprise as Nightingale wasn't a great user of emails. As ever, Valerie didn't bother with greetings or formalities, and the email consisted of just one paragraph, giving details about the fourth name on the list, Olivia Taylor, including her date of birth, address and the events surrounding her death. She had tied her skipping-rope round her neck, fastened the other end to the bannister and jumped over. Death had been instantaneous, and yet again, the police found no evidence of anything suspicious.

He was about to close the mailbox when he noticed that another email had just come in, also from Valerie. It was headed Timmy Williams, and he clicked to open it.

Timmy Williams was the fifth name on Wainwright's list. The boy had been eleven, and Valerie had obtained his Memphis address and his school details. He'd been killed that afternoon in a traffic accident. Somehow Valerie had managed to find a witness report, which said the boy had just ignored a DON'T WALK light and walked straight out under the wheels of a truck. Police had ruled out DUI for the truck driver, and had made no arrest. They were treating it as an accident.

Five dead kids, and all of them could have been suicide. It made no sense at all to Nightingale. All of the deaths had come after their names had been written on the list that had been sent to Wainwright, so how could anyone predict suicides? Or, worse yet, how could someone or something be causing young kids to kill themselves?

Worst of all, how in the name of sanity was Nightingale meant to stop them?

He lay down on his bed and stared up at the ceiling, trying to come up with a plan. If the list maintained its logic, he had just eight days to save Wainwright's niece, and nine to save Sophie Underwood. But that still left seven more potential victims, seven kids who would be on his conscience, unless he could find a way to save them. Was that what was this was really about, forcing him to watch helplessly while innocent children died? If this was aimed at him, then it must be the work of someone who knew his weakness, knew that there was nothing that would eat away at him more than to see kids hurt.

Proserpine?

He knew she still craved his soul, the one that had been pledged to her, and she had promised him that one day he'd offer it to her again. Was she waiting for him to summon her and offer his soul in exchange for sparing the children's lives? It seemed unlikely, the kids were strangers to him, why should he make them his responsibility? Except for Sophie, of course. Sophie, that was a tough one to explain. If this were the work of one of the former Apostles, they probably wouldn't have learned about Sophie. The Met had never publicised his role in her rescue, it was just another successful operation. He hadn't needed to give evidence at the subsequent court case, especially since they'd kicked him out by then.

He badly needed a lead, and he had no real idea where to find one. Claiming to be a journalist and trying to ask the parents questions was unlikely to get him very far. The police weren't going to be helpful either. All he had was a list of dead kids, which he could have got from anywhere, and another list of potential victims. Showing the rest of the list to a police officer wouldn't get any kind of reaction, not until one of them actually died. When that happened it was ten to one that instead of helping him investigate the police would throw him in jail as the number one suspect.

There must be some connection between the kids on the list, beyond the obvious geographical and age links. Since he couldn't ask the parents or the police, and he didn't much want to risk summoning Proserpine and hope she felt like answering questions, that really only left one avenue of investigation open to him.

The gentlemen of the Press. Or gentlewomen. If there was such a thing.

CHAPTER 11

In fact it did indeed turn out to be a lady of the Press who agreed to see Nightingale the following day. He'd taken a good look through the morning's Memphis Herald and had found a three paragraph report on Timmy Williams's death, under the by-line of Kim Jarvis, so that was the name he'd asked for at the newspaper office reception desk. As ever, reporters were always far more interested in talking to him than the police were, and he was pointed in the direction of her third-floor desk after just a perfunctory call from the girl at reception.

Kim Jarvis turned out to be a slim blonde in her early twenties, who didn't rate an office, just a desk in the bullpen. She was dressed in blue jeans and a low-cut white top under a grey jacket. Nightingale winced as he noticed the half-dozen silver earrings in each ear, the silver stud in the side of her nose and the small metal ring through her upper lip. He never understood body piercings. She looked up from her computer screen and pushed her green plastic-framed glasses onto the top of her head as Nightingale found his way to her desk.

'Jack Nightingale, right?' she said. 'Sally said you wanted to see me personally. Have we met before?'

She wrinkled her nose, tilted her head to one side and looked at him quizzically. He smiled and shook his head. 'Not in this life,' he said. 'I was wanting to talk to you about a story you wrote.'

'Well, that narrows it down, they don't use my name on most of them. Which of my Pulitzer-winning scoops are we talking about here?'

'The kid who was hit by a truck yesterday. Timmy Williams.'

Her smile disappeared instantly. 'Sit,' she said, borrowing an empty chair from the next desk and pulling it round for him. 'That was awful. Pretty much a coincidence, I was heading back here when I heard the sirens and followed it up. Kid never had a chance.'

'Your report said the truck driver wasn't arrested.'

'No, that's right. The cops breathalysed him as a routine thing, but there were plenty of witnesses to tell them it wasn't his fault. The kid was standing next to his mother at the lights, and he just walked straight out under the truck. She didn't have hold of his hand or anything.'

'Would a boy of eleven let his mother hold his hand in public? It's plenty old enough to know how and when to cross a road, surely?'

'You'd think, but not this time. As I said, the witnesses say he just walked straight out.'

'He wasn't on his phone was he? Distracted?'

'No. He was looking straight ahead, his mother said. Anyway, tragic for the family, but it's a road accident. So who are you, and what's your interest?'

'Well, you know the name. As for my interest, well...can we just say I take an interest in the unusual?'

'Say what you like, but what's unusual about a road accident? They happen all the time.'

'But, from what you've told me, it wasn't an accident. The boy deliberately walked out into the truck's path.'

She shook her head. 'No, the witnesses said he just walked out without looking, but there's a big difference between careless and deliberate.' She frowned. 'You seem to be suggesting he actually wanted to get himself killed.'

'Maybe I am suggesting that.'

She sat back in her chair. 'Oh come on. Why would he want to do that?'

'No idea, maybe there was something in his family background. Did you go into it?'

'We did not. The police called it an accident, we weren't about to start prying into the family history, they have enough to deal with. We're not vultures, there's no story here. Now come on, what makes you think this kid wanted to die?'

Nightingale pulled out a sheet of paper on which he'd written four names, and passed it across. Jarvis looked at it, frowned and then looked back up at him.

'I've heard another one of those names, Olivia Taylor. Recently. ' She frowned. 'A day or two ago, right? A young girl hanged herself.'

Nightingale nodded.

'What about the other two?' asked Jarvis.

Again, Nightingale told her what he knew. She nodded along with his sentences.

'So that's four kids in four days who appear to have killed themselves in Tennessee?'

'Five if you include Timmy,' said Nightingale. 'It certainly looks that way, and that would be pretty unusual, right.'

'True enough,' she said. 'Even one would be very unusual, teenage suicide isn't rare, but with primary kids it almost never happens. And five in five days? How do you come to cotton on to this?'

Nightingale hadn't been looking forward to that question. 'Tell me, Kim, what are your views on the supernatural?'

She looked around the bullpen. 'I'm due a coffee break around now, so what do you say we take this across the street.'

'Fine with me, I skipped breakfast.'

The reporter took him across the road and into the Three Kings bar. 'Hope you don't mind, but you can smoke in bars not coffee shops,' she said.

'I'll cope,' said Nightingale. He ordered a black coffee and a Danish to go with his Marlboro. Jarvis went for a doughnut, a cappuccino and a Camel.

'So,' said Nightingale. 'You care to answer my question now?'

She blew smoke and watched it curl upwards. Nightingale recognised the technique, she was buying time while she thought. 'I'm interested in the supernatural,' she said eventually. 'I have friends who are Wiccans, but I'm not sure that's the way to go. A lot of people assume I'm some kind of vampire anyway when they see all this.'

She took off her jacket, to reveal two complete sleeves of tattoos.

Nightingale widened his eyes. Kim's tattoos had obviously taken a lot of work. The colours were vibrant, and the designs well-executed. He picked out dragons, wizards and witches, and a variety of Occult symbols.

'I tend to wear jackets or long sleeves at work,' she said. 'But I love them, and the metalwork too.'

'Didn't the piercings hurt?'

She smiled. 'The ones you can't see hurt a lot more.'

Nightingale winced and tried hard not to imagine what she meant.

'Ouch,' he said.

'Don't knock it till you've tried it,' she said 'You should get yourself a piercing down there. The girls go wild for them.'

'No thanks,' said Nightingale, 'I'll stick to flowers and chocolates.'

She shook her head. 'Dull, dull, dull. So you got no tattoos either?'

'Just the Pink Panther on my ass,' said Nightingale.

'Huh, more of that British humour.'

'Could be. So, anyway, about the Occult...'

'So anyway, I don't dismiss the Occult at all, and I'd like to know more about it. Are you going to tell me why you asked?'

'I was given a list two days ago, with some names on it. The first four were the four I showed you in the office.'

She got the point straight away. 'Two days ago? But the last two weren't even dead then.'

'I know, and I can't prove what I say, but believe me, the list was made before any of the kids on it died.'

'Well I'm guessing the police would be pretty interested in talking to the guy who gave you that list. Who is he?'

'Friend of mine. But he gave me the list. He didn't make it.'

'Who did?' she asked.

'That's the problem, he doesn't know and nor do I. But whoever did make the list is behind the death of these kids.'

'Why would you say that?'

'Well, how else could he know in advance?'

'Come on now, Jack, even if I accept that someone made a list of dead kids before they died, that doesn't mean they killed them. Weather forecasters and stock market analysts predict the future, but they don't create it.'

Nightingale paused to think about that. It was a fair enough point from someone who didn't know his background and Wainwright's, but he didn't believe the idea of a prophet unconnected with the deaths. Thirteen unexplained deaths would be pushing it for even the most gifted seer. 'I don't think so,' he said eventually. 'That would still leave us with the unexplained deaths. Five in five days.'

'This is a lot to swallow,' she said. 'What do you plan to do about it?'

'I don't really know,' said Nightingale. 'It's too weird to go to the police with, I was just trying to find a way to get a little closer to the kids, maybe ask some questions, find a common factor, figure out what's going on. You're not convinced, are you?'

'Not really. But you could convince me easily enough.'

'How?' he asked.

'Just give me the next name on the list.'

'I suppose that could work.'

'It could, though you'd better make pretty sure you're nowhere near him or her when it happens. If it happens, I mean.'

Nightingale gave her the next name, and she wrote it in a small notebook. David Robinson. 'Now,' she said. 'How about a little background on you? So far I know you're English and you 'take an interest in the unusual'. My nose says cop, or ex-cop, so let's have some more details. Why should I even be talking to you?'

Nightingale tried his best winning smile. 'I was a cop, in a previous life. I was in the Metropolitan Police, once upon a time.'

'That's London, right?'

'Yeah, I was a police negotiator. Now I'm not. Now I work for someone who pays me to look into unusual things.'

'And he's the one who got the list?'

'That's right.'

'And does he know someone on that list? Is that why you're in town?'

Nightingale nodded. Kim Jarvis was pretty sharp.

'So are you going to give me his name?' she asked.

'He likes his privacy.'

She nodded thoughtfully, then looked at her watch. 'Time I was somewhere else,' she said. 'Give me your number, if I hear anything, I'll call. Same goes for you, if you think of anything else, call me. If there's a story in this, I'm in. Meanwhile I'll see if I can turn up anything to connect these kids. Maybe I can nose around their schools, people are more likely to talk to me than some middle-aged English guy.'

Nightingale winced inwardly at the 'middle-aged', but gave her his mobile number. She put it into her phone, then called his, so he could store her number. 'Okay, I'll be in touch,' she said. 'Thanks for the coffee.'

Nightingale took the hint and counted out some bills as she headed for the door.

When he was back in his car he phoned Wainwright. His call was answered almost immediately. 'You got anything, Jack?'

'Not much. I managed to talk to the reporter who wrote the story about the latest kid who killed herself. I told her this was the fifth suicide, and mentioned the list. I gave her the next name.'

'You did what? She'll think you're insane.'

'Maybe, unless a kid with that name dies today. And besides, judging by the tattoos she's covered in, she's something of a believer in the Occult. Ever heard the name? Kim Jarvis?'

'Not that I know of, I tend to move in different circles for my...activities. That's kind of lucky, the woman who wrote the story, and the first person you talk to in Memphis is a keen Occultist.'

'Isn't it though, what are the chances?' Nightingale couldn't keep the sarcasm out of his voice.

'Coincidences happen.'

'Sometimes they do,' said Nightingale. 'Sometimes we get pushed in the right direction. I'll see how it plays out. I don't have many other ideas. Look, Joshua, the only thing I can think of doing is to put a cordon around your niece.'

'We can't do that without telling my sister and Matthew, and I can't see them believing a word of it. He doesn't trust me. Guess he can maybe sense I'm in the opposite camp. But I'll do what I can do.'

'Meanwhile I guess I'm waiting for the next name to be crossed off, see if it throws anything up. Plus I suggest we try to do something at the source.'

'Meaning?'

'Meaning we both have some contacts in the Occult world, it's time to use them, try to find a pattern behind this, see if there's any more information available on Abaddon, figure out who might want to get at us through hurting kids.'

'I'll get to work. Can you think of anyone?'

'The ones who chased me out of England, The Order Of The Nine Angles. They specialised in ritual child killing. And they worshiped Proserpine.'

'You have kind of a direct line to her, don't you?'

Nightingale paused and lit a cigarette, in direct contravention of Hertz rules. He'd never told Wainwright the full story of his connection to Proserpine, and didn't plan to.

'She's been known to communicate with me, but it's usually on her terms. It could be a last resort, but I'm not about to summon her in a hotel room. I'd prefer to deal with people who can't blast me into Hell on a whim.'

'Makes sense. Besides, if she's part of this, she's not likely to tell you how to stop it.'

'Probably not. Though she does have a tendency to be playing all sides at once.'

'Okay. I'll see what I can do. I'm in Haiti right now. A very good place to do some finding out that won't involve Google. Stay in touch, Jack.'

Nightingale started the car and headed back to the Peabody. At the moment he was stuck, and when that happened he usually tried a beer.

CHAPTER 12

Dudák lay in bed, next to the strange creature that slept now, after its exertions. Dudák had once again diffused a little energy into the creature, and it had reacted as it always did, writhing in paroxysms of frenzied pleasure and pain, before finally collapsing, sobbing and spent, into an exhausted sleep.

Dudák had felt nothing, a different kind of energy would have been necessary for that, but the creature was useful, and needed to be kept compliant. It could have been forced to do Dudák's will, but, it was simpler if it co-operated freely.

First, of course, the creature had made its report.

The first target had arrived, as expected, and been pushed in the right direction. It seemed to suspect nothing, not that it would make any difference. Its course had been decided, and it would not be possible to change it, even should it try.

There was no sign of the second target, and it might prove more difficult to ensure its presence, but Dudák was confident in the arrangements which had been made. Not that the arrival of either target would affect his enjoyment, but it was important that the plan succeed. Failure might have unpleasant consequences, even for one as powerful as Dudák.

Dudák needed no sleep, and was not conscious of the passing of time while the creature slept on. At a new time, it would wake and be given fresh instructions.

The creature was his slave.

But Dudák too was little better than a slave in all this.
There would always be those with more power.

CHAPTER 13

Nightingale still had half of his bottle of Corona in front of him when he finished his meal in Huey's Burger. He'd asked the concierge at the Peabody to recommend a nearby place with no live music and Huey's fitted the bill. He'd chosen the 'Heart Healthy Mahi-Mahi Plate' since he had a tendency to bolt down too much fast food, or forget to eat altogether, if a case got hectic. Fresh fish seemed a good idea.

A waitress in a black t-shirt whose name-badge identified her as Diane arrived as he finished the last mouthful. She looked around twenty years old and radiated waitress charm. 'Everything okay for you there?'

'My heart's never felt better,' said Nightingale, and then, seeing her puzzled expression, 'Joke.'

'Oh, right. Still, I guess you need to take care of yourself, don't you. My dad checks his blood pressure and cholesterol almost every day. But he still smokes, we all hassle him about it. What can you do? Can I get you another beer? Dessert?'

Nightingale sighed, and wondered if he really looked as old as Diane's dad. It must be the stress. 'No thanks, just a cup of coffee, please. Regular, with milk.'

'Have that right up for you,' she said, and departed with his plate.

Ten minutes later his heart still felt fine, the coffee was gone, and his attempts at thinking had got him nowhere, so he paid the bill, with an extra twenty percent for Diane, despite her making him feel old.

He headed back to the Peabody. As he walked through the entrance, a pretty black woman in a red coat almost bumped into him.

'Why, Mr Nightingale,' she said. 'There you are.'

He gave a puzzled frown, before recognition dawned. It was Wainwright's sister. 'Mrs Fisher, sorry, didn't recognise you with your hair down.'

'It's a good disguise, huh?'

'Certainly is.' he said. 'Are you visiting someone?'

'I'm visiting you. Just about to give up waiting too. You care to buy me a drink? If Joshua's paying you, you can certainly afford to pay for a poor old preacher's wife.'

She laughed at that, and Nightingale assumed that no sister of Wainwright's would be left short of money. He returned her smile. 'Oh I don't know, should a poor old preacher's wife risk being seen with a dashing young Englishman?'

She looked him up and down. 'If I let you have the 'dashing' and 'young', do I get the beer? I think my reputation can stand to be seen with you. Besides, I could always claim you were a homeless guy who'd asked me to buy you some new shoes.'

Nightingale looked hurt. 'Hey, don't you start in on my Hush Puppies. I get enough grief from your brother about them.'

'Quite right. Is it even legal to sell those things in Tennessee?'

'I like them, they're comfy.'

'I'll assume that's a good thing. Anyway, I didn't come down here to offer you fashion advice, so let's sit.'

Making a mental note that Sarah Fisher could be every bit as direct as her brother, Nightingale followed her to a table. A tall waitress in a black uniform was with them almost immediately.

'I'll take a cappuccino,' said Sarah Fisher.

'Sounds good,' said Nightingale, 'same here.'

Their coffees arrived almost immediately. Sarah Fisher took a sip of her coffee and leaned forward in her chair.

'Well, I can't say I was expecting a visit,' said Nightingale. 'What can I do for you, Mrs Fisher?'

'Sarah.'

'Jack.'

'Well, it's not exactly a social visit, Jack. I have a few questions I'd like answered.'

'I'll do my best. What's on your mind?'

'Well, first of all, and hoping it never reaches my husband's ears that I said it, what in the Blue Hell are you doing in Memphis?'

Nightingale made a surprised face, and hoped it looked genuine. 'Well, I told you Sarah, I'm looking...'

'...for books, you said. Bullshit. You don't look like the reading type to me, and, let me warn you now, I am very good at telling when somebody's lying to me. You were and you are. Why exactly did Joshua send you up here?'

'You're pretty direct,' said Nightingale. 'Must be the Brownsville upbringing. Joshua's like that too.'

She sniffed, and looked daggers at him. 'I'm also very good at spotting someone changing the subject. Answer the question.' She forced a smile. 'Please.'

Nightingale always hated lying, it was so difficult to remember everything and keep it up. On the other hand, Wainwright had been very clear that Sarah and her husband should not be told the truth, even if there was any chance they'd believe it. He improvised desperately, in the face of her penetrating look. 'It's nothing sinister, he knew I was coming up here, so he asked me to drop by and say hello.'

She was shaking her head. 'No. My guess is you're bought and paid for, and if you're up here it's because he told you to come, and visiting us wasn't incidental, it's the reason you came. Now why?'

Nightingale was out of ideas. 'I'm sorry, Sarah, that's all there is to it. I can't tell you anything else.'

She put her coffee cup down sharply and clicked her tongue at him. 'Can't, or won't? Comes to the same thing. Guess you know who's pulling your strings and who's paying the bills. Let's try this another way. How long you worked for my brother?'

Nightingale smiled, glad to be back on firmer ground, if only for a while. 'About three years,' he said.

She nodded. 'Not so long,' she said. 'And how long you known him altogether?'

'Maybe five years.'

'I see. Well, Mr Nightingale, I have known him nearly thirty-five years now. So maybe listen a while, and I'll tell you a few things about Joshua Wainwright.'

Nightingale smiled and nodded. He decided he might find it interesting to have some of the blanks filled in on the billionaire man of mystery. 'Go right ahead,' he said. 'I'm a good listener.'

'Good, because so far I haven't been impressed with your talking. You know we're from Brownsville, right?' Nightingale nodded as she took a sip of coffee. 'One of the poorest cities in America, they say, though I hear things are getting better these days, what with the port expanding,' she continued.

'Yes, I think he told me once that his father ran off before he was born and his mom used to take in laundry.'

She gave a contemptuous snort. 'Took in washing? In 1982? Even in Brownsville they had washing machines. Next you'll be telling me he used to pick cotton. The man was messing with you. He likes to do that.'

'Yeah, I knew that,' lied Nightingale.

'Sure you did. Anyway, Brownsville wasn't too bad to us. I don't get back there much, probably not at all anymore since my folks died. 'On the border, by the sea' they say about it, it's the last city in the USA before you reach Mexico. My dad had a good office job at the port and mom taught Junior High, so we did okay. Josh is two years older than me, and always took care of me. We were pretty close, until he got to be sixteen. Then he changed almost overnight.'

She paused and waved at the waitress for another coffee. Nightingale had barely touched his.

'Changed how?' he asked.

'I don't know how to explain it. Up until then, he'd been a typical Brownsville kid, for good or bad. Had some friends my parents didn't approve of, there'd been the odd whisper that he'd been seen drinking, maybe taking a few small things from stores, not much of a student. But then he suddenly got a whole lot more serious, and all that kind of thing stopped.'

'What do you mean by serious?'

'He started reading a lot more, bringing home a lot of books from the library and sitting up reading them in his room. He dropped all his old friends he used to run around with, took up with some of the weirder kids at school.'

'How weird?' asked Nightingale.

'Oh not the gun-nuts or the religious ones, but maybe the Goths and the Dungeons and Dragons crowd. But then after a while, he dropped them too, and became very solitary and quiet. And he dropped me too.'

'How?'

'Well, there was no fight or anything, but we'd always been close and we shared everything. But he just seemed to close down and move away from me. Almost as if something in him had gone missing, and the warmth wasn't there anymore. And then he hit it big.'

'Hit it big?' said Nightingale, puzzled.

'He never told you? On his eighteenth birthday, as soon as it was legal, he bought a Texas lottery ticket, and won a Jackpot share. A million dollars.'

Nightingale raised his eyebrows. 'I never knew that.'

'Well, like I said, it was shared, six or seven people, I guess, so he didn't make the news, but it was big for us. He paid off my parents' mortgage, put enough in a fund to pay me through college, and then he was gone.'

'Gone?'

'Pretty much. He left High School and bought himself a place in Houston, and went into whatever it is he went into.'

'Which was?'

'I don't know, nobody did. All we know is that he made an obscene amount of money at it very quickly. If we ever asked him about it, on the rare occasions when he visited, he'd say he was in property. He must have been damned good at it. These days, I guess the money makes money for him. Funny thing, though, his name never got mentioned in any kind of deals, or business. You never see him on rich lists. You try Googling him, and it comes back with no hits.'

Nightingale nodded. 'I know he doesn't like any kind of publicity.'

'We barely see him now. He came to our wedding, sat through the service, staring into space, then went missing for the photographs. I saw him for about ten minutes, he gave me a huge cheque, but there was no warmth in him, Jack. Like I said, still that something missing from the kid I used to know.'

Nightingale thought he might be able to shed some light on what was missing, but that wasn't his choice to make. 'So you don't see much of him now?'

'Almost never. Matthew never really approved of him. He seemed to like the guy fine, but there was always a barrier of some kind between them. He calls every couple months, always asks after Naomi, but he usually seems to call when she's out. Shame, the few times she met him, she loved him.'

She took a long sip of coffee. 'Which brings us back to square one, and you. My brother sends you up here to see us out of the blue, he never visits himself, much less sends a so-called friend. What's happening, and what are you here for?'

Nightingale shook his head. 'Sorry, Sarah, I only know what I told you. I can't help you any more.'

She gave him a look that seemed to pierce right through to his soul, and Nightingale stared over her shoulder. She dropped her voice almost to a whisper.

'Funny,' she said. 'I got a bad feeling about you, like you're bringing a lot of trouble to me and my family. At the same time, I get the feeling that you're a good man, and you don't want to hurt anybody. Maybe you bringing trouble without meaning to. Maybe you making some bad decisions here. Maybe you need to give some thought about what you doing and who you doing it for, Jack Nightingale.'

Nightingale said nothing, but still couldn't meet her searching gaze, She got up, fumbled in her purse and left a ten dollar bill on the table.

'And maybe it's better I buy my own coffee,' she said, and headed for the door. 'I wouldn't want to be in your debt.'

CHAPTER 14

David Robinson turned off his iPad. He had been looking at it under his bedclothes, placed it on the floor by his bed, then swung his legs out, and headed for the door, a happy smile on his freckled young face. He walked carefully down the stairs from his bedroom, tip-toed across the hall, his Nike sneakers muffling his footsteps, and opened the front door without a sound. Once outside, he walked past the garage, then down the side of the boundary fence to where he'd hidden his bike behind a bush just after dinner. He wore his black jeans and his white 'Memphis Grizzlies' t-shirt with the bright blue bear's head on the front. It was a chilly night, but he paid no attention to the temperature, just straddled his bike and set off into the empty, moonlit street, at a steady, unhurried pace. He had plenty of time.

The journey took him just over twenty-five minutes, through side-streets and quiet suburban roads until he was close to his destination. The old building on Main Street still stood where it had for over a hundred years, though these days its original purpose was almost a sideline, with much of it converted into meeting areas and condominiums, as part of the renovation of the downtown area in which it stood. But still, twice a day, it performed the role it had been built for, and David had just ten minutes to wait.

He propped his bike up against a tall lamp in the parking lot. There was a lock hanging round the saddle, but he paid it no attention, and stood under the lamp, staring with unfocused eyes into the distance. Nobody seemed to notice him in the few minutes that he stood waiting there. Finally he saw the light moving towards him, and started to walk.

Prompt at ten pm, the City Of New Orleans train pulled into Memphis Central Station, nine and a half hours after leaving its home city, and with over ten hours and five hundred and thirty miles to go until it reached its destination in Chicago.

Every other day except this one.

This night witnesses saw the young boy in the Grizzlies tee shirt walk quietly from the parking-lot onto the platform, stop for a moment, nod at a blonde woman who stood a few yards away from him and then walk straight off the platform and under the huge grey and blue diesel locomotive as it inched its way into the station.

The train was barely moving at the time, its brakes slowing it to a halt a few moments later, but speed wasn't a factor. A hundred and thirty-four tons of metal rolled over David's body before the first passenger even had chance to scream. It took another thirty seconds before anyone pulled out a mobile phone and frantically punched 911.

The first police car arrived three minutes later.

Nobody paid any attention to Dudák, leaning back against the station wall, the blue eyes rolled up so that only the whites showed, the red flush slowly creeping up the neck. Then the eyes closed, and a muffled sigh of satisfaction escaped the closed lips.

It was good to feed.

CHAPTER 15

Nightingale's alarm was set for 7.30, but the ring tone of his mobile phone woke him a good hour earlier. The caller ID showed Kim Jarvis's mobile number. 'Jack? Kim Jarvis.'

Nightingale's voice was thick and dry with sleep and the previous night's cigarettes. 'You're up with the lark,' he said, sitting up and running a hand through his hair.

'I'm a reporter, we never sleep. Turn on the local news, WMC-TV5 or Fox-13. Then get back to me.'

She cut the connection, and Nightingale groped for the TV remote on the bedside table pointed and pressed. He found the WMC channel first and watched their outside broadcast, from what was obviously the local train station, judging by the huge blue and grey train that filled half the screen. The subtitle feed underneath the picture gave him the full story faster than the solemn female reporter's voice could hope to.

A 'so-far-unidentified male child' had fallen under the wheels of the City of New Orleans as it was pulling into Memphis Central last night, and been pronounced dead at the scene. Police were still at the station, though the paramedics had long since left with the body. There was an appeal for any witnesses who had not yet been traced and given statements to contact the Memphis Police Department.

Nightingale winced, reached for his cigarettes, remembered the hotel's no smoking policy and picked up his mobile phone instead. Before he had chance to return Kim Jarvis's call, the ringtone sounded again. This time it was Wainwright. Nightingale muted the television and pressed the answer button on the phone.

'Jack, you seen the news?' asked Wainwright.

'Watching it right now. That reporter woman called me.'

'David Robinson's name was crossed off the list at just about the time that kid hit the rails. I saw the name go, but the story took an hour or two to break over here.'

Nightingale didn't waste time asking where 'over here' might be. Wherever Wainwright was at the moment, chances were high that he'd be somewhere else inside a few hours.

'The TV news didn't give a name, Joshua. Could be a coincidence.'

'Sure it could, But it isn't. I guess it's not that easy to ID a kid, they don't carry passports or a driver's licence. And they'll be needing to contact the family first. Probably waiting for some mom to find her kid doesn't show up for breakfast and call the cops. And I'll bet my boots the lady's name will be Robinson.'

Nightingale's eyes were still on the television screen as he listened to Wainwright. The subtitles changed.

'Joshua, they're saying that witnesses saw the kid walk straight under the train. He didn't fall and there was nobody near him when it happened. This is crazy. How can somebody know in advance about a suicide?'

'I'm guessing whoever is doing this made it happen, rather than knew about it.'

Nightingale's thoughts flashed back to a few forced suicides he'd encountered in his early days of being dragged into the world of the Occult. He could think of at least two entities that could be making this happen. And if there were two, there could be many others. He'd even seen Wainwright himself use the force of his will to make people follow his orders. 'What about hypnotism, Joshua? Like you used on Judas in San Francisco?'

'That was a parlour trick compared to this. We were lucky my will was stronger than hers and I was a lot more advanced. But even so, it was all I could manage to get a little information out of her. This is in a whole different league, the control must be incredibly strong to force someone to kill themselves. The resistance to that would be huge. I doubt there's an adept in the USA who could do that, especially not at a distance.'

Maybe a Shade, thought Nightingale. Or something even more powerful. Something that already held a grudge against him, and maybe against Wainwright too.

'Jack, we may be talking about something that's not human. Or more than human.'

'A demon? An Elemental?'

'Elementals don't work that way, Jack. They're not capable of logical planning, they just feed and destroy.'

'So what might I be looking for?'

'I just have no idea. They don't write books about this stuff, or if they do, I've never read one. And I don't know anyone who has. You said there were people you might be able to talk to?'

'Could be, but I've got so little to go on. Just a list which seems to be predicting suicides, and a few dead kids. Plus it seems to be aimed at you and me. At the moment, I'm just waiting for kids to die and struggling to find a handle on this.'

'I know, Jack. But time's a-wasting. I need to call in some favours here, maybe speak to a few people who aren't that easy to contact. Could be time you did the same. I always get the feeling you have a source or two you don't talk about.'

And won't be talking about, thought Nightingale. He and Wainwright had been on the same side a few times, but Nightingale had learned not to give his trust easily. He preferred to keep his life compartmentalised as much as possible, and Wainwright didn't need to know about many areas of it.

'Okay, get back to me soon, Joshua. I know it makes no sense, but I'm starting to feel responsible for these kids.'

He cut the connection and phoned Kim Jarvis..

'Took you long enough,' she said.

She sounded irritated. 'Something came up, sorry,' he said.

'You saw the news report?'

'Sure. Is it David Robinson? Is that why you called?'

'Seems the kid rode to the station on his bike. Memphis PD ran the serial number through the National Bike registry and got a hit. They're not releasing the name till the family have been informed and had some time. But I have a source and he gave me the info.'

'So this is your dramatic pause moment? Tell me.'

'Bike's registered to a family called Robinson. They have a son called David, aged eleven. Look, Jack, I know there's a huge story in this, and I want in on it all the way. Let's do breakfast.'

'Breakfast it is,' he said. 'Name the place.'

CHAPTER 16

Dudák lay on the bed, his eyes wide open, staring into the darkness but able to see things that no human ever could. The feeling of fullness was satisfying, more so after so many centuries of emptiness. The hunger within was not the basic need to refuel that the creature sleeping on the other side of the bed would feel when it awoke. Dudák could survive infinitely with the cravings unfulfilled, but once the hunger had been re-awakened, it grew stronger by the day. And food had been plentiful lately, with the prospect of much more to come.

The creature slept fitfully now, seeming to be suffering from the dreams that plagued its kind during times of rest. Dudák had wasted no time in attempting to satisfy its needs tonight, there were more important matters to be considered, and, besides, the feeling of satisfaction inside was all-consuming and needed to be savoured.

The creature had been unhappy, complaining, but Dudák had sent it to sleep once it had completed its task. Dudák was not prone to anger, nor even irritation, and the situation would be addressed dispassionately. The creature had been useful, had performed the tasks required of it, and would continue to do so for a little while longer. But the time was fast approaching when its usefulness would be at an end, when it might become an inconvenience, and would therefore be disposed of.

Dudák would take no pleasure or satisfaction from the disposal, but nor would there be any hesitation, pity or mercy.

What needed to be done would be done, Everything had been mapped out well in advance, and there could be no deviation from the plan which had been set out for Dudák.

CHAPTER 17

Kim Jarvis's choice of breakfast venue was Brother Juniper's on Walker Avenue, a fifteen minute drive from Nightingale's hotel and a similar distance from her newspaper's office. Nightingale guessed she didn't want any of her colleagues to see them together, and was clearly taking him a lot more seriously than the previous day.

The restaurant was made of whitewashed wooden boards, with high triangular roof gables which put Nightingale in mind of a small town church. Its sign advertised the 'Best breakfast in Memphis', and, once he'd entered, it struck Nightingale as a fairly typical American diner. There were several patrons perched on stools at the wooden counter, and quite a few more sitting on plain varnished chairs around the bare wooden tables in the room. Nightingale took a seat at a table at the back, with his seat giving him a clear view of the door. He wasn't expecting trouble, but being careful had gotten to be a habit in recent months.

He'd arrived on time, and Kim Jarvis followed him in less than a minute later, scanned the room, caught his eye and headed for his table. Her long blonde hair was pulled up, and her collection of earrings was also hidden under a black-leather, peaked motorcycle-cap. Her jacket was also black and looked as if it had been borrowed from a slightly larger biker boyfriend. Her Levis were tight, blue and sported the obligatory knee-rips. Today her glasses were large, round and dark enough to hide her eyes completely. She took the chair opposite Nightingale.

'Incognito?' he asked, trying his best winning smile.

'Something like that,' she said quietly. There was no answering smile. 'You order yet?'

'Just got here,' said Nightingale, and as he spoke a waitress arrived bearing menus. She wore an apron over a white t-shirt, gave her name, Sammy, took their coffee order and left them to study the menus. Each one bore a cartoon of a friendly looking monk at the top, with his hands clasped over an ample stomach.

'What do you recommend?' he asked.

'No idea, never been here before. That was a big part of the attraction. What'll you have?'

Nightingale applied himself to the menu. It had been quite a long time since he'd needed to pass the Metropolitan Police physical exam, and it wasn't as easy to stay in shape as it had once been. Smoking and a diet of takeout would catch up with him eventually, so when he had time to think about food, he tried to keep it healthy. Or at the very least, add some healthy ingredients to the mix. Today that meant adding a bowl of oatmeal and blueberries to his order of eggs, bacon and sausage. Kim Jarvis chose scrambled tofu with vegetarian sausage, and Nightingale decided to keep his thoughts on that to himself. Sammy took the orders, flashed them a beaming smile and left them to their coffee.

Kim Jarvis kept looking around the restaurant, finally decided there was nobody there she knew or who could overhear their conversation, and spoke just above a whisper. 'You really need to tell me what's going on?' she said.

'I wish I knew.'

'There's a ten-year-old boy squashed flat by a train, and you knew about it all of twelve hours before it happened. Tell me how that's possible.'

'I told you as much as I could, pretty much all I know, yesterday.'

'Oh sure, you had some magic list given to you by some mysterious old wizard, whose name you didn't dare to mention. What's really going on here?'

'I really don't know. How much have you told the cops?'

'Nothing yet. Do you know how many psychos show up at the office every day? We humour them, just in case maybe they're the one in a thousand who actually might have a useful lead. The only people who get more of them are the cops.'

'You think I'm a psycho?'

'The jury's out on that.'

'It did occur to me that you might be a serial killer getting his kicks by sticking his nose into the investigation,' she said. 'But there is no killer at work. These aren't killings, they're suicides. The cops have solid witnesses who saw that kid walk out in front of the truck, a whole platform full of people who'll swear that David Robinson was nowhere near anyone else when he jumped in front of the train. And no evidence at all that the girl who hanged herself was pushed. And I don't see you as Mandrake the Magician, or some Jedi Knight waving your fingers in the air and persuading random kids to kill themselves.'

'Good to know. So where do we go from here.'

'Maybe you give me some kind of genuine explanation for what's going on here, and where you come into it.'

'It's complicated. I doubt you'd believe it.'

'Try me.'

The waitress arrived with their orders and they kept quiet until she had walked away.

Nightingale nodded slowly. 'Alright, maybe you are entitled to know a little bit more about this. I told you before that I was working for someone, the man who had that list, though he didn't make it.'

'Well, that's progress, at least you're admitting it's a man. Give me a name.'

'That's not happening. Not now, probably not ever. He'd be very unhappy if his name was brought into this, and he's not a man you'd want to upset.'

'So you're giving me nothing?'

Nightingale sipped his coffee. 'Maybe a little more. I told you before I'd been mixed up in some strange stuff lately. Did you ever read about the gang of Satanists that the cops claimed to have discovered operating out of a mansion in San Francisco?'

'I did. There were all kinds of crazy rumours about ritual killings, child abductions, some pretty well-known names apparently involved, though nobody seemed to know exactly who. Then the whole thing seemed to go quiet. No charges yet, no court cases, and no big stories.'

'That's the one. Well, believe me, some of those rumours were true, except they didn't go anywhere near far enough. A lot of people ended up dead, and I was involved in breaking up the ring. But it seems those involved had more power than we thought, a lot of strings got pulled. Most of them are still walking around.'

'And I'm guessing they're pretty pissed at you.'

'At me and the guy who put me onto them.'

'So they know who he is?'

'Yes, his name got involved in the whole thing.'

'So this is all about revenge?'

Nightingale realised again just how sharp Jarvis was. She had a knack for connecting the dots. 'Maybe. At the moment that's about the only theory we have.'

She leaned across the table towards him. 'But come on, if they just bear a grudge against you, why not just shoot you? It's the American way.'

Nightingale grinned. 'Yes, I'd noticed. At a guess, I'd say that just killing one or other of us isn't enough punishment. They want to destroy us psychologically before that happens. Or maybe even something worse...'

'What could be worse than driving you nuts then killing you?'

'You don't want to know.'

'Maybe not.' She used her fork to hack off a piece of vegetarian sausage. 'You said that some of the names on this list are people who are important to the two of you?'

'Yes. The last two. Whoever's doing this wants us to suffer while the names get ticked off, one by one, knowing that each one brings us closer to a personal loss.'

'So the first names are just to establish the pattern?'

'Maybe. But each name crossed off is a kid that should be alive now, a set of parents whose lives have been destroyed, and we get the burden of knowing that it's all our fault.'

She sat back in her chair. She seemed to have forgotten about her breakfast. 'But that's ridiculous, you're not the ones doing the killing.'

'But it's because of us, and what we did, that these kids are dying. You try living with that.'

'Yeah, I get that. But even if this theory of yours is true, how are they doing it? You can't just make someone kill themselves to order.'

'Seems as if you can.'

'But how?'

'If I knew that, maybe I could start figuring out a way to stop it, while there are still some people on that list left alive.'

She put a forkful of scrambled tofu into her mouth and chewed. Nightingale had never eaten tofu and never planned to. He'd read somewhere once that tofu always contained rat. It was something to do with rats being partial to soy beans. They were so partial to it that they would burrow into sacks of soy beans and then die of suffocation. The soy beans were processed into tofu and the rats along with it. Nightingale wasn't sure if the story was apocryphal or not, but he always found the irony of vegetarians eating rat meat to be amusing. It wasn't something that he would tell the reporter, obviously. At least not while she was eating. 'It's an awful lot to take in,' she said eventually. 'And an awful lot to try to believe.'

'I know. Some days I don't believe it all myself.' He shrugged. 'But now, in words of The Monkees, I'm a believer.'

She sighed. 'Okay, let's assume I take it on board. Where do we go from here?'

'I'm getting a sense of a pattern coming together here, and maybe I've got enough of one to take it to an expert I know and see if they have any ideas which could help. Meanwhile, there's something I need you to do. The next name on the list is Charmaine Wendover. It's a pretty unusual name. Maybe you could find out who she is, maybe find a way to get close to her, maybe get me close to her, so we could try to protect her.'

'Or so you could try to kill her?'

It was hard to tell if she was joking or not, so Nightingale decided to take what she'd said seriously. 'It seems I haven't entirely convinced you that I'm the good guy here.'

'Let's just say I'm keeping an open mind. At the moment the only thing connecting you to any of these deaths is that list of yours. And if it's accurate, Charmaine Wendover is due to die sometime today. Doesn't give us much time.'

'I don't think we're meant to have much time. Or to stop any of this. It's not a game, whoever's doing this has stacked the odds in their favour. I'm meant to watch it all happen and be unable to prevent any of it. Will you help?'

She nodded cautiously. 'On one condition.'

'What?'

'We can't do this one name at a time. Give me the rest of the list, I can be tracking down as many names as I can.'

It was a reasonable request, Nightingale decided, and it might help. 'Okay. Give me a pen.'

Nightingale wrote down the original eleven names on Wainwright's list in her notebook, from memory. She took it back and glanced through it, her lips counting them off.

'Eleven.' She frowned. 'But didn't you say there were thirteen?'

'I know who the last two are, and where to find them.'

'And I'm guessing you don't want me to go looking for them?'

'You guess right.'

They finished their breakfast, Nightingale paid the bill, and went back to his car as the reporter returned to her office.

Nightingale had a bad feeling about his conversation with Jarvis but it wasn't until much later that he remembered what was wrong.

CHAPTER 18

Nightingale was back in his hotel room by midday, a 'Do Not Disturb' sign on the door, and was ready to consult his favourite 'expert' in Occult matters. Her name was Alice Steadman, she was a tiny old lady who might have been anywhere between sixty and eighty, white haired and with a trick of holding her head to one side which always reminded Nightingale of a thoughtful bird. As far as most of the world was concerned, she was a harmless good-natured soul whose day-job was running the 'Wiccan Woman' store in one of the less fashionable areas of London. Nightingale knew her to be far more than just an old shopkeeper, and had referred to her on more than one occasion as an angel. Whether that was literally true, he had no idea, but he just knew that she had been of immeasurable help to him in his past dealings with Dark Magic. But only if it had suited her purpose to do so, since there had been other times when she had been unwilling, or unable, to offer him any help at all. According to what she had told him, her role was to maintain 'The Balance' whatever that might be at any given time. It was yet another concept that Nightingale had never quite grasped.

Still, since Wainwright seemed to have no ideas at the moment, Mrs Steadman would be Nightingale's first, and best, and possibly only, hope. For a variety of reasons, he rarely stored important numbers in his mobile phone, but he had quite a few of them written in his own special code on a card in his wallet, so he punched in the number of 'Wiccan Woman' and waited for it to ring.

Three minutes later, the number was still ringing and still unanswered. Nightingale checked the time and added six hours. It would be just after 6pm in London, and the shop would only just have shut. He'd always assumed that Mrs Steadman lived on the premises, but maybe she'd had an appointment. The store was the only number he had for her. If she owned a mobile phone, she'd never spoken about it, or offered him the number.

He checked the store's website on his phone, and clicked on the 'contact' section. Under the address and phone number appeared an e-mail address. He sent a fairly generic message asking Mrs Steadman to contact him as soon as possible. He didn't dare add any further information, since he had no idea whether it might be opened by her latest shop assistant.

The trouble was, he had no idea when, or even if, she might receive it, and he had no time to waste. Every minute lost was another minute closer to the death of another child, it seemed.

There was another way of contacting her. But he needed to make a few purchases first.

CHAPTER 19

Dudák stood before the creature and projected the full force of the will into its weak mind. The creature's own will was now a blank slate on which Dudák could write the necessary instructions. But they had to be precise, to cover any eventuality, so that the creature would have no room for error. Dudák spoke in the creature's own language for nearly thirty minutes, but it was the silent force of will which would compel obedience, and which ensured the words were engraved firmly on the opened mind.

At the end of that time, Dudák woke the creature from its state of trance and smiled at it. As ever, the pitiful besotted thing looked back with a mixture of worship and lust on its foolish face.

'Wow,' it said. 'Feels like I dropped off for a while there. Been a long day I guess. And still so much to do. Guess I should be going pretty soon. But maybe we might just have time for a little fun before I go? All work and no play, you know?'

Dudák had no need to glance at the clock on the wall to know that the creature was correct. There would be time.

Dudák smiled, said a few words in the creature's language, then walked to the bedroom door, holding it open for the creature to enter first. Was there perhaps some small, unsuspected grain of kindness in Dudák that was showing itself after all these centuries? Or was it just another opportunity to learn more about these creatures and their strange reactions? Or perhaps Dudák's own needs and hungers aroused some understanding of the different needs and hungers in others?

In any event, thirty minutes were available, and it would be the final time for this one.

CHAPTER 20

Nightingale lay on the bed in his hotel room and tried to relax his body totally, while keeping his mind focused on his destination. It was just after 9pm, so it was the early hours in London and Mrs Steadman would almost certainly be asleep. So far as he knew, she would have to be sleeping for the connection to be made.

The various herbs that Nightingale had bought from the Spiritual Emporium in Whitten Road were still burning in the small copper dish, and the specially-blended dark-blue candle he'd paid forty dollars for was burning nicely.

The gentle smells combined to help him drift away to sleep, as he concentrated on relaxing his body from toes up to the top of his head, all the time focusing on the image of Alice Steadman in his mind, his lips silently repeating her name.

It still seemed that he was fully awake, but gradually he began to feel himself lift from the bed, towards the ceiling of the room. He turned to look back downwards for a moment, and saw his own naked body still lying on top of the counterpane, the chest rising and falling with each shallow breath. Then he was up and through the ceiling, looking down now at the million lights of Memphis, as he passed upwards towards the uncountable light of the stars, heading for the Astral Plane.

Then the lights were gone, and a light mist surrounded him, and he felt that he had stopped rising. He could feel grass under his bare feet, and a warmth on his back as the mist cleared. He saw that he was walking across a park, towards a figure, dressed in black and sitting on a bench. He looked down, and saw that he was wearing a dark suit, and his trademark Hush Puppies.

He could see her silver hair now, and make out the loose black dress, the ribbed black tights and the black patent shoes with the gold buckles. She put her head on one side, in the familiar way, and patted the bench next to herself. 'Sit down, Jack,' she said in her soft, soothing voice. 'I heard your call, why have you summoned me?'

Nightingale sat at the far end of the bench from her. 'Long time, no see, Mrs Steadman. You're looking well.'

She smiled. 'Everyone looks well up here, Jack. We can't bring our ailments up with us. Where are you now?'

'Tennessee,' said Nightingale. 'In trouble again, and in need of your help again.'

She smiled. 'And you know I'll always help you. Now, just relax and tell me everything you know.'

Nightingale looked into her eyes and frowned. There were no pupils. No irises, just dark pools of impenetrable blackness. A feeling of dread washed over him. Something was wrong. Something was very wrong.

She seemed to sense his hesitation and smiled, except it was more of a snarl than a smile and the parting of her thin lips revealed yellow, sharpened teeth. Whoever had joined him on the Astral Plane, it wasn't Mrs Steadman.

He started to get up but as he moved his arm was clutched in a grip like steel. He looked down to see a wrinkled claw of a hand fastened on to it, the fingernails long and yellow, like the talons of a raptor. He cried out in pain, trying vainly to break the grip with his left hand. The old woman gave a hideous laugh, and Nightingale stared at her in horror. Mrs Steadman's friendly features had disappeared, and in their place were those of an even older woman, her skin paper thin and horribly lined, dark patches under her eyes, and the light of madness shining from them. She wore the same tweed overcoat and purple headscarf that he remembered from the last time he'd seen her. The pursed, bloodless lips parted, and the voice that spoke was little more than a whisper.

'Edward, Edward,' rasped the woman. 'Stay with me. Stay with me.'

Despite himself, tears sprung to Nightingale's eyes at the sight of Rebecca Keeley, the birth-mother he'd never known, and who had thought him dead until the final day of her life. 'Rebecca...Mum...stop it, let go,' he stuttered. 'I can't stay here.'

'You must Edward,' she said, using the name she'd wanted to give to the child she'd been told was stillborn. 'I lost you for so long, now stay with me. Stay for ever.' Her grip tightened on his arm.

Nightingale closed his eyes, trying desperately to focus on some kind of reality. Whatever this thing was, it couldn't be Mrs Steadman, or Rebecca Keeley, but its purpose was clear. To keep him here, until... Until what? Nightingale had no idea how long a person could remain on the Astral Plane with his body empty of its essence and consciousness. He assumed it wasn't possible indefinitely, he needed to get back. He opened his eyes wide and stared into the old, wrinkled face. 'You are not my mother,' he said, stressing every word. 'Let me go.'

He tore frantically at the clawed hand holding his arm and stood up. The figure of Rebecca Keeley shimmered and lost focus as he managed to pull his arm away. He ran back in what seemed to be the direction he'd come from. Behind him he could hear the old woman start to scream, as if she was being burned at the stake, the same anguished screaming he remembered from the first time he'd met her, a wrecked and ruined figure in a Basingstoke care home.

Nightingale kept running, though he had no idea where he was heading. He just knew he needed to get away.

'Where you off to in such a hurry, Bird-man?'

Nightingale stopped running and looked up at the huge shaven-headed black man who stood in his path. He was dressed in a blue Nike track-suit, with a grey padded jacket on top. He was also holding a Glock pistol, pointed unwaveringly at Nightingale's chest.

'T-Bone,' said Nightingale.

'In person, Bird-man. Or as much in person as anyone could be who had his guts ripped out on your account.' He grinned showing a gold tooth.

'You know that wasn't me. It was the Nine Angles, payback for their guy that you shot.'

T-Bone shook his massive head. 'That's not the way I see it, Birdman. And let's face it, it's not the way you see it either, or I wouldn't be here. It's pay-back time.' His huge finger tightened on the trigger.

'Wait, T-Bone,' shouted Nightingale, 'this won't work, it's a dream, you can't shoot me up here.'

The big man smiled, but his gun hand was rock-steady. 'You don't think so? Maybe depends what you believe. Maybe I kill you up here, maybe you die down there. Let's give it a shot, pardon the pun, Birdman. Bye.'

Nightingale hurled himself sideways and heard the explosion of the gun, then he was off and running to his left, if directions had any meaning on the Astral Plane. He heard no pounding feet behind him, it seemed T-Bone had gone, for the moment at least. He stopped running. He needed to focus, and get himself off the Astral Plane before it was too late. He'd been in contact with Mrs Steadman before on the Astral Plane but she had summoned him and she had sent him back. Now he was trapped and it seemed, someone had a strong interest in seeing that he never made it back to the sleeping shell of his body in his hotel room. He racked his memory to try to think of something, anything, he'd read or heard which could help him get back.

'You're not going back, Jack,' said Robbie Hoyle, and Nightingale spun round to face him.

'You're not Robbie,' said Nightingale, as he gazed into the pale, sad face of his dead best friend. 'You can't be.'

The figure smiled wistfully. 'Why can't I be, Jack? We're in your dream now, and you know it's your fault I'm dead.'

'Robbie, don't say that. I never meant for that to happen, you have to believe that.'

'What difference does it make what you wanted? If it hadn't been for you playing silly games with things you didn't understand, Anna wouldn't be a widow, and my kids would still have a father. It's all your fault, Jack. Why is that? Why do your family and friends always end up suffering because of you?'

Nightingale tried desperately to think of something to say, but he knew that Robbie – or whatever was pretending to be Robbie - was right. So many people close to him had died, how could it not be his fault? Sure, he hadn't intended it, and hadn't killed anyone, but the responsibility hung so heavily on him that it couldn't be pushed away.

'Robbie, I...'

'And what about us?' said a horribly familiar voice behind him.

Nightingale couldn't help himself, he had to turn round again, though he knew what he'd see.

His Uncle Tommy and Aunt Linda stood there, the way he remembered them in life, not horribly mutilated as they'd been when he'd discovered their bodies. They gazed at him, and both shook their heads reproachfully. 'It's your fault we're dead too, Jack,' said Aunt Linda. 'Torn to pieces, just so you could save your miserable soul.'

'That wasn't how it happened,' said Nightingale. 'I never even knew about my soul being pledged when I found you dead. It wasn't my fault, I couldn't have stopped it.'

Uncle Tommy shook his head again and held up a reproachful finger. 'Now you know you don't believe that, Jack. You know you blame yourself, and so you should. But now the time's come to make amends. You're to stay here, and join us. You're not going back.'

'Yes, stay with us here.'

Again Nightingale turned round and saw a young, small, Chinese woman, wagging her finger reproachfully at him.

'Amy, Amy Chen. You can't be here, you're not dead.'

She frowned at him. 'Can't I? How would you know, Nightingale? You left me behind to sort out the mess you forced me into. How was I supposed to stand alone against a coven of Satanists? And look at these children.'

There were six children standing around her now, all shaking their heads at Nightingale.

'Six of them, so far,' said Amy Chen. 'Six children, dead because of you. You need to stay with us here, you need to suffer with us.'

'No,' said Nightingale, 'I never meant...'

'Mr Nightingale. Look at me.'

Uncle Tommy and Aunt Linda were gone, there was no sign of Robbie Hoyle, Amy Chen or the children either. Just a tiny, white haired old lady, wearing a knee-length black dress over dark leggings and buttoned boots. Alice Steadman. Nightingale shook his head at her. 'You won't fool me again, whatever you are,' he said.

The old woman frowned in exasperation. 'Listen to me, Mr Nightingale, you're in terrible danger, and you must get back to your body. You should never have tried to come here by yourself, it's far too advanced and dangerous. There are people here who want to harm you, and who are using your own dreams and memories against you. They are trying to stop you from returning. Your body cannot survive for very much longer without you.'

'Why should I believe you? You're just another one of them, another ghost from my past. If you're real, send me back.'

She shook her head sharply. 'I can't do that, since I didn't summon you. Only you can do it.'

'How? Why should I trust you?'

'You have to. You need to wake. Focus on something mundane, this will sound ridiculous but...'

A mist had grown up from nowhere between Nightingale and the figure of the old woman, blocking her from his sight, and stopping him from hearing her final words clearly. All that seemed to come to him was, 'Toe...big toe.'

But that couldn't be it.

'Mrs Steadman,' shouted Nightingale. 'Come back, help me.'

He heard the sound of a dog barking in the distance, getting rapidly closer. It didn't sound at all a friendly noise, but it was impossible to tell from which direction it came, until the animal came into view, directly ahead of him, and what seemed like fifty feet away. It was a black and white collie, and Nightingale recognised it at once, though there was no sign of its owner.

'Oh no,' he said, aloud. 'Not you. Not now.'

The animal raced towards him, seeming to grow bigger as it approached, until it was almost the size of a bull. As Nightingale watched in horror, its outline shimmered, and all resemblance to a sheepdog was gone. In its place stood a creature straight from Hell, with three gigantic heads roaring threats from the huge red mouths, the long, pointed fangs ready to tear and disembowel their victim. The giant front paws reared up and the razor-sharp claws were unsheathed, as the powerful hind legs tensed to spring at him. Nightingale's skin started to burn as the creature's hot breath fell on it.

Could it have been true? Could she be trusted? Had he heard it right? Big toe? Nightingale closed his eyes, and focused all his attention on the big toe of his right foot, desperately trying to move it, just an inch or two,

The animal roared, and pounced.

CHAPTER 21

Charmaine turned off her tablet, put it back in the desk, checked that everything was ready and set off. She didn't have any trouble in sneaking out of the apartment. It was long after dark and her mother had fallen asleep on the sitting room sofa after the second bottle of wine. Mom hadn't always been this way, thought Charmaine, as she walked down the stairs, but ever since Dad had walked out on them for a younger model, she had struggled to cope, money had gotten tighter, and the pills and the wine had provided a way to numb the pain, and shorten the hours in the day when it had to be endured. Soon Mom wouldn't need to worry about having a daughter to feed, clothe and get to school.

Charmaine's expression changed as she pushed open the door to the street. A look of determination came into her eyes, her jaw set and she started on her last walk. It wouldn't be long now. She pulled the hood of her zipper jacket up over her blonde hair, feeling the small bottle in each side pocket as she did so, and feeling the larger bottle in her backpack bouncing against her spine with every step. The streets weren't too busy at this time of the evening, and nobody paid any attention to the small slim figure in black as she strode confidently towards her final destination. It was almost as if she were invisible, or under some form of protection.

She didn't have so far to walk, just over twenty minutes and she arrived in plenty of time. The gates should have been locked at sundown, but someone seemed to have neglected their duties, and she pushed them open just enough to squeeze herself through, before shutting them behind her. She walked along the paths, through the gardens, meeting no security guards along the way, until she came to the place that had been chosen for her. This too should have been locked, but, strangely, it wasn't. She pushed open the entrance door and walked unhesitatingly into the darkness. All around her was breathtaking beauty, just waiting to reflect any light that might shine, but she never saw any of it, as she made her way to the far wall and sat down.

The bottle in her left pocket had a 'child proof' cap on it, but any child capable of understanding arrows could have opened it, and she'd watched her mother do it often enough, so the darkness proved no obstacle. She put the first two pills into her mouth, then unscrewed the top of the second bottle, took a mouthful and swallowed hard. Her first ever taste of vodka should have burnt her mouth and throat, but she showed no reaction, as she repeated the process until the first pill bottle was empty. Then she started on the second. When that was finished, she poured the remaining vodka straight down her throat.

It took her very little time to die, with the sudden intake of a large amount of alcohol causing what the coroner later described as 'ventricular ectopic activity increasing electrical instability in the heart, leading to sudden cardiac arrhythmia and death.' Her body had never had chance to absorb any of the tranquillisers.

Outside, Dudák leaned against a convenient stone, feeling the energy of the child's last moments feed the hunger within. Again, the eyes rolled up until only the whites were visible, and the red flush rose up the neck and throat. It had happened much sooner than expected, but Dudák had shown enough foresight to follow the child, and be at hand to feed at any moment.

Dudák sat down behind another stone, hidden by the darkness of the moonless night, and awaited the coming of its creature, and the culminating part of the night's plan.

CHAPTER 22

Nightingale awoke with a jolt, still feeling the hot breath of the Hellhound on his skin, holding his arm across his face in a last attempt to protect himself. It took him almost a minute to realise that he was alone, in his bed at the hotel, with the big toe of his right foot still twitching in response to his desperate attempt to re-anchor himself in the world of reality. The room was in darkness, as the candle had burnt out. His phone was ringing and he picked it up. Nearly five hours had passed in the real world, whilst his trip to the Astral had seemed to last just minutes. He wondered how much longer his unoccupied body might have survived.

He focused on the caller display now, saw that it was Kim Jarvis and slid his finger across the green icon. 'Jack, where were you? I've been calling for nearly two minutes. I was getting scared that something had happened to you.'

'Call of nature, love,' said Nightingale. 'What's happened?'

'I found the girl, Jack. Simple, I just called every Wendover in the book and asked to speak to Charmaine. As soon as I got someone who asked who I was, instead of who Charmaine was, I hung up and started stake-out duty outside the apartment. She lives with her mother, Elise Wendover. I don't know how she got out of the apartment without her mother knowing but I followed her down here. She's okay so far, but God knows what she's planning, Can you get here now?'

'If I knew where 'here' was, maybe I could.'

She told him. 'Memphis Memorial Park cemetery. It's on Poplar Avenue.'

'You're joking,' said Nightingale. 'A cemetery? At night?'

'No joke, Jack. Look for the Crystal Shrine Grotto. Get here as fast as you can, I don't want to be alone down here.'

'I'll be with you as soon as the GPS can get me there.'

'You at the Peabody? Should take you twenty-five minutes.'

Nightingale made it in thirty-five minutes. He parked outside the cemetery, climbed out of the SUV and lit a cigarette as he looked around. There was no sign of Kim. The gates were unlocked, and he walked through easily enough, pushing them closed behind him. The road outside had been empty, and so was the cemetery. There was enough moonlight for him to follow the signs to the Crystal Shrine Grotto. He couldn't help noticing how well-tended the whole place was, with the flowers and trees making it feel more like a park than the English cemeteries he was used to. The place was almost completely silent, with just the occasional sound of a vehicle passing in the streets outside.

Nightingale followed a final sign that took him over a rustic wooden bridge, across a small lake, and then he stopped in front of what looked like a small part of an English castle set into rocks, with bushes behind them. A large, dark wooden door was set into the stonework, with the left part of it ajar. Nightingale took the time to read the sign outside, which told him that the Crystal Shrine Grotto was a unique cave that had been constructed eighty years earlier by a Mexican artist called Dionicio Rodriguez. Natural rock and quartz crystal collected from the Ozarks had been used to construct a background for nine scenes from the life of Christ.

No light came from inside, so Nightingale pulled his mobile phone and switched it on, then put it in flashlight mode. He pushed the door gently, to open it far enough for him to squeeze through.

The light from his phone illuminated the walls and Nightingale gasped at the beauty of the artist's work. The bland sign outside hadn't prepared him for the vast numbers of crystals in a dazzling variety of colours, which clung to the walls and ceiling as if they had all grown there. Placed around the walls were the various scenes of Jesus's life, but Nightingale barely gave them a glance, as the light shone onto the one thing there that didn't belong to this world of beauty.

'Oh, no,' he said, picking himself up from the ground and walking over to where the tiny figure sat propped up against the wall. The beam of light darted over the two medicine bottles and the empty fifth of vodka, then Nightingale bent to push back the hood, lift the hair and feel for the carotid pulse.

The temperature of the girl's neck told him at first touch that it was useless, as did the blank eyes staring at him from another world. He closed the eyelids and stood up straight, trying hard to reconcile what he was seeing with what he'd been told.

The lights went on, and Nightingale spun round, his eyes screwing themselves shut automatically, then opening, blinking, and finally focusing on the figure that stood in the doorway.

'Move away from her, go and stand over there.' The figure accompanied the words with a gesture from the gun in the left hand. Nightingale complied.

'Evening, Kim,' he said. 'You're not really dressed for this weather, are you?' He slid the phone into his pocket.

She wore a khaki exercise bra-top, and a pair of denim shorts, with desert boots on her feet, exposing the tattoos which he could now see seemed to cover every visible inch of her body below the neck. Despite himself, Nightingale couldn't help admiring the artistry of the dragons, cats, witches, cauldrons and Occult symbols, old and new. The colours were vibrant, almost pulsing, as if they were all fresh.

'Just thought you might like to see the full effect for once. And it will be only once. It's nice to let the world see too.'

'Impressive,' said Nightingale. 'Must have hurt.'

'What's a little pain, Jack? Sacrifices have to be made, as you can see.'

'If you say so.'

He took a half-step forward, but she shook her head. 'No. Back you go, or I might decide to shoot off some part of you that you'd miss. I'm very good with a gun.'

Nightingale believed her. He'd negotiated at gunpoint before, and the calm, controlled ones had always frightened him the most. They always gave the impression of having nothing to lose by firing. The excitable ones wanted an excuse not to pull the trigger. He nodded at the body of the child, propped against the wall.

'You did that? And the others?'

She laughed, more in contempt than genuine humour. 'She was dead long before I got here.'

'So who did kill her?'

'She did, all by herself.'

'Why? You expect me to believe that a ten-year-old girl would take her own life like that? What's happening here, Kim? Who's doing this?'

Again the mocking laugh. 'You've seen way too many movies, Jack. This really isn't like that. The villain isn't going to explain it all to the hero, just so he can kick the gun away and good can triumph over evil. All you need to know is that this is much bigger than you, and this is where you bow out.'

'You're not going to shoot me here in cold blood. You...'

'You'll never get away with it? Oh, come on. The last words of yours I'll ever hear, and that's the best you can do? No, I'm not going to shoot you, that would be far too easy.'

Her voice sank to a whisper. 'Bye, Dude.' She put the gun in her mouth, pulled the trigger and blew the top of her head off.

CHAPTER 23

Dudák heard the sound of the shot from inside the cave and nodded in satisfaction. It hadn't been necessary to wait by the wooden bridge after all, but there was always the possibility of the unexpected. The creature had done as instructed, and with perfect timing. Already the sirens were responding to the summons that Dudák had sent as the creature had entered the cave. There was no point in staying now. Dudák could not feed here, and an encounter with the police would be unwelcome. Dudák melted silently and swiftly into the darkness, and was half a mile away by the time the first police-car arrived.

CHAPTER 24

Nightingale took a full minute to process what he had just seen, gazing in horror at the body of the journalist, who had collapsed on the floor in a grotesque heap, the gun falling from the limp fingers. Her blood was already staining the floor of the cave. He could hear the sirens getting closer by the second. Somebody must have called the cops. What had happened had obviously been well planned and part of that plan involved the cops turning up.

If this had been London, he might have risked making a run for it, but in the United States of America, with all the cops armed, running was not a good idea. With a woman and a little girl lying dead on the floor, there might be a tendency to shoot first and ask questions afterwards. He got down on his knees, put his hands behind his neck, and waited.

The first cops arrived at the grotto two minutes after he first heard the siren.

There were two of them, both overweight, in their thirties and with the tired eyes of men who had seen everything and were no longer surprised at the way human beings treated each other. One of them went over to Kim's body while Nightingale felt a gun barrel pushed against the back of his head.

'Just keep your hands exactly where they are, Sir. Don't make any kind of move at all.'

Nightingale was impressed but not reassured by the 'sir.'

More cops came into the grotto. Someone grabbed his arms, pulled them smartly behind his back and fastened the handcuffs round his wrists.

'Just you stay right there for a while, Sir, while we see what's what here.'

Nightingale felt hands running over him, seeking a weapon that wasn't there, then removing his mobile phone, wallet, cigarettes and lighter, which was all he had in his pockets. Meanwhile, he could hear another officer calling in the suspected double homicide, announcing they had a suspect in custody and requesting backup from the Memphis Homicide Bureau.

Nightingale was pulled to his feet, and found himself facing the two patrolmen who had first entered the grotto. One was black, the other white. There were now a dozen or so cops crowded into the grotto.

The black officer looked up from examining Nightingale's wallet. 'Jack Nightingale. This you?'

Nightingale nodded. 'Yes, Sir.'

'Well now, Jack Nightingale, I am arresting you on suspicion of murder.'

'I understand.'

'I don't plan to start an interrogation, that'll be someone else's job, but I reckon I'll read you your rights anyway, make sure you've heard them.'

Nightingale had heard the set speech many times on TV shows, and once or twice in person since arriving in the USA, so he said nothing, merely answering yes when the officer asked him if he understood his rights.

Routine took over, quickly and efficiently. Homicide detectives arrived, followed swiftly by the medical officer and the CSI team. Nightingale's clothes and shoes were taken from him and he was given a paper suit and paper shoe covers to wear, before being placed in a patrol car and driven to what he assumed was the nearest police station. A desk sergeant booked him in, and he was taken to a holding cell, where the handcuffs were removed.

Nightingale sat on the bed and tried to make some sense of the last hours. It was clear that Kim Jarvis had been lying to him all along. Pretty obviously she'd been a 'forced card', pushed on him so that she could lead him wherever he was meant to go. By the look and feel of the child, she had already been dead when Jarvis had called him. As he digested that fact, he remembered something else, and mentally kicked himself for missing it the first time.

'Thirteen names,' he muttered to himself. 'She knew there were thirteen names on that list. And I'm damned sure I never told her that. So who did?'

CHAPTER 25

Nightingale sat in silence in the interview room once he'd requested permission to go outside to smoke and been refused. The woman with the light-brown skin and the navy-blue suit had also sat in silence, occasionally checking her mobile phone. Her younger white male colleague with the cheaper grey suit and red tie had just sat and drunk his coffee very slowly. Nightingale thought it must be stone-cold by now. Nobody had offered him a cup. If this had been the UK he would have been offered a drink and a sandwich and asked if he needed a social worker or a lawyer. But this wasn't the UK, this was America, the country with the world record for the number of people it had put behind bars. Two million and counting. Nightingale knew that he was going to have to tread carefully if he was going to avoid being added to the number. The paper suit he was wearing was scratching his skin but he knew there was no point in mentioning it.

They'd all been waiting twenty minutes when the door opened and a young blonde woman in a well-cut black skirt-suit was shown in. She was carrying a brown leather briefcase and a carrier bag containing clothes. She took the seat next to Nightingale.

'Pamela Hutton, Chalmers, Ketty and Douglas,' she said to the detectives. 'I understand my client was arrested last night on suspicion of murder. Who exactly is he meant to have murdered?'

She was a lawyer? Nightingale hadn't asked for a lawyer, mainly because he doubted that there was anything a lawyer could say or do that would get him out of his current predicament.

'Sergeant Bonnie Parker,' said the female cop. She nodded at her colleague. 'This is Detective Campbell. Your client was apprehended...'

'My client was NOT apprehended,' interrupted the lawyer, 'since he was not a fugitive, and had committed no crime. He was wrongfully arrested.'

Parker frowned and pursed her lips. 'I really don't think so. Your client was...discovered in a tourist attraction out of hours, along with two dead bodies. I think any judge would agree that the arresting officer had probable cause for the arrest.'

'Maybe we'll ask a judge about that soon. Is my client being charged with murder.'

Parker shifted a little in her seat, and drummed her fingers on the desk. Nightingale thought he recognised a fellow smoker, deprived of her addiction for the moment. Having been nearly seven hours without a cigarette, he knew the feeling..

'No, Ms. Hutton. He isn't,' said Parker.

'Because?'

'Because we currently have no evidence that any murder was committed.'

'So why is my client still here? Is he being charged with anything?'

'Maybe trespass. Obstructing the police.'

Hutton laughed and shook her head. 'I don't think so, my client didn't break in to the Grotto, and caused no damage. And he hasn't refused to co-operate at any stage with the police.'

'He's refused to answer questions or tell us what he was doing there.'

'Nonsense, he's merely exercised his constitutional right to silence, until such time as he'd conferred with a legal representative.'

Nightingale realised that the lawyer hadn't even looked at him since she had sat down.

'Witnesses don't have a right to withhold evidence,' said Parker.

Hutton shook her head again. 'My client was arrested on suspicion of murder, not requested to give a witness statement. Did you advise him that he was no longer under arrest?'

Nightingale was impressed with how much the lawyer knew, bearing in mind he had never spoken to the woman in his life.

Parker looked at Campbell again, who gave a small shake of his head, which the lawyer didn't miss. 'I see,' she said. 'Seems you were trying to railroad my client a little. I think we're leaving.' She nodded at Nightingale and motioned at the door the way a shepherd might instruct his dog.

'Maybe not,' said Parker. 'I can still hold him as a material witness.'

Hutton smiled again, as if this were all too easy for her. 'Material witness to what? Suicide isn't a crime, there'll be no criminal investigation here. Now, do you want to file charges for trespass, or can we leave?'

Parker knew when she was beaten, She held her hands up, and dropped the belligerent tone. 'Okay, Ms Hutton. Your client is facing no charges, but I really would like to ask him some questions. He was ap...he was discovered in the Crystal Grotto last night, along with a child who appears to have committed suicide. As you may be aware, there has been a spate of suicides of young kids over the last week, and we would love to know if they're connected in some way. And then there's the question of why a young, pretty, well-respected reporter for the Memphis Herald decided to shoot herself in the same place. Also why the gates of the cemetery and Grotto were unlocked, when the security company swear they locked them and were patrolling as normal last night, yet saw nobody enter. Any information your client might have would be very welcome.' She flashed the lawyer a sarcastic smile.

Hutton turned to look at Nightingale for the first time. He nodded. 'As a law-abiding guest in our country, Mr Nightingale is, of course, anxious to help the police in any way possible.' she said. 'But I point out that he had no sleep last night, and has not eaten for quite a while. He is currently staying at the Peabody Hotel, and has no immediate plans to leave. You may interview him there later today. Please call me first, since I shall wish to be present.'

Parker sighed. 'Very well. Could we maybe say at 3pm? Gives your client plenty of time to eat, sleep and take a bath.'

'That will be fine.'

She rose, nodding with her head at the door. Nightingale preceded her, flashing a friendly smile at Parker on the way out.

The Sergeant didn't return it.

CHAPTER 26

The carrier bag the lawyer was holding contained jeans, a shirt, socks and a pair of trainers in his size. He used the men's room to change out of his paper suit. His mobile phone, wallet, car keys and, more importantly, his cigarettes and lighter were all returned to him, and he lit up as soon as he left the police station. From the disgusted look Pamela Hutton shot him, he deduced that he'd be wasting his time offering her one. 'Thanks, ' he said. 'That was very efficient.'

She raised an eyebrow, perhaps wondering if Nightingale was being condescending, but then seemed to give him the benefit of the doubt. 'You're entirely welcome, just doing my job.'

'And the clothes were a nice touch. How did you know my shoe size?'

'I was given a full briefing, Mr Nightingale.'

'I guess you'll want to know what it was all about?'

'Not at all, Mr Nightingale. My instructions from my Senior Partner were to be present at any and all police interviews, make every effort to have you released from police custody, and provide legal advice on any question you might be asked. That's all I know, and all I need to know, it seems. Though I will say I am glad you didn't turn out to be a murder suspect.'

'Did your partner happen to mention who was paying?'

'She did not. And I didn't ask.'

Good old Joshua, thought Nightingale. Always playing his cards close to his chest. The Senior Partner would probably be on retainer to one or other of Wainwright's faceless shell companies. He wondered in how many cities around the world Wainwright could just pick up the phone and get immediate action. Probably most of them. He smiled at her. 'Can I offer you coffee? Breakfast?'

'Perhaps some other time,' she said, leaving the 'perhaps not' unsaid, but clearly implied.

'Fair enough,' said Nightingale. 'I'll pick up a cab and find my car.' She nodded.

'So,' she said, 'I'll be at the Peabody just before three.'

Nightingale gave that some thought. There seemed no danger of his being charged with anything, and it occurred to him that the detective might loosen up and perhaps give Nightingale some useful information if the formidable Ms Hutton wasn't there to approve every question and answer.

'Maybe that won't be necessary,' he said. 'Seems I'm in the clear, and I should be able to cope with giving a witness statement. Why not take the afternoon off?'

She sniffed. 'I'm a very successful and hard-working attorney, Mr Nightingale, and I plan to go as far as possible in my field. I won't be doing that by taking afternoons off. Rest assured, I shall find something to fill my time, profitably. Entirely your decision, of course, but call me if you change your mind.' She handed him a business card, spun round quickly and walked away with a clatter of heels and without a parting smile.

CHAPTER 27

Nightingale walked into the closest diner to the police station and ordered a substantial breakfast from a large, blonde woman in a gingham apron. According to the menu, it was called Stan's Café and certainly seemed a step down from Brother Juniper's yesterday, but Nightingale was too hungry to be critical.

He checked the display on his mobile phone while he waited for his order to arrive. Three missed calls from a number in London, which he recognised as the Wiccan Woman store, and three more from Wainwright. Nightingale called Wainwright and the Texan answered almost immediately. 'So, you're out?' said Wainwright.

No greeting, and no warmth in the man's voice. Seemed the stress was really getting to him now, and Nightingale couldn't wonder at that.

'I'm out. Nothing to keep me for, though they'll have some questions later.'

'Tell me,'

Nightingale ran through the events of the previous night.

'Yeah. I got some of that from the news, some of it I got from...other places. What the hell is going on, Jack?'

'Joshua, I genuinely have no idea. Apart from another name crossed off.'

'Yeah, that's right. Happened around midnight.'

'Interesting,' said Nightingale. 'The kid died a couple of hours earlier. Guess whoever's doing this didn't want me tipped off.'

'But you still have no ideas?'

'Maybe I do have the start of one. I'll be needing to make a call or two.'

'You keep saying that, Jack, but time's a-wasting here. We're running out of days.'

'And kids are running out of life.'

Wainwright's voice hardened. 'Jack, kids die every day, lots of them. They mean nothing to me. There's just one on that list who does, and you need to stop this thing before it gets to her. If you can't, maybe...'

'Maybe what, Joshua?'

'Maybe I need to find Plan B, and soon.'

'Let me know if you think of one, I need all the help I can get. I really thought Kim Jarvis might be part of the solution, turns out she was a huge part of the problem. That'll be my next stop, try to find out what kind of people she knew, who might have been controlling her.'

'Get on with it, Jack. There are only five days to go.'

'Yeah, and five kids likely to lose their lives.'

'Like I said, only one that matters.'

'Only one that matters to you,' said Nightingale, but Wainwright had already gone.

Nightingale finished his breakfast and paid. By the time he was on the street again, he'd forgotten what he'd eaten. But he had remembered that he needed to pick up his car from the cemetery. The guest information pack at the Peabody had warned him that hailing a cab on the streets of Memphis was pretty difficult, so he found and called the yellow cab number, and was picked up outside Stan's just as he was finishing a cigarette.

CHAPTER 28

Eighteen hundred miles away, the woman in the wheelchair sat at her window and watched the sun rise after another night of very little sleep and constant pain. Her tolerance to the drugs was increasing, and they were less and less effective with each night that passed. Most nights now, she didn't even try to manoeuvre her weak and broken body into bed, but just caught what sleep she could in the chair. She knew that would cause more stiffness in the leg muscles, probably lead to pressure sores soon, but she hadn't felt anything below the waist for many months now. It was the back that hurt her most, and the many operation scars, most with adhesion scar tissue growing inside them as they had healed after the extensive abdominal surgeries she'd needed. The doctors said the only remedy was to open her up again and remove them, but they would probably grow back again soon after.

What would be the point?

She turned the powered chair from the window, and drove it across to the other side of the room, where a large pine desk stood against the wall. The desktop computer with its large flat monitor screen was her real window on the world these days. She rarely left the house, apart from medical appointments, and her only human contacts were the two live-in carers and the domestic staff who cooked and cleaned for her.

She touched the mouse, with her stronger hand, the left, and the screen sprang into life. She clicked back onto the news-site from Memphis, and her pale, thin lips twisted into a smile.

'Another,' she said to the screen, 'and the slave too, though she didn't matter. There will be others. A shame he was released so quickly. I'd hoped he would be out of the way until the end. Powerful friends. But they'll be powerless to stop it.'

She read the full story, then clicked back to reports from previous days. The child who'd thrown himself under the train, the one who'd walked off the sidewalk under a truck, the one who'd hanged herself at home. The earlier ones had barely rated a mention, but they were becoming more public now, and reporters were starting to ask questions about a possible connection. Of course, they would never get near the truth. Their minds could not have comprehended it, and besides, there was so little time left to them. They were no threat.

And as for the man Nightingale, what could he do either? Just be pushed around the board like a lost pawn, always reacting to events, but never able to control or anticipate them, until it was all far too late. Until the whole plan had come to fruition, and everything had been lost.

It was a good plan, born from hatred and the overpowering need for vengeance. It had sparked into life on the first day after she had awoken, been fed and fanned into a flame during the long months of operations and recovery. It was hopeless, of course, and they had left her as a badly-patched ruin, and with little time ahead of her. But her hatred had never wavered, maybe it had even given her the strength she had needed to fight through the treatments.

She'd been left with a clear plan of action, but with no means to put it into practice. Those she could once have called on to carry it out for her unhesitatingly, never came near her now, and they would have lacked the power anyway. Her own power was horribly diminished by her ordeal, so there was only one way to get the help she needed.

She'd taken the final irrevocable step, pledged all that she had left and made the ultimate sacrifice, all for hatred. The promise had been made, the pact signed, and she knew it would be carried out. What might happen to her after that was not a consideration. Nothing mattered but the hatred and the need to destroy.

She read the latest news report from Memphis once again, then clicked on her personal diary, brought up the previous day's date, and typed in two words.

Charmaine Wendover

Then two more underneath.

Kim Jarvis.

Then she scrolled down to that day's date and again the cruel smile played over the thin lips.

Would there be another one today? How would it happen? It must be all part of the pledge she had signed, what other reason could there be for it? And how desperate must HE be getting now, watching it all happen, and slowly beginning to realise that he was powerless to stop it.

The pain suddenly shot through her, but this time she bit back the cry of anguish, and concentrated on what lay ahead. She had been promised that she would see it through till the end, and she planned to enjoy every day that was left to her.

The hatred would see her through.

CHAPTER 29

The taxi dropped Nightingale a block or so east of the cemetery, and he walked along to the side street where he'd left his car. As he approached his car from the opposite side of the road, he was pleased to see that it looked just the way he'd left it, but when he walked round to the driver's door he flinched at the sight of a black and white collie dog urinating against the front wheel. 'Oh no,' he said out loud. 'Not again.'

She stepped out from the front of the car and smiled serenely at him.

'Hello, Nightingale. Going somewhere?'

This time she'd changed her hair. The spiky fringe was gone, and her jet black locks were brushed backwards and upwards to form a halo around her young, dead-white face, She was wearing a calf-length leather coat over black leather shorts, torn, black fishnet tights and long studded black boots. Her t-shirt was black, with Born To Lose printed across it in bright red letters. Inverted crucifixes hung from her ears and there was a spiked dog collar fastened around her neck. A large silver ankh hung from the collar. The dog finished spraying Nightingale's car and walked over to lick her hand.

Nightingale could never get over her eyes. They were jet-black, the irises merging completely into the pupils, and always devoid of expression, let alone warmth. He shuddered.

'Give me a cigarette, Nightingale. Unless the American health lobby have managed to persuade you to give up.'

'Not yet,' said Nightingale. 'Catch.'

Taking out his pack, he tossed her a cigarette. It would probably have been safe to hand it to her since he hadn't actually summoned her, but who knew the rules with Hell-spawned demons, even if they did show up looking like teenage Goths. Better safe than sorry. She caught it in her left hand, gazed at it and watched it light by itself. She took a long drag then smiled at him through the smoke. 'In a hurry, are you?'

'I'm guessing you know as much about that as I do.'

She gave him an amused smile and rolled her dark eyes. 'Now what on Earth makes you say that, Nightingale?'

'I just thought I recognised one or two of your signature touches lately. What are you trying to do this time? I assume it's nothing good.'

This time she laughed. It wasn't a pleasant sound. Like someone swallowing broken glass. 'The Great Detective has been doing some detecting. And by the way, Nightingale, I do things, I don't try to do them.'

'You failed at keeping my soul. You had it and I got it back. So it's not as if your success rate is a hundred per cent, is it?'

The laugh was a little less cruel this time. 'File that under "unfinished business", I think, I had more important fish to fry at the time, and you were quite useful to me. And what are these signature touches you've been so busy detecting?'

'People keep killing themselves. You've been known to make that happen.'

Her smile was gone now, and she took a step closer to Nightingale. He flinched backwards, a pure reflex action. 'Oh yes, you know all about that don't you, Nightingale? Poor Uncle Tommy and Aunty Linda. Then that Harrison character, and your poor dear, dead dad's driver. Now what was his name...'

'Alfie Tyler,' said Nightingale. 'I've often wondered, why did you do all that? All you needed to do to take my soul was just turn up on my thirty-third birthday and collect it. Why all the dead people? Why all the warnings to put me on my guard?'

Her eyes seemed to grow bigger very quickly, until he was gazing into two huge pools of darkness that seemed to draw him in and down below their surface. 'Because I can, Nightingale. And because maybe your miserable soul isn't actually the most important thing in the known universe. Maybe it was never about you. Maybe you were just a very small cog in a very big machine.'

'And is that what's happening now? I'm being played again?'

She chuckled. 'Same old Nightingale. It always has to be about you. There are far more important things going on here. Don't get in the way any more.'

'Or what?'

'Or maybe you'll wind up as a suicide statistic too. You said it, you know it's a little talent of mine. There's a bus due along that road in four minutes. Would you like to know what it's like to walk in front of it?'

'You wouldn't. You've said before that you don't want me just dead, you want my soul.'

'Oh I do. And I plan to have it. Unless something more important comes up. As the song says, 'You can't always get what you want'.'

'Which song?'

She raised one of her thick black eyebrows. 'You don't know? Before your time, I suppose. I forget about your sort and time. As I said, Nightingale, this isn't about you, and you'd be very well advised to keep out of it. It would be a shame if you ended up dead. Or worse.'

He flashed her what he hoped was a confident smile, 'Maybe I feel lucky.'

She raised a warning finger, then put it to her black-painted lips. 'Hush now, You've got quite a long way on sheer dumb luck so far, but it can't last. You need to be very lucky every time, if you're not...'

'I can't pull out. There are children's lives at stake.'

'Ah, the old weakness, you're just a big Santa Claus, aren't you? Full of love for kiddies everywhere no matter whether they're naughty or nice. You may have noticed that seven of them are dead so far, you're not doing too well.'

Nightingale shrugged. 'I'm doing my best.'

'I'm sure that'll be a comfort to their parents. And the parents of the ones to come.'

'Why are you doing this?'

Again the mocking laugh. 'Who said I am? Maybe I just like to watch you run around in circles.'

'But you know what's happening. Help me here.'

This time the laughter seemed to come from genuine amusement. 'Oh Nightingale, you are such an infant. You persist in this idea that I'm on your side. How many people that were close to you are dead now? Why on earth would you expect me to help you? That bus is due now, shall I make you walk under it?'

Nightingale held his hands up in surrender. 'Okay, I get it, you haven't come to help.'

'Nobody will be helping you, Nightingale. You and Wainwright have danced your little jig, and now it's time to pay the piper.' She grinned. 'That's what this is about, Nightingale. Paying the piper.'

'Looks like I'll be going then.'

'You'll go when I've finished with you, and I haven't yet. Listen carefully now. I don't plan to visit Tennessee again any time soon, and I've got rather tired of being summoned whenever you think of a question. So don't do it. I'm not your personal phone-a-friend.'

'I thought the rule was that you had to come if you were summoned. You have no choice in the matter.'

'Oh we have to come when we are summoned. But the whole purpose of summoning our kind is to make a deal. There has to be something in it for us. With you, there hasn't been lately. So I'm making my own deal. You summon me to Memphis and I'll have to come. But when I go, I'll be taking someone back with me when I leave. It'll cost you a life, Nightingale. The life of someone you care about.'

'There aren't any of those left.'

She smiled cruelly and fingered the ankh that hung round her neck. 'Oh really? Not dear little Jenny? Maybe Amy Chen? Didn't Robbie Hoyle have a wife and kids? What about your long-lost sister? I'll think of someone. I mean what I say, Nightingale. Don't even think about summoning me here. If you do, you'll regret it for the rest of your short, miserable life.'

Nightingale shuddered. She was right, he was always disarmed by the harmless appearance, but beneath it lurked one of the most powerful Devils in Hell. She had told him what would happen, and he knew from experience that he needed to believe every word. He nodded.

'Looks like I'll manage without you,' he said.

'Probably not too well, is my guess. Remember, this isn't the movies. The guy in the white hat doesn't always win.'

The air around her flickered and seemed to fold in on itself, and she and the dog were gone.

Nightingale's hand was trembling as he lit a cigarette.

CHAPTER 30

Nightingale had the horrible feeling that he was back at square one again. The one source he had was now dead and had seemingly been part of whatever was happening. If Proserpine was behind it all, it could get even nastier than a bunch of dead children. But if she was orchestrating what was happening, why would she show up to warn him off? At the moment it was all far too complicated to think through, and he needed more information in a hurry.

He waited until he was back in his hotel room and had showered and changed before phoning Mrs Steadman again. A familiar precise voice answered him. 'Mr Nightingale? How good to hear from you. I'd been rather worried.'

'I'm fine, Mrs Steadman. Thank you for your concern.'

'I am so glad you got back safely from the Astral Plane. You really should never have tried anything so dangerous by yourself. It's so easy to find false visions planted in your mind, and for those who want to harm you to block your return.'

'The big toe thing worked.'

'Yes, it sounds ridiculously mundane, but focusing on a small, easily visualised piece of reality will usually work to bring someone back. You should never have tried to contact someone on the Astral by yourself, it's a very advanced technique.'

'I think I realise that now, 'said Nightingale. 'But I couldn't contact you by traditional methods.'

'No,' said Mrs Steadman. 'I am rather busy at the moment.'

She didn't elaborate, so Nightingale didn't ask. He'd long ago discovered that there was far more to Mrs Steadman than met the eye. 'Sorry,' he said, 'I'm just stuck, big-time, and I didn't know who else to ask. At least I've finally got hold of you.'

'Ask about what?' she said. 'What are you involved with now?'

He gave her a condensed version, leaving out Wainwright's name. Mrs Steadman listened in silence as he ran through what had happened to the children, and he told her about Kim Jarvis killing herself in front of him. As he spoke, he could visualise her in the back room of the store, surrounded by her Wiccan candles, crystals, pots, jars and herbs, with the kettle perhaps just boiled for her tea. He missed the warmth and welcome of that room.

But that was all in another life.

When he described that morning's visit from Proserpine, she gasped. 'Oh dear me, no, She is still pursuing you?'

'Seems so. Closer than ever this time. Seems I might be on her bad list, and so is Wai...' He choked off Joshua's name, but it was too late.

'Ah, so you are still working for him,' she said. 'I think I told you before that I didn't exactly approve of that idea. He is definitely of the Left-Hand Path, and may well not prove as good a friend as you might think. He does not have your best interests at heart. I really wish you wouldn't consort with him, Mr Nightingale.'

'Yeah, I remember you telling me that,' said Nightingale. 'At the moment he seems to be riding with the good guys. He's horribly scared for his niece. Seems she's the last name on the list.'

'And you seem rather scared yourself, Mr Nightingale, though probably not for his niece. I think there's something else that you've chosen not to tell me.'

Nightingale closed his eyes and sighed. 'Might have known I wouldn't be able to pull the wool over your eyes, Mrs Steadman,' he said. He opened his eyes again. 'You remember Sophie Underwood?'

'The little girl you lost and then saved? Of course.'

'She's the thirteenth name on the list.'

There was another gasp, and then she clicked her tongue. 'Oh dear, oh dear. It really does seem as if someone has rather a grudge against the two of you. I'm not sure that I will be able to help with this.'

'Why not? There are children at stake here, Mrs Steadman.'

'Well, yes. But again this all seems to result from something you and Mr Wainwright have done. Someone is trying to revenge themselves on you through these children. You are paying the price for interfering in someone else's activities. In a sense, they are restoring the Balance, and as I have told you before...'

'It's your job to try to keep the Balance, not disturb it.'

'Quite. But still... Do you think you could remember precisely what that awful creature Proserpine said to you? Her exact words.'

Nightingale cast his mind back, visualised the scene, then tried to put his police training back to work, and remember the conversation verbatim. When he'd finished, she was silent for a moment before asking her question slowly and carefully.

'And you're quite sure those were her words? 'You've danced your jig and now you need to pay the piper'?'

'Yes, I am.'

'And remind me of the young lady reporter's last words.'

That was much easier, and Nightingale told her everything Kim Jarvis had said in her last moments.

'Oh dear me, I really hope not. For everyone's sake.'

'What is it?'

'I may be wrong, and as I say, it isn't my place to do anything about it, I think Proserpine knows that, too, when she said there would be nobody to help you.'

'But...'

She interrupted him firmly.

'No, Mr Nightingale. I really am sorry, but I can't be of any help to you with this. It's not my place to interfere, and what happens, happens. If it is meant to be, then so it will be. But I shall watch what happens with interest.'

Nightingale tried to protest again, but it was too late, she had cut the connection. It wasn't the first time that Mrs Steadman had declined to help Nightingale, but it was still a serious setback. He was pondering his next move when the room phone rang.

'Jack Nightingale? Bonnie Parker, I'm down in the lobby. Any chance you could come down?'

'You're a little early.'

'I was just passing, thought I might save myself a little time later.'

'Just passing?' said Nightingale. He didn't believe that for one minute. 'I'll be right down.'

'Right down' might have taken a little longer than Sergeant Parker would have expected, since Nightingale took the stairs down from the twelfth floor.

Parker looked surprised to see him emerge from the stair door, rather than one of the bank of elevators. 'Did you need the exercise?' she asked.

'Nah, just don't like lifts.'

'We call them elevators. You don't look the claustrophobic type.'

'I'm not. Just don't like them.'

Parker nodded and let it pass. She'd obviously managed to find time for a change of shirt since their previous meeting, and the current one was light blue. She looked to be wearing the same suit.

'You were just passing then,' said Nightingale. 'Nothing to do with trying to talk to me before Ms Hutton showed up?'

Parker frowned at him. 'Mr Nightingale, that's an awful thing to say. You're perfectly at liberty to call her, and not say a word till she gets here.'

Nightingale grinned. 'Actually I gave her the day off. Can we go someplace where I can smoke a fag or two while we talk?' He grinned, knowing that she would pick up on the slang. Smoking a fag was what he did in the UK, to the American ear it was a criminal offence.

Parker seemed to ignore his attempt at humour and just nodded. 'Let's take a little walk to Beale Street. I'm sure a tourist like you wants to see the home of the Blues.'

'Just so long as it's home to an ashtray or two,' said Nightingale.

A stroll of a few blocks through the heart of downtown Memphis brought them to the city's most famous street, though at this time of the day it was pretty quiet. Ryan O'Rourke's Bar might have been a little too mock-Irish for Nightingale's tastes at night, with too many shamrocks and leprechauns painted on the walls, windows and menus, but it came with patio seating, his favourite Corona beer, and that all important permission to smoke. He proved his theory correct when Parker accepted one of his Marlboro to go with her coffee. 'I thought I recognised a fellow smoker,' said Nightingale.

'Not often,' said Parker. 'My husband thinks I quit.'

'Bet he doesn't.'

'Maybe not. Talking of recognising things, I smell cop on you.'

'Guilty as charged. Metropolitan Police, London. Negotiator and firearms officer.'

'Really? Most of you guys are still not armed?'

'That's right. But I'm not "you guys" anymore. I left years ago.'

'And what brings you to Memphis, Mr Nightingale? And specifically to the Memphis Park Cemetery last night to witness two suicides?'

'So much for small talk,' said Nightingale.

The detective shrugged but didn't say anything. It was an interrogator's technique around the world – leave a silence and wait for the person being questioned to fill it.

Nightingale took a long drag on his cigarette, then blew smoke upwards and watched it rise. As ever with the police, he had three choices. Tell them the plain, unvarnished truth, which they would never believe, and which would probably get him arrested or committed. Try to make up some convincing lies, which would mean trying to remember them all, improvise quickly, and hope they stood up to scrutiny. Or stick as close to the truth as possible, but not all of it, and not all at once. As cops went, Parker seemed a pretty straight kind, so Nightingale decided to try option three.

'Well, first of all, I only witnessed one suicide. The kid was dead long before I got there.'

'Charmaine Wendover. She deserves her own name.'

Nightingale nodded. 'She does. I'm sorry. Well, as I say, Charmaine was dead long before I got there.'

'You checked?'

'I did. She was cold. Probably a couple of hours before.'

'What brought you to the cemetery?'

'I drove,' he said, but the look of contempt that flashed across her face showed that she didn't appreciate his attempt at humour. 'A phone call from Kim Jarvis. We'd been working together...sort of...on the spate of kids committing suicide here in the last few days.'

'Might make sense for her, as a reporter, but what's your interest?'

'Shall we say I'm interested in the unusual? And young kids committing suicide in public is pretty unusual.'

Parker shook her head. 'That's not gonna fly, Nightingale. The Peabody says you checked in three days ago, that's a day before the Robinson boy died at the station. And two deaths isn't a spate.'

'What about Olivia Taylor, Timmy Williams, Madison Moore, Susan Johnson, Martin Brown?'

'I caught the Olivia Taylor case. Little girl hanged herself with her skipping rope from the balustrade of her parents' house. Suicide for sure. But who are the others?'

'Timmy Williams ran out under a truck while walking with his mother. Madison Moore drank drain cleaner. Susan Johnson jumped out of her apartment window, and Martin Brown cut his wrists in the bath.'

Parker pursed her lips, took a sip of her coffee and made a disgusted face. 'That's a lot of suicides.'

'And nobody connected them?'

'Why would we? Suicides generally don't connect. Yes, it's pretty unusual, but there's no suggestion anyone else was involved in the deaths, right?'

'True enough.'

'Anyway, we're wandering from the point. What made you show up in Memphis, all the way from London, in response to two kids killing themselves?'

Nightingale laughed. 'Nice try. You know full well I didn't come from London. I've been working over here for quite a while. Didn't you check my immigration status?'

'Might have. So who do you work for, and what's their interest?'

'I might take the Fifth on that one,' said Nightingale. 'Let's just say I work for some people with an interest in the unusual.'

'You have a licence to work as a Private Investigator in Tennessee?'

'I'm guessing you know the answer to that one, too.'

'You guess right. So tell me about Kim Jarvis. Where does she fit in?'

Nightingale recognised Parker's sudden switch of topic, hoping to wrong-foot him. He bought himself some time by lighting another cigarette, and signalling the waitress for two more coffees. 'Unless you're in a hurry?' he said to Parker.

'I can go one more. Not like I have a homicide to worry about.'

'So why are you here?'

'Something smells wrong, and I'm off duty until three. Now, you're doing a fine job of trying to change the subject, but tell me about Kim Jarvis.'

Nightingale grinned. Not much got past the detective. 'I barely knew her. Met her two days ago, I showed up at her office because it was her by-line on the story about Timmy Williams. When I told her about the other suicides, she seemed interested in the possibility of a connection.'

'I don't buy any of that. For a start, how did some out-of-town guy even get to hear about the other three? They would never have even made the local papers. And why would an experienced reporter try to make a connection between suicides? She'd have thought you were a nut, and sent you on your way.'

'Maybe she should have,' said Nightingale. 'Unless I wasn't telling her anything she didn't know.'

'What do you mean?'

'Well, she was pretty much on the spot when Timmy Williams stepped in front of the truck, and she knew where to find Charmaine. The stuff she fed me about following her to the Crystal Shrine was nonsense, the girl had been dead for two or three hours before Kim turned up. And why kill herself? In front of me?'

'A good question, ' said Parker. 'Why not talk me through that?'

Nightingale obliged, covering every detail as accurately as he could, but leaving out her final sentence. 'So that was it? She says "Bye Dude" and then she shot herself?'

'That was it.'

'And she wanted the world to see her tattoos. You know anything about Black Magic?'

The question came out of nowhere, and Nightingale couldn't stop his face from betraying his surprise. 'Why would you ask that?' he said.

'Maybe you didn't get a good look at them. I did. All kinds of wizards, witches and mythical creatures. Weird writing in languages nobody in our Department can read. A bunch of symbols they tell me might mean something in Occult circles...and one more little thing.'

Parker lit another cigarette to emphasise her dramatic pause. Nightingale kept quiet.

'Back of her left shoulder, there was a goat's head, and a seven pointed star.'

Nightingale kept his face as expressionless as he could. 'So?'

'Does it mean anything to you?'

'Should it? Why pick that one out?'

'Because it wasn't just another tattoo. It had been branded into her skin with some kind of hot iron.'

Nightingale gazed intently at the glowing end of his cigarette, and tried to keep his hand steady, as his memory reeled back to the nightmare that had been his final case in England. Followers of The Order Of Nine Angles often had a brand on their body of a seven-pointed star.

'Branded, eh?' he said. 'Must have hurt. Is that kind of thing common over here?'

'Not much,' said Parker. 'I've seen it used as an initiation for some street gangs, but nothing so elaborate. And yes, the ME said it would have hurt like hell. But it wasn't recent. It had been there a few years.'

Nightingale nodded. 'Anything else?'

'Not really. We found her coat and purse in her car near the cemetery. Bag had the usual stuff and in the pocket of the raincoat was a list of names. Guess who?'

'Not difficult. The dead children?'

'Got it in one, plus Charmaine Wendover, and by rights she couldn't have known she was dead until she'd left the car and gone to the Grotto. So how did she know she was dead, and how did she know the girl's name? She wasn't carrying any ID. And why did she call you forty minutes before she died? And who the Hell is Julia Smith?'

Again, Nightingale kept his face as expressionless as he could. 'Who?' he asked.

'Julia Smith,' repeated Parker. 'The list in her coat pocket. Martin Brown, Sue Johnson, Madison Moore, Olivia Taylor, Timmy Williams, David Robinson, Charmaine Wendover and Julia Smith. Seven of them are dead, all apparent suicides. So I'll ask you again, what does that list mean, and who is Julia Smith?'

'I have no idea,' said Nightingale. 'You'll find it easier than I will to locate her.'

'Oh we located her, all right. Or rather them. There are more than a dozen of them in the Memphis area and forty that we've found in

Tennessee, and that won't include all the kids, who may not be registered. People move around a lot. And even if we do find them all, so what? Do we drop by and see if they're feeling like killing themselves?'

'Might be difficult,' agreed Nightingale.

'Might be. You know, Nightingale, I get the feeling you know a whole lot more about this than you're spilling. So I'll ask you again, what brought you here, and what's linking these suicides?'

'I was sent here, as I said. The people I work for flagged up the deaths, it's the sort of thing they look for. I'm here trying to find a link, and stop it.'

'Bullshit. Maybe I should run you in again, make you tell me where you were at the time of each death.'

Nightingale shook his head. 'It'd be a waste of time, and you know it. I can prove an alibi for all of them, and even if I couldn't, so what? There's no suggestion of a crime about any of them, they've all been classed as suicide.'

'But why are they killing themselves? asked Parker. She banged her fist on the table which rattled the cups and drew a few curious glances from other patrons. She shrugged her shoulders and looked a little guilty. 'Sorry,' she said. 'But children just don't kill themselves like this. What is it, some kind of mass hysteria, or hypnosis?'

Nightingale nodded. 'You might be onto something there. Maybe ask an expert.'

'If I knew one. That's odd...'

Something over Nightingale's shoulder appeared to have caught the detective's attention. Nightingale turned around, but just saw a few people on the far sidewalk.

'What?'

'The kid in the St Richard's uniform. She's a long way away from school at this time of day.'

Nightingale saw the young black girl in the green school blazer, bright white shirt and green tie, the knee-length grey plaid skirt and the white socks. She had a school satchel on her back. He turned back to face Parker. 'You don't work as the Truant Officer as well, do you?'

Parker laughed. 'Guess not. And St Richard's girls aren't usually the truanting type. Their parents pay enough to make sure they show up all the time.'

Nightingale felt the hairs stand up on the back of his neck, and he spun round in his seat in response to the warning sign.

The little girl was standing still on the sidewalk facing Ryan O'Rourke's, staring intently across the road at them, Her satchel now on the floor at her feet, and she bent down, undid the straps, darted her hand inside and straightened up again.

'Get down!' shouted Nightingale. 'She's got a gun!'

Instantly the whole patio was in uproar, with tables being pushed over, cups and glasses hitting the floor, men shouting and a woman screaming as the patrons dived to the ground. The girl looked blankly at the scene and then started pulling the trigger. The screaming intensified, to be joined by cries of agony and yet more screaming, as it seemed some bullets found a target. Nightingale dropped and rolled behind one of the tables. The shots kept coming, and the screams grew even louder.

Now Parker was shouting. 'Put it down. Put it down kid, or I'll shoot.'

Two more shots came, this time from very close to Nightingale's head, and then no more. Just a groan, and a stream of curses from Parker. 'Police Officer,' she shouted, and got to her feet. 'Everybody stay down. Do not move.' She was holding her gun that she had pulled from a holster on her hip.

Nightingale watched her as she walked across the street to where the small crumpled figure lay on the sidewalk, blood now covering the white shirt, and spreading rapidly onto the concrete, He saw Parker bend down, touch the girl's neck, then straighten up, and throw up against a lamp-post. Nightingale took out his mobile phone and punched in 911 for an ambulance, but stopped when he saw that Parker was already calling it in on her radio. The screaming had stopped now, though the groaning and cries of pain from behind him continued, along with a rising buzz of confused voices.

Nightingale got to his feet and looked around. There were groups of people gathered round what he assumed to be the casualties, and it didn't look as if he could help much. He walked across to where Parker was still talking on her mobile phone, then bent down to look at the girl. She was clearly dead, Parker's two shots had taken her in the chest and punched big holes through vital organs. Her face was untouched, and showed no fear or pain, just a look of incredible calm.

Her satchel had fallen over on the sidewalk, and Nightingale bent down to look at it, staring at the little plastic window that held the piece of card with the name written on it, though he already knew what he'd see.

'Julia Amanda Smith,' he whispered. 'Class 4B. Suicide by cop.'

CHAPTER 31

The next two hours were an exercise in chaos, as the Memphis PD tried to deal with the situation, interview dozens of witnesses, arrange medical attention and ambulances for the wounded, while keeping one of the city's most popular tourist destinations shut and dealing with the complaints of dozens of inconvenienced citizens, bar owners and people who seemed to be trying to organise a spontaneous protest, based on the wild rumours which were no doubt circulating that the killing had been racially motivated.

Nightingale hadn't seen Bonnie Parker since the shooting, and assumed she'd been taken away from the scene in a police car as quickly as possible, to start the process of inquiry at Police headquarters. Nightingale gave a witness statement to a uniformed police sergeant, telling him everything he'd seen from the arrival of the young girl on the sidewalk opposite, up to the point where Parker had shouted her warning, fired twice, then run across to try to help the victim. He hoped that other witnesses had seen the same and would back up the story, otherwise Parker was likely to be hung out to dry. Shooting dead a ten-year-old black child on the street, in a city with an over sixty percent African-American population was not going to play well on the news, unless the full story was given quickly.

A lot of people were going to be looking for some kind of explanation, and Nightingale doubted they'd be getting one that made any sense. Random spree shooters tended to be white, male and middle-aged, except for the school and college students who suddenly snapped, who were generally white, male and younger. Black female children spraying bullets just didn't happen. Until today.

Having given his statement and contact details, Nightingale was permitted through the police cordon and started the short walk back to the Peabody. His mobile phone rang before he'd got two hundred yards. It was Wainwright. 'Jack. Julia Smith just got black-lined here. I'm hearing there's a kid shot dead on Beale Street.'

'I know, I was there. She showed up and started firing, maybe at me, maybe randomly, and a cop took her down. She shouted warnings, but the kid just kept shooting. Like she wanted someone to kill her. The name on her school bag was Julia Smith.'

'What the hell is going on? You've noticed these things are getting more and more public?'

'I had. It started off with domestic incidents, but the last three will have made the national news. Almost as if whoever is doing this is upping the ante with each one.'

'That makes sense. Nothing these people, or whatever they're using here, like more than a little fear, panic and chaos.'

'Lord of Misrule,' muttered Nightingale.

'There is that. Something else that's pretty obvious too.'

'Yeah,' said Nightingale. 'They're pulling me into it. I found the Wendover girl's body. Kim Jarvis's suicide was all for my benefit, and today this kid knew exactly where to find me. I assume she'd never fired a gun before, otherwise I might not be here now.'

'Maybe,' said Wainwright. 'Unless they want you around for the big finish, want you watching it all and knowing you can't stop it.'

'Sounds like the kind of torture that somebody with a huge grudge might enjoy,' said Nightingale.

'And remember, the grudge works on both of us.'

'Have you been able to find out anything about what's left of The Apostles?'

'Not a thing,' said Wainwright. 'They're all deep undercover. The singers aren't singing, the sportsmen all retired, the bankers quit, they're holed up in mansions behind bigger security than Trump. Not a word on Abaddon, or Margaret Romanos. No morgue or funeral home knows anything, and no medical facility received her, alive or dead.'

'But she'd fit the bill.'

'Not by herself, this kind of control would be out of her league.'

'What are you telling me, she might have set some kind of demon on these kids?'

'That could be, but I've never heard of one working this way.'

'So what do I do next?' asked Nightingale.

'What about the people you said you could ask for help?'

Nightingale didn't care to mention Proserpine, since that was something he had never fully shared with Wainwright. Also she had a serious dislike for her name being 'taken in vain' as she'd once put it. Wainwright didn't know much about Mrs Steadman either.

'They came up with nothing,' said Nightingale.

'Then you need to find the next ones on the list and stop them killing themselves.'

'Will that break the spell, if they miss a victim?'

'Who knows, they're probably making up their own rules,' said Wainwright. 'You find them, I can put security on them. I've already got my niece under guard, without telling her parents.'

'I thought you weren't going to do that?'

'I didn't think I'd have to. The game is changing, Jack, we're running out of options.'

'To be honest. I'm not sure what good security's going to do, there are any amount of ways a kid could kill itself at home, in school, in the street, long before anyone could stop it.'

'Thanks for that, Jack, makes me feel a lot better,' said Wainwright, his voice loaded with sarcasm. 'But it's all I've got at the moment. I'm gonna try a few things with some books, maybe see if I can find out if there's something evil hanging over my niece. Maybe get rid of it.'

'That's possible?'

'Who knows. Better than nothing. I'll be in touch.'

Nightingale put his phone away. He walked into the Peabody and asked for his key. The receptionist handed it over, together with an envelope containing a phone message. Nightingale tore it open. Neither the number, nor the name rang any bells, but the word Urgent got his attention, so he took out his mobile phone and called Professor Wilhelm Schiller.

The voice that answered sounded rather too young and female to be the Professor, but he was put through after listening to a little classical music for a minute or so. The Professor's voice was old and cracked with a fairly strong accent, which Nightingale supposed was German, in keeping with his guess about the name. 'Ach, Mr Nightingale. It seems it is most urgent that I speak to you. Can you come to my home this evening? Shall we say after dinner, at eight?'

'Could you tell me what it's about, Professor?'

'It is not a subject for discussion on the telephone. Shall we say that a certain lady contacted me, and suggested you were in very great need of assistance, and that I might be best placed to provide it, in the matter of the children'

'True enough, if she recommended you, then I'll certainly be there. Let me have the address.'

The Professor dictated it, and gave him directions. His home was a short drive away. 'Very well, Mr Nightingale. I will see you at eight, I hope. And please be very careful, you may be in danger.'

'When am I not?' thought Nightingale to himself as the Professor ended the call. As he headed up the endless stairs to his room for yet another change of clothes, to replace the ones he'd torn and dirtied rolling around Beale Street, he offered up his thanks to Mrs Steadman. Then realised that there was more than one 'lady' in the case, to whom the old man could have been referring. He hoped it was indeed Mrs Steadman that the Professor was referring to.

CHAPTER 32

There were times when Nightingale asked himself whether his dislike of elevators didn't provide him with too many problems, and the trip up and down to the twelfth floor of the Peabody was definitely one of them. On the other hand, it did provide him with a little extra thinking time. The result of that was deciding that he would get nowhere trying to track down the remaining children who had been marked down for death. The names were too common, and, even if he did find the right one, he couldn't hope to get near enough to protect any of them without the parents calling the cops on him. He'd have to try another angle.

The late Kim Jarvis.

He headed for the offices of the Memphis Herald again, but this time he had no name to give the girl on reception.

'I'd like to speak to someone about Kim Jarvis,' he told her. 'Is there anyone here who knew her well, had worked with her a lot, maybe a friend?'

The receptionist looked extremely suspicious. 'I'll try, I'm not sure I'll be able to find anyone to discuss her with you,' she said. 'It all came as a shock. What's your name?'

'Jack Nightingale. I'd been helping her with a story. I was with her when she died.'

The girl opened her eyes wide, then picked up a phone and pressed a number. 'Peter Mulholland? There's a guy down here says he was working with Kim and was with her when she...when she died.

Name's Nightingale. Uh-huh. Okay. Fine.' She hung up, and gave Nightingale a smile. 'Peter Mulholland will be right down. Please take a seat.'

Nightingale returned the smile. 'Thanks for your help,' he said.

Nightingale walked away from the desk and took a cursory look at one of the framed, historical Herald front pages, which hung around the walls, above the black leather sofas which he could have chosen to sit on. At the moment he was the only visitor. He hadn't read more than a couple of headlines from 1972 when the elevator doors to his left opened, and a short, fat man who looked about forty stepped out. He was wearing a dark blue suit, with the coat unbuttoned to show a large expanse of blue shirt that strained to cover his stomach. The knot of his blue and yellow striped tie was hanging around the second button of the shirt, with the collar undone. The sandy hairline seemed to start nearer the back than the front of his head now, and he seemed to be compensating by growing it as long as possible, so it fluffed upwards and outwards in loose curls. He'd grown a matching walrus moustache, which could have used a trim. He smiled at Nightingale, exhibiting some no doubt costly shining white crowns, and held out a chubby hand to Nightingale as he approached. 'Peter Mulholland,' he said. 'You knew Kim?'

'I was with her when she died, at the cemetery,' said Nightingale. 'The name's Nightingale. Jack Nightingale.'

He held out his hand and Mulholland shook it. There was very little firmness to Mulholland's grip, and Nightingale guessed he spent far more time in bars and restaurants than in gyms.

'Australian, huh?'

'English,' said Nightingale. 'Manchester, originally.'

'Sure. You know, we been trying to find you, maybe see if we could set up an interview, but the cops wouldn't even give us a name so far. And now you walk in...' He grinned, flashing his too white teeth again. 'Must be my lucky day.'

'I'm not really here to give you a story, I was just wondering if I could get some background information about Kim Jarvis.'

Mullholland pulled his lips in and frowned. 'What? Why? Are you a reporter?'

'No, I'm an investigator. There's been some strange things happening here the last few days, and Kim had been helping me to look into them, until...'

'Until she became part of the strangeness, I guess,' said Mulholland.

Nightingale nodded. 'That about sums it up.'

Mulholland rubbed the back of his neck as if trying to ease the tension there. 'Okay,' he said. 'How about we head across the street to the Three Kings, have us a drink then you can ask your questions and I'll ask mine, and we'll see who's best at getting answers.'

'Works for me,' said Nightingale, holding the door open.

The Three Kings hadn't changed since Nightingale had been in there with Kim Jarvis three days before, and the two men took a booth near the rear. Peter Mulholland ordered a Wiseacre beer and some nachos, Nightingale settled for coffee and a muffin. He hadn't eaten since breakfast, but the events of the morning had left him without much appetite. He hadn't lost his taste for nicotine, so lit a Marlboro, but Mulholland shook his head at the proffered packet.

'No thanks, I quit five months ago.'

He looked as if he were expecting Nightingale to offer congratulations, but that didn't happen. Nightingale did wonder if quitting had triggered the weight gain, but asking that didn't seem a great idea. Instead he got straight to the point. 'Had you known Kim Jarvis long?'

'I guess around three years, that's when she started here. She came in from a smaller paper in Mississippi somewhere, I think.'

Nightingale noticed he had his hand in his coat pocket quite a lot. 'Peter, it would probably be a lot easier if you just put the recorder on the table. We can always switch it off if I need to.'

Mulholland shrugged his shoulders and blushed a little, then put his digital recorder on the table between them. 'No offence,' he said. 'But I've got a living to make.'

Nightingale nodded. He could hardly expect the reporter to spend his time giving out information with nothing in it for him. 'I'm happy enough for you to have the story, just don't use my name,' he said. 'I'll tell you everything I know, but treat it as off the record.'

The reporter nodded.

'So you were on local news, same as Kim?' asked Nightingale.

'At first,' said Mulholland, and we weren't a bad team on one or two of the bigger stories, but the last year or so, I've been more desk-bound, moving into opinion pieces. But we always got on well, so I used to see quite a lot of her in and out of the office.'

Nightingale said nothing, but raised an eyebrow. Mulholland raised his hands and shook his head. 'No, no. Nothing like that. We just got on well. Had some interests in common.'

'Like what?' asked Nightingale, trying not to sound too interested.

'Well, craft beer,' said Mulholland, holding up his glass. 'Smoking, before I quit, heavy Metal music...'

Nightingale must have looked surprised. 'Yeah, I know, I don't really fit the image these days, but I still like the music, even if I don't fit into leather and denim so well. And we were both big Titans fans, saw a few games together.'

Nightingale nodded. 'That's the Memphis football team, right?'

Mulholland looked at him in mock horror. 'Wow, you really are not from around these parts. Memphis is pretty badly served for major league sports, no football or baseball teams, just the Grizzlies in the NBA. Titans are based in Nashville, which is where I'm from way back. I took her a few times when we got tickets.'

'And did you share an interest in tattoos?'

'You saw those? Nah, not my scene. I'm not big on pain, and it's kinda like wearing the same shirt every day of your life. Not that I have that many. But Kim just lived for hers. She'd have grown another couple of arms if she could, just to have more of them done.'

Nightingale forced a laugh. 'Yeah, I saw most of them. You heard she was in sports gear when...it happened?'

'Yeah, I heard that. Christ, Jack, that was the damnedest thing. She always seemed a happy enough person. What the hell would make her do that, and in the Memphis Cemetery for Christ's sake? It makes no sense.'

'Not to me either, even though I'd only known her a day or so.'

'Seriously, she wasn't the suicidal type. And the dead kid too. What's been happening with kids lately? That's about the third or fourth youngster killed themselves in the past few days. And today half the office is up on Beale, some little girl pulled a gun and started firing, till a cop shot her.'

'Yeah, I heard,' said Nightingale. He thought it best not to say that he was there when the little girl was killed.

Mulholland shook his head. 'Going to be Hell to pay for that, little black kid getting shot.'

Nightingale tried to pull the conversation back on track. 'From what I saw, a lot of Kim's tattoos were Occult themed, witches, dragons, mystic symbols. Did she take a lot of interest in that kind of thing?'

'Not that she ever talked about to me. Mostly they were kept under wraps, she wore long sleeves almost all the time. I only saw the arms now and then. Don't remember ever seeing the legs, she wasn't one for skirts. I just heard from a cop contact that they were pretty much everywhere on her.'

'Did she ever talk about a favourite one, or one with a special meaning?'

'Not that I ever heard. I know she must have had a complicated one done on her shoulder a couple of years back, because she always seemed to be rubbing it. She laughed it off when I asked though. But that was a while back.'

'Did she have family? Close friends?'

'I think her folks were dead. She never mentioned friends from outside work, maybe she liked to keep things separate. I'm pretty sure she went through a few room-mates, but I never met any.'

'Would you have a home address for her?'

Mulholland nodded. 'Guess I could give you it,' he said. 'Couple of things might persuade me. First of all, another one of these.' He held up his empty glass, and Nightingale waved at the barman and pointed at it. Mulholland smiled as the fresh drink arrived, and took a good swig. 'Second of all, how about a story for me?' He pointed at the recorder. 'Come on, Jack, let's have the full story of last night.'

'Was it only last night?' said Nightingale. 'Seems like a lifetime ago.'

He talked Mulholland through a careful selection of the events leading up to Kim Jarvis's suicide. Mulholland was silent throughout the story, but then had plenty of questions, to most of which Nightingale pled ignorance.

'So that's it? She just says "Bye, Dude" and puts the gun in her mouth?'

'That was pretty much it,' said Nightingale. 'Did you know that she owned a gun?'

'Never talked about it if she did. Fact is, I'm surprised, every time there was a big shooting on the news, she'd talk about needing to get guns off the street. Never figured she'd own one. The cops know it was hers, do they?'

'The cops didn't seem to want to share too much with me, once they accepted I hadn't killed anyone, I was out of there.'

Of course, it hadn't been quite that easy, but Nightingale figured that Mulholland had enough for a reasonable few columns, and he doubted that the reporter could tell him much more.

'So, about that address,' said Nightingale.

Mulholland took a business card from his wallet and scribbled an address on the back before handing it to Nightingale. 'I was planning on going myself,' said Mulholland. 'I'm following up the story.'

'Why don't we go together?' asked Nightingale.

Mulholland finished the last inch of his beer in one swallow, then nodded. 'Well, it looks like I'll be needing someone else to drive.'

They went out to Nightingale's car and climbed in. Nightingale put the address into the SatNav and they headed off.

'So what is it you do, Jack?' asked Mulholland, as Nightingale drove through the city.

'I guess you could just call me an investigator,' said Nightingale. ' I get called in whenever my organisation comes across something that doesn't seem right.'

'And who might they be? The FBI? CIA? The X-Men? The X-files?'

'None of the above,' said Nightingale. 'Just some people with a lot of money and a social conscience.'

Mulholland grunted, clearly not convinced, but fell silent since they had just pulled up in front of Kim Jarvis's home.

The house was bigger than Nightingale was expecting, built of brown brick and set behind a lawn that had evidently been mowed comparatively recently. It was all on one floor, and in Britain Nightingale would have called it a bungalow, but he had no idea if Americans would understand the term. The roof was high pitched and constructed in an arrangement of sideways and forward-facing triangles in grey slate. The biggest triangle, over on the left, covered a built-in double garage. The whole building looked to be relatively modern and in good repair.

'Nice place,' said Mulholland as he heaved himself onto the sidewalk. 'Maybe she had more money than just a reporter's salary.'

'You've never been to her place before?' asked Nightingale.

'I was never invited,' said the reporter.

'She ever say anything about another job, or maybe an inheritance?'

'Nope,' said Mulholland. 'She was pretty tight-lipped when it came to personal stuff.'

They walked down the path and Mulholland pressed the doorbell.

A few seconds later, they heard a female voice. 'Who is it?'

Nightingale nodded to Mulholland. 'Name's Peter Mulholland, I worked with Kim Jarvis at the Herald. Wondered if I could come in and talk for a few minutes.'

Mulholland moved towards the door and held his press-card up to the peep-hole. They heard the sound of bolts and deadlocks being unfastened.

The door opened, and the owner of the voice proved to be a slim but athletic-looking young blonde woman. Nightingale guessed she would be over twenty-five, but probably not yet thirty. Her straw-coloured hair hung in slightly messy waves down to her shoulders, and her dark blue eyes were a little red around the lids. She was wearing a long, blue UCLA sweater over some black footless leggings, and no shoes. A pretty girl, thought Nightingale, and with an air of innocence and inexperience of life about her. It looked like her room-mate's sudden death had upset her quite a bit.

Mulholland introduced himself and asked who the woman was.

'My name's Carol Goldman,' she said. 'I shared the house with Kim.'

She looked inquisitively at Nightingale. 'Jack Nightingale,' he said. 'I was with Kim when she .....' He smiled awkwardly, not wanting to finish the sentence,

She opened the door wider and invited them in. They walked by her into the entrance hall. She shut and bolted the door behind them, and showed them into a good-sized sitting room. There wasn't a great deal of furniture, and what there was of it was black and white. Two black leather chairs and a matching sofa were placed around a black wooden coffee table, with black floor lamps by the side of each one. A black wide-screen television hung on one white wall, with black bookshelves to either side of it. These were about half filled with books and magazines. Nightingale took a quick glance, the books were mainly reference books on journalism and novel-writing, the magazines dealt with writing too, but there were also plenty focusing on football, baseball, motor-cycles and tattoos. Another wall was taken up with a run of black display cabinets, but these were pretty much empty, apart from a few ornamental bowls and vases. The whole place looked as if the occupants had recently moved in. There was no music system that he could see, and no DVD player to go with the television.

Nightingale agreed with Mulholland's opinion that it looked rather more expensive than he would have expected for a junior reporter, but he supposed it could have been a rental. Carol waved them to the sofa, but remained standing herself, near the kitchen door. 'Can I get you anything?' she asked. 'Coffee? Juice? Herbal tea? Maybe a beer?'

The two men shook their heads. 'I'm good, thanks, don't want to take up more of your time than we need to,' said Mulholland.

Carol sat down on the edge of the armchair nearest them. 'So how can I help?' she asked.

'Well, first of all, please accept my sincere sympathies,' said Mulholland. 'Kim was a good friend of mine, and I'm sure you're going to miss her just as much as we all are.'

'I guess you probably knew her better than I did,' said the woman. 'Fact is, I only met her a couple months ago when I answered her ad to share the house. I'd been travelling abroad, and needed a place, and this was the first one I saw. We hit it off, I guess, but I wouldn't say I'd gotten to know her all that well. She was pretty private, and our work timetables meant we didn't see all that much of each other.'

'You're not a reporter?' asked Nightingale.

She smiled and shook her head. 'Not me, at the moment I'm just scraping by as a substitute teacher and helping out in a bar downtown from time to time. Good thing I had some savings, as my income's not what it ought to be.'

'You can't find a full-time teaching job?'

'Not yet. Fact is, I have a bachelor's degree, but not my teaching licence yet, so I can only fill in for the same vacancy for twenty days at a stretch. It's a pain, but it's the law here in Tennessee.'

Mulholland nodded, but was keen to move on. 'Kim's death came as an awful shock to us, as I said. Especially since she'd seemed perfectly normal in the days leading up to it. Had you noticed her being depressed?'

'Not at all. From what I saw of her, she seemed pretty happy. The last few days she'd said she was working on a story that might turn out quite big, though she couldn't say what it was, until it broke.'

Mulholland nodded. 'So, no reason you could think of for her to kill herself?'

'None that I saw.'

'Did she own a gun?' asked Nightingale.

'A gun? No. I don't think so. She never mentioned having one.' Carol frowned. 'Actually, I'm sure she didn't. Couple of times she'd been pretty vociferous about how much she hated them, usually set off by some story on the TV. I have no idea what she might have been doing with one, or where she got it.' She took a deep breath to steady herself. 'Do you know what happened?' she asked. 'The police didn't give me much in the way of detail.'

'I was there, when it happened,' said Nightingale.

'Please tell me,' she said, hugging a cushion to her chest.

It was about the fifth time inside twelve hours that Nightingale had needed to tell the story, so he had it off by heart now, though he again left out a detail or two, just as before. Carol Goldman listened in silence until he reached the end.

'That's awful,' she said. 'I can't believe she'd kill herself.'

'We're all in shock,' said Mulholland. 'What about you? What will you do, stay here?'

'No, I doubt if I could anyway, it's Kim's place, we just had a pretty informal arrangement where I paid rent and a share of the bills. I guess her family will own it now. There's a couple places I can go until I get somewhere settled.'

'Do you know anything about Kim's family?' asked Nightingale.

'Not really,' said Carol. 'She never talked about them, but you just sort of assume there had to be someone. I guess I'll find out soon enough.'

Nightingale got up from the sofa. 'I was wondering if I could have a little look round the place,' he said. 'Just maybe get a feel for the kind of person she was?'

'Sure,' Carol said, 'I can give you the grand tour, but I'm not sure what you'll get from it. I think she'd only just moved in before she put the ad in.'

Nightingale would have preferred to have looked round on his own, but he couldn't come up with a convincing reason why Carol should allow a stranger to wander round her home, so he followed her through the kitchen and bathroom first. Neither of them contained anything that struck him as unusual, though his experience of female bathrooms had been pretty limited recently. Everything was neatly put away, with both rooms having been very recently cleaned.

Carol indicated a closed door next to the bathroom. 'That's my room,' she said. 'I guess you don't need to see in there? It's a little messy, you know?'

Nightingale would have liked to see inside, but again couldn't come up with a convincing reason. He wasn't a cop, there hadn't been a crime, and Carol Goldman wasn't a suspect.

He smiled at her. 'No, that's fine. Maybe just Kim's room now?'

She opened the door to Kim's bedroom. The room was immaculately tidy and spotlessly clean. There was a king-size bed in the middle of the room, with a black and white striped counterpane and black pillows. A black wood drawer unit stood on either side of the plain black headboard. The bookshelves to the left and right of the window were also of black wood, looking slightly higher quality than flat pack units, but they were completely empty, no books, ornaments, magazines or CDs.

The wall opposite the bed was completely filled with black built-in wardrobes. Nightingale nodded at them. 'Do you mind?' he asked.

'Go ahead,' she said.

He opened the right-hand door, and was again surprised by how little was inside, and how immaculately organised it all was. There were half a dozen office-style suits in various dark shades, then a collection of jeans in black and denim blue, shirts and sweaters on shelves, all neatly folded, and boxes of shoes, each one with a photograph of the contents taped to the outside. The drawers at the bottom held underwear, which seemed functional rather than playful, but he didn't feel like searching through it with Carol standing behind him.

The wardrobe on the left held more casual and dressy clothes, with an emphasis on black leather, lots of pants, jackets, skirts and boots. Plus a variety of sportswear, sweatpants, t-shirts and a few more shoe-boxes, with photos of sneakers on the outside. No guns, cartridges, church candles, inverted crucifixes, black and white chickens. If Kim Jarvis had any connection to the Occult and Satanism, she hadn't brought it home with her.

Either that or someone had taken great care to remove it.

Carol showed them back into the sitting room. She looked at them, as if expecting more questions, but there were none. Nightingale looked at Mulholland and they both shrugged their shoulders. Nightingale handed the girl one of his cards, which just bore his name and a number that would be diverted to whatever mobile phone he was currently using. 'We're as puzzled by all this as you are, Carol. If you think of anything that might shed any light on it, please call me. Any time at all.'

'I will. But look, what has this all to do with the dead little kid? Seems she had no reason to kill herself either. What happened, Mr Nightingale? What caused all this? It makes no sense at all.'

Nightingale nodded. 'It's a complete mystery,' he said. 'I wish I had some ideas.'

Mulholland was already at the front door, so Nightingale followed him, and Carol let them out. Mulholland stopped at the sidewalk. 'Not sure why we bothered,' he said. 'There was hardly anything of her in the place. No music, no movies, not a photo of her or anyone else.'

'Well, seems like she hadn't long moved in,' said Nightingale.

Mulholland grunted and looked up the street. 'I think I could be done for the day,' he said. 'I can e-mail my story in. Won't be up on the site till tomorrow morning anyway. You can leave me here.'

Nightingale followed his gaze, saw Red's Bar across the street and nodded. He felt like a beer but he had an appointment with the mysterious Professor. He shook Mulholland's hand and walked away. He had no way of knowing that it would be the last time he would see the journalist alive.

CHAPTER 33

Hundreds of miles and a time-zone away, in a darkened room in what had once been a church, four large black candles were burning, one at each corner of a heavy mahogany table, which stood in the middle of a nine-pointed star, chalked on the floor. At each point of the star stood copper bowls, filled with fresh chicken's blood. In between the points of the star were brass bowls, in which precisely measured mixtures of herbs burned, giving off an acrid green smoke, which filled the room. The smoke seemed not to affect Joshua Wainwright, who stood before the table and breathed in the fumes through his nose and out again through his mouth. He was naked, except for a belt made of twisted grass around his waist, from which hung long leaves, to make a green skirt which reached down to the middle of his thighs. His torso had been painted with a reversed swastika on each breast, a five-pointed-star on his stomach and two words of power in a long dead language across his collar bones. His forehead bore two crescents, one above each eye, and executed in the same pale yellow liquid that he had used on his chest.

He pressed a button on the wall and the throbbing, insistent sound of voodoo drums filled the room. He knelt before the table, held his hands up with the fingers spread, gazed up at the giant, inverted golden crucifix which stood in its centre, and started to mouth words in the same long-dead language as he'd used to paint his collar bones. The prayer took five minutes to finish, and he repeated it twice more, his body motionless except for the movement of his lips, his eyes never wavering from the crucifix.

When the third prayer was finished, he rose from his knees, walked to the left-hand side of the table, and picked up a china bowl which held communion wafers, previously blessed by a priest. He walked to each of the burning bowls in turn, spat on a wafer, broke it in two, then threw it into the bowl. The embers of the herbs in each bowl roared into green flames as the desecrated wafers touched them. He returned the china bowl to the table, then slowly walked back to each bowl and shook drops of his own urine into them, to make the blasphemy complete.

Back at the table, he chanted a Latin phrase thirteen times, then stared intently at the small clay doll which stood in front of the crystal ball, in front of the mockery of the crucifix. It was dark and crudely made, the arms and legs just stumps, and the head a round featureless ball. With his left hand, he picked up a razor sharp copper knife, ran it along the palm of his right hand and a line of blood sprang out. He put the knife down, rubbed the blood onto the doll's head, then picked up a lock of black hair from a brass plate, and pressed it into the still-soft clay on top of the head. Finally he spoke in English.

'Lord Legba, Lady Ayida, keepers of the time to come, show me what awaits this one. Let the darkness be put aside, let the light shine for just a moment, that I might tell the fate that may await.'

He closed his fist on the doll, squeezing it into a shapeless mass with all the strength he had in his hand, feeling its essence mix with his own, as the two fates became entwined, despite the other being thousands of miles away. His eyes opened as wide as they could, the whites almost straining to their limit, as he gazed fixedly at the crystal. A pink vapour grew slowly from the bottom of the ball, and slowly filled the whole of it, then, even more slowly, began to clear.

A small figure seemed to walk across a grassy, shallow hill, at first smiling and strolling happily, but then it seemed to take fright, and started to run. Wainwright's face ran with sweat as he watched the figure run faster and faster, looking behind it in terror, A larger figure came into view, a horribly misshapen thing, shuffling along on three or maybe four legs, its skin covered in scales which shifted colour at every moment. It seemed to move very slowly, yet with each step it grew closer and closer to the small running figure. Just at the moment when it caught up with its quarry, the thing turned its face towards the watcher and roared in triumph from its ghastly toothless mouth. Simultaneously, its prey screamed a high-pitched death cry of pain and terror. The monster paused to leap, but at that instant, another figure appeared, too obscure to see features, but recognisably human. The monster lurched back in surprise, the new figure advanced...and the crystal was suddenly pitch black.

Wainwright screamed too, and swept the crystal ball off the table with one savage back-handed blow. The glass smashed into a myriad fragments, and the four black candles flickered and died, plunging the room into darkness. The beat of the drums stopped, and the room fell silent.

'Not going to happen,' Wainwright in a throaty whisper. 'Just not going to happen.'

CHAPTER 34

Peter Mulholland drained the last half-inch of his latest Wiseacre and set the glass down on the bar, next to the empty bourbon glass. The last three beers had all come with chasers, and even an experienced and weighty drinker like him had taken far too much, even though he didn't show it to the outside world. The barman nodded at him. 'Same again, buddy?'

Mulholland shook his head, pulled out a tired black leather billfold and counted out enough money for his tab and a decent tip. 'I'm done,' he said, 'Been a bad day, not sure that all those drinks were the best idea, but I didn't have a better one.'

'Sorry to hear that,' said the barman, his face not showing much sorrow at all.

'Yeah, lost a good friend. Makes no sense.'

'Life rarely does. But I'm sorry to hear about your friend.'

'You probably already heard,' said Mulholland. 'Kim Jarvis. At the Crystal Grotto.'

'Shit yeah, I did hear. The damnedest thing.'

'Yeah, 'said Mulholland, 'the damnedest thing is right. She blew her own brains out. Why would a person do that?'

The barman shrugged. 'Want I should call you a cab, buddy?'

'Nah, I'll walk a while, maybe clear my head, then I'll call one when I'm done walking.'

Mulholland tapped his pockets to check he had his phone, wallet and cigarettes, then remembered he didn't smoke anymore. Old habits died hard. He slithered off his stool, wobbled to the door, then wandered unsteadily out onto the street, turned left and started walking in the direction of his apartment.

Across the street, the watcher stood in the shadow of a closed shop doorway. The wait would have seemed a long one to anyone else, but time in this place meant nothing. The vigil and what was to follow were probably unnecessary, even Nightingale didn't know the importance of what he had learned, and this fat creature much less so, but there was just a chance that the story might be printed and strike a chord with someone who might understand. Even then, there would be little chance of the arrangements being interfered with. But it was important to deal with what could happen, rather than what was likely.

Mulholland shuffled on, his eyes barely registering the street names, until he arrived at a crosswalk. The red DON'T WALK glared at him, and he stood unsteadily on the sidewalk, until the green WALK flashed on. He had taken three steps before the watcher stared hard at the signal, and it turned back to red, but Mulholland was too intent on placing his feet in front of each other to notice. He had taken another two paces before the watcher called to him.

'Hey Peter, got a light?'

The reporter span round, a puzzled look on his face and he took a half-step back before the dark blue SUV drove through the green light at 30mph and killed him.

The driver was a woman coming home from her yoga class, stone-cold sober, whereas Mulholland was three times over the driving limit. The CCTV showed he'd crossed against a red signal. The woman told police she thought she'd seen someone standing on the sidewalk, near the signal on the opposite side of the road from Mulholland, but no witness ever came forward, and the CCTV showed nothing.

The woman was told a few days later that she would face no charges, the drunken pedestrian had been at fault. Sometimes accidents happened and people died. It was the way of the world.

CHAPTER 35

Nightingale checked the clock on the dash of the car, which showed he was five minutes early for his appointment with Professor Schiller as he parked outside the address he had been given. The house stood back from the street, behind a large and well-tended lawn, with equally well-kept flower beds on both sides. The gravelled driveway led to a large garage, and then continued round to the house itself. Unlike a lot of the properties he'd seen in Memphis, this one was two stories high, the first floor being made of red brick, and the upper floor clad in the same white planking he'd seen at Brother Juniper's restaurant. It looked to be a decent-sized house in a fairly desirable area, but it didn't speak of any great wealth. Nightingale had no idea of what a professor might earn, but it seemed it didn't run to a mansion.

He walked up the drive, but didn't need to ring the bell as the door was opened for him before he reached it. His arrival had obviously been noted. A dumpy, middle-aged woman in a black dress stood on the doorstep. She had chin-length blonde hair that wasn't her original colour, judging by the darker strip at her centre parting. She wore brown-framed spectacles with tinted lenses so Nightingale couldn't see her eyes. Her lips were painted bright red, probably too young a shade for her, and there were stray grains of powder in the wrinkles on her face.

Then she smiled, and Nightingale warmed to her. It gave her the look of a benevolent grandmother, ready to dispense candy to her little ones.

'What name, please?' she asked.

Her accent seemed to match what Nightingale had heard of the professor on the phone. 'Jack Nightingale. Professor Schiller is expecting me.'

'Please come in. May I take your coat?'

'No thank you,' said Nightingale. 'I'll keep it with me.'

She nodded her head again, as if agreeing that it was a wise choice. 'Very good. This way please, my husband is in his study.'

Mrs Schiller led Nightingale down a wood-panelled hall, towards the back of the house. The place looked like the viewing room of an auction-house, with a plethora of antique tables, chests, bookshelves and stands, most of them filled with historical pieces that looked as if they dated back centuries. Wood carvings and bronze figurines stood next to plates, china ornaments and thick old books. Nightingale was no expert, but the majority struck him as of European origin, there was no American work to be seen.

The house seemed larger inside than it had appeared from the street, and there were several rooms opening off the corridor. Nightingale had a glimpse of a sitting room and dining room through open doors, as the woman continued smartly down the hallway, with him following two steps behind.

She stopped at the last door on the left, a sturdy piece in old oak, with a black metal key plate and a large dark wooden doorknob. She knocked and waited.

'It used to be he didn't like to be disturbed while he was writing,' she said with a conspiratorial smile. 'These days, it's to wake him up if he's sleeping. He often drops off after dinner.'

There was a short pause, before a voice spoke through the door. 'Herein.'

Mrs Schiller turned the knob, pushed the door open, then stood aside to usher Nightingale into the room. 'Willi, here is your visitor, Mr Nightingale,' she said.

Nightingale stepped through the doorway, and the woman shut it behind him. He gazed round the large room. It seemed like a continuation of the corridor, with antique objects everywhere, with yet more tables, stands and cases to hold and support them all. Every inch of wall-space was devoted to bookshelves, from floor to ceiling, and every space on them was filled with endless volumes, ranging from obvious modern printings to hand-bound works which must have been many centuries old. Nightingale noticed that quite a few titles were in German. The floor was covered in a deep-pile red carpet, which stretched from wall to wall. At one end were French windows, leading out onto a back garden. At the other end of the room were two large square windows with red curtains drawn across them.

Nightingale's eyes finished their tour of the room, and settled on the huge mahogany desk that dominated the far end of the room. It was also covered in figurines, bowls and small plates, and piles of papers. In the middle of it all stood a computer keyboard and monitor. Behind the desk, in a leather chair, sat a thin old man, patiently waiting for Nightingale to finish his inspection. He must have been well over eighty, his thin face heavily lined, and his hands covered in prominent blue veins. He seemed to have modelled the style for his wild, white hair on the late Albert Einstein, though there was no matching moustache. His eyes were blue and watery, but stared at Nightingale with a fierce intelligence, through gold half-moon spectacles.

'So, Jack Nightingale,' he said, in his reedy, heavily accented voice. 'I am Willi Schiller. You will forgive me not getting up or shaking hands, but I suffer with arthritis, so the fewer movements I need to make, the better.'

'No problem, Professor.'

'I don't suppose you speak German?'

'I'm sorry, no.' Nightingale was about to make a joke about not needing to seeing as how England won the war, but realised that not everyone appreciated his sense of humour so he just shrugged.

'Never mind,' said the Professor. He waved Nightingale to a seat in front of the desk. It looked too modern for the room, so Nightingale assumed it had been brought in and placed there in anticipation of his visit.

'So where do you teach, Professor?' asked Nightingale as he sat down.

'Hah,' said Schiller, 'I am actually an Emeritus Professor of the University of Memphis now. Too old to be teaching now, though they still keep an office for me for the rare occasions I care to use it. These days I keep busy giving talks in schools about the Holocaust. Make sure it's never forgotten.'

Nightingale nodded. 'So "Emeritus" means you've retired?'

'Indeed. A very polite way of saying "Put out to grass". Still, forty years were enough.'

'And what did you specialise in?'

'Medieval German History, with a sideline in traditional folklore, myths, legends and old religious beliefs.'

'You're from Germany originally?'

'Of course, my family escaped in 1935, when I was just a child. As you might imagine, many of my relatives died in those dreadful times, and I have never wished to return. There were many invitations to conferences, and symposia, but I refused them all. I am proud to be American, even though my accent places me firmly in Europe. My parents always spoke German at home.'

Nightingale nodded. At any other time, he'd have been pleased to hear the Professor's life story, but there was a clock ticking in his head, and he had no time to waste. 'So you studied German History?'

'Indeed so. I am fascinated with the history of my Fatherland, but not its descent during modern times.'

'You mentioned myths and legends?'

'Indeed so, I am an expert on the old beliefs, I even know some who still practise them.'

'You mean witchcraft?'

'Pah. It is one word for it. Traditional beliefs, folk remedies, witchcraft, mostly it was harmless old women making potions. Legends of creatures from the mountains and forests. Fairy stories to be told to children. The same as you might find throughout Europe many centuries ago.'

'But not always?'

The Professor was silent. He opened the top drawer of his desk, and took out an old Meerschaum pipe, richly carved and yellowed with years of use, and began to fill it with tobacco from a wooden box on his desk. 'You wish to smoke?'

Nightingale needed no second invitation and lit a Marlboro. The Professor finished loading the pipe, lit it with a match from a stand on his desk, and drew deeply on it. 'My wife says smoking is very bad for me,' he said, 'But at eighty-seven I think I know enough to make my own decisions. Just getting to eighty-seven shows it can't be all that dangerous.' He coughed heavily, to prove his point, and fixed his blue eyes on Nightingale through the cloud of blue smoke. 'I suspect you are a man in a hurry, Mr Nightingale, and have no time to waste on an old man's stories.'

Nightingale nodded. 'I wouldn't have put it quite like that, I'd be very interested to chat some other time, but, as you say, time is pressing. I've been here four days, and I'm still pretty much in the dark. Any light you could shine would be gratefully received.'

The Professor blew more smoke. Nightingale felt his eyes prickle. Whatever was in the pipe was strong stuff. 'Let us put our playing cards on the table, Mr Nightingale,' he said eventually. 'I am not a practitioner, of the Dark Arts, nor even of their whiter variants, but I have amassed a considerable knowledge of their use in Europe, and of the beliefs which underpin them. It was suggested to me that my knowledge may be of help to you, in your current predicament. The lady who contacted me, suggested that it is a very serious matter. It would be best if you were to be completely frank, DO not fear that I shall think you mad, I too have seen things which defy rational explanation.'

'So, Mrs...'

The Professor cut him off with an upraised hand. 'No. We will mention no names, please. Not even here where we seem to be alone. What is it the proverb says, "Least said, soonest repaired", is that not correct?'

Nightingale nodded. 'Then I'll be as brief as I can. I've been working for someone who certainly is a practitioner of what you call the Dark Arts, though, as far as I know, he only uses them for his own knowledge and enrichment, he doesn't do much harm.'

'Hah,' scoffed the Professor, 'that is just what he would want you to think.'

'Maybe,' said Nightingale. 'He's been anxious in the past to stop some people using the Occult to bring harm to the world, to prevent them exposing things that should be kept hidden, to ensure they don't gain too much power.'

'He will have made enemies. So will you, if you are his cats-paw.'

'Well, I wouldn't have chosen that term, I prefer to think of myself as an assistant. '

The Professor slapped his hand down on the desk. 'Cats-paw. For a foolish vigilante. Such people are dangerous, and will make dangerous enemies. Proceed to the current situation. It deals with children, no?'

'Yes. As you said, it appears that we've made some pretty powerful enemies. A few days ago, he received a list...'

The old man sat in silence while Nightingale related the story of the cursed list, his only movements being to nod his head, puff out more clouds of smoke, and occasionally widen his eyes in astonishment or horror. Nightingale was now running through the list of children, and their suicides, when Schiller interrupted him. 'Excuse me, there is not the possibility, however slight, that these children could have been murdered?'

'Seems not, The police have called them all suicide, and I'm inclined to agree, seems no way they could be anything else. Well, except Julia Smith this morning, she was clearly shot by a cop, but she'd worked very hard to bring that situation about.'

'A policeman shot her?'

'A policewoman. A detective. But she had no choice. The child was holding a gun and could have killed a lot of people. It was what the media calls "suicide by cop", where someone wants to die but gets the authorities to do the dirty deed.'

The Professor nodded. 'This seems very bad, but so far, it is just what you might call the hors d'oeuvre, no? The main course of the feast is yet to come.'

'It seems that way. I doubt my boss would even have noticed this happening at all if someone, or something, hadn't gone to a lot of trouble to bring it to his attention. The last two names on the list are plainly directed at him and me, they're people we care about, and it was obvious that we would put our heads above the parapet to save them.'

'But this is so complicated, children killing themselves, magical lists, just to bring you here. If someone has a grudge against you and your principal, why not just shoot you? Or slit your throat? Or put poison in your morning coffee? There are much simpler ways to get revenge, no?'

'Maybe whoever is behind this can't arrange that. But more likely, just killing us isn't enough. Maybe they need to put us through Hell before we die. Or maybe...'

He paused, blew a smoke ring and watched it widen out as it drifted upwards.

'Maybe what?' asked the Professor.

'Maybe they want to back us into a situation where we'll offer them something even more important than our lives for the kids to be spared.'

The Professor peered at Nightingale over the top of his spectacles. 'Such as what?'

'Souls are currency in certain circles.'

'So they might think you would sacrifice your own soul to save a child?'

'They might.'

'And what about your principal? Would he too make such a bargain?'

'I'm not sure. I'm also not sure if he's in a position to offer it.'

Nightingale remembered the one occasion that he'd asked Wainwright direct if he'd made a pact with a Devil, exchanged his soul for his huge wealth and influence. 'That's not something you ever ask someone,' had been Wainwright's response.

The Professor put his pipe down on a small ivory stand next to the computer monitor, and pressed his fingers together. He closed his eyes for a few seconds, then opened them suddenly and stared into space, past Nightingale's shoulder, as if he could see something there.

'But surely,' he said, 'if they wished such a bargain, it would be simpler to threaten the children directly, rather than arrange this complicated system of suicides?'

'Maybe, or maybe they want to prolong the agony, make us suffer.'

'Why should you be suffering at the death of strangers?'

'Maybe because they know I've always felt sympathy for children in danger.'

The Professor stared at him with watery eyes. 'And can you honestly say you are terribly upset by these recent suicides?'

Nightingale took another pause. 'No, not really upset, or hurt. I have no connection to them, I never knew any of them alive. Except the last two. Those two are personal. But personal or not, I need to stop them from dying. I need to put a stop to whatever is happening.'

The Professor picked up his pipe again, inhaled deeply and let out more smoke. 'What if the deaths of these children serve a purpose in themselves, apart from prolonging your discomfort and assuring you that they are serious?'

'What other sort of purpose might the deaths of innocent children serve?'

'Let me give that some thought,' said the Professor. 'In the meantime, you have more to tell me, I think. About the suicide and the visit you had from the demon who calls herself Proserpine.'

It was clear that he had been well briefed so Nightingale held nothing back from the Professor. He told him everything about Kim Jarvis's suicide and the police discovery of the brand of the Nine Angles on her shoulder.

'You have come across this brand before?' asked the Professor. 'You know what it signifies?'

Nightingale had no wish to recap on his various encounters with the Order of The Nine Angles, which had been the final reason for his faking his own death and leaving England, so he just nodded. 'Yes, I do. And I know it ties her in with the visitation I had from Proserpine.'

'Tell me everything the demon said.'

Nightingale gave him a verbatim account of the encounter with Proserpine.

'She would not use words idly,' said the Professor. 'She said you had both danced your jig, and now it was time to pay the piper?'

'Exactly.'

'I see. And now, to go back to the reporter. Tell me again what she said before she killed herself.'

'She said "Bye, Dude" and then she pulled the trigger.'

'Hmm. This is sometimes how the young people address each other. Though, perhaps an odd choice of word to an Englishman in the last seconds of her life. Unless she was not addressing you.'

Nightingale was puzzled by that. 'I was the only one there.'

'Maybe.'

The Professor pulled off his glasses and stared straight into Nightingale's eyes. 'Think hard now, think, remember. Is it possible she did not say "Dude". Is it possible she said "Dudák'? What do you think? Is that a possibility?'

Nightingale felt the hairs on his neck rise again, for no reason that he could have given. 'Maybe,' he said. 'But who or what is "Dudák"? It's not a word I'm familiar with.'

The Professor replaced his gold glasses on his nose, and leaned back in his chair. 'My friend,' he said. 'What do you know of Hameln?

CHAPTER 36

A thousand miles away, the Gulfstream had been cleared for take-off and Joshua Wainwright sat back in his white leather seat, fastened his seat-belt and stubbed out his cigar as the plane prepared to race down the runway. Amanda was strapped into her seat in the rear of the cabin. With the exception of the two pilots, they were the only people on board that night.

Wainwright was on his mobile phone as the plane's wheels left the ground. 'Any report from the security team outside the house? Nothing? I guess that's good. No, no new instructions and I know it's tough not being more specific. Just keep the car outside her house, and two teams to follow the little girl everywhere she goes. The trackers are on both cars, no? No, no need to follow either of the adults, like I said, unless the girl's with them. Don't let anything happen to her, and watch her like a hawk. And don't get seen. Yeah, I know it's impossible, but just get it done.'

He cut the connection and instantly dialled another number.

'I'm on my way. No, he doesn't know. Yes, for sure. Very pissed, but it's not his call any more. No, I don't think he's got that far yet. How could he? I can't stay away, I know what I saw, and I think I know what it means. Get everything ready, I may need you, and it, at no notice at all. Don't let me down on this.'

Again he cut the connection, again he dialled a new number straight away. 'Valerie? Coming in as discussed. The hire car will be ready for pick-up in the name I gave you? Yeah, I got the licence and credit cards. And I'm booked in at the Crowne Plaza in the same name. Nothing fancy, just a room. Nah, I don't know why I'm bothering to call really, when did you ever forget anything? But this is just so damn important.'

This time he put the mobile phone back in the pocket of his jacket, picked up the half-smoked cigar, relit it and smoked for a while. Amanda brought him a large Glenfiddich, which he managed to make last for thirty minutes. He looked at his watch and figured he had two hours before landing, so closed his eyes and willed himself asleep.

It might be his last chance to rest for quite a while.

CHAPTER 37

'Hameln?' repeated Nightingale. 'Nothing at all, who, or what is it?'

'It is a "what", a place,' said the Professor. A small town of fifty thousand people in what is now the Lower Saxony region of Germany. Famous for only one thing in its entire history. The Rat-Catcher.'

Nightingale frowned. 'Hameln? I thought it was Hamelin.'

'Trust me, my friend, I know how to pronounce it.'

'Tomato, potato,' said Nightingale, but it was clear from the look of confusion on the Professor's face that he had no idea what he was talking about. Nightingale shrugged. 'So you're talking about the pied piper?'

'Indeed.'

'But that's ridiculous, it's a myth, a fairy story.'

The Professor shook his head. 'There are many things in history which now have the status of myths, legends or fairy stories,' he said. 'Some of them are just that. But in other cases, the legend has grown up to hide an appalling truth. It is so in this case. Tell me what you know of the story.'

'Same as everyone else, I suppose,' said Nightingale. 'The town was overrun with rats, the townsfolk had no answer, when along came this bloke to offer to get rid of all the rats for a purse of gold or something. He played his magic pipe, the rats all followed him and ran into the river. The townspeople welched on paying him, so this time he played a different tune and all the town children followed him into a cave or something, and were never seen again.'

'Indeed so. Now, focus on the main point of the story. What actually happened?'

'The kids followed him, did what he wanted. And they were never seen again.'

'Where do you think they all are now, Mr Nightingale? Playing happily in Paradise?'

'I suppose they're all dead, aren't they?'

'They are. And they died because Dudák wished them to be dead. And then he fed from them.'

CHAPTER 38

Sarah and Matthew Fisher watched in horror as the news bulletin showed the CCTV footage of the shooting in Beale Street that morning. The scene was total confusion, chairs and tables overturned, customers diving for some sort of cover, all played out in silence, apart from the commentary by the reporter over the top. 'The latest casualty figures are three dead, including the shooter, and two wounded, one seriously. Police have not released names of those killed or injured at the moment. Witnesses say that the shooter was wearing a school uniform, and appeared to be quite young. Police have stated that the shooter was shot and killed by a plain-clothes police officer, after ignoring several warnings to drop the weapon. The name of the officer has not been released. Representatives of Black Lives Matter have met with the police and the Mayor's office, but have released no statement so far. The Mayor has appealed for people to stay calm. On Beale Street, flowers have been left at the scene of the shooting.'

The picture showed scenes of two men walking towards the small body on the sidewalk, and then cut out. The scene changed to a report from a woman in the street outside Memphis City Hall, covering an upcoming special election, and Sarah pressed the mute switch. She looked across at her husband, at the other end of the sofa.

'You saw him too, didn't you?' she said to her husband.

He nodded. 'It certainly looked like him,' he said.

'It was him. Same raincoat, same haircut, same old shoes. Nightingale, the man who was here three days ago. The one who seemed so interested in Naomi.'

'Oh, that's pushing it a little far, honey. The man was barely here twenty minutes, just a friend of your brother's, a quick social call. And Naomi liked him, she was the one who wanted to show him her room.'

'Oh, I'm not saying he's a danger to her, he seemed perfectly nice. But you know what people are saying about this morning's shooting?'

'What's the word on the street, honey?' asked Matthew with a smile.

'Time and a place for humour, this ain't it,' she said dismissively. 'People are saying the shooter was a kid in a St Richard's uniform. Naomi's school. And Naomi says one of the girls in her class was missing after morning recess. Julia Smith, you know, Councilman Smith's daughter.'

'Oh, come on, Sarah. That's a pretty big leap, and it's all just gossip. Ten-year-old girls at private schools don't suddenly turn themselves into spree killers.'

'No,' said his wife, 'I'll grant you that's not normal. But there've been a few kids that age not exactly acting normal in Memphis these last few days. Look at that boy who cycled all the way to the train station just to walk under the train. And the kid who killed herself in the Crystal Grotto. And now this.'

'If it happened that way.'

'It happened that way. And that English guy was right there. And he's a friend of Joshua.'

'Why would that be a bad thing? What would Joshua or his friend know about kids in Tennessee?'

'Well, nothing I guess. But, you know, you've never exactly been a fan of Joshua.'

Matthew Fisher held up his hands in protest. 'Now, honey, you know that's not true. I've got nothing against your brother. Fact is, we wouldn't be in this house now without that generous wedding gift from him. But he's never been interested in my line of work, in fact I always got the feeling he disapproved a little of you marrying a priest. And, you know, there's always been something a little unusual about him. He's a hard guy to categorise. All that money from who knows where, always travelling the world, never in one place for very long, no real friends that we know of, nothing in the way of relationships, he never talks about himself. But he's never been anything but kind to us, and to Naomi. I'm sure he wouldn't have sent his friend up here to cause any harm to children. Much less Naomi. She's his niece, remember. She's his blood.'

'Oh I know Joshua would never hurt us, and the same goes for any one he trusted. But I have a bad feeling about all this. There's something not right, and it's coming our way, I'm sure of it.'

'One of your feelings again?'

'Maybe,' said Sarah. 'I know you don't believe in them, and most of the time I don't myself. But sometimes they've been right. Look at that time I got a feeling about Mrs Laurence, and told you about it. Next day she had a stroke. And the Hunt family. I have the same kind of feeling now, but this time it's for us.'

Matthew Fisher shuffled along the sofa, put his arm round his wife and gently drew her towards him. 'Sarah, honey, it'll be alright. I don't have second sight, I'm not sure you do, but I have faith in the Lord, and he's not about to let anything happen to us. We can give Joshua a call in the morning, and I'm sure he'll tell us there's nothing to worry about.'

She nodded. 'You're probably right. Let's do that. And one more thing...'

'Yes?'

'When you go in to check on Naomi tonight, just for me, give her your Mother's gold cross to wear, and say a prayer over her, just for God to keep her safe.'

He nodded, and the shadow cast by the lamp hid his frown from her. It was rare for Sarah even to pay lip-service to her husband's religion. Something had got her genuinely worried.

Across the street, fifty yards or so down from the Fisher's front drive, the two large men in the dark sedan sat watching the door and sipping the last of the coffee they'd brought with them in the thermos. The clock on the dash showed they'd be relieved in another hour, but they were experienced professionals, so there was no slackening in their concentration. Their eyes were peeled for anyone suspicious approaching the house. It seemed unlikely that the little girl would be leaving home at this time of night. She was probably fast asleep, and the men outside would see she came to no harm.

Neither of them noticed Dudák, who had passed within twenty yards of them, smiling and satisfied.

CHAPTER 39

Nightingale stared at the Professor in astonishment. He could barely comprehend what the Professor had said, let alone believe the man. 'He fed from them?' he said. 'You mean this thing's some kind of a cannibal?'

The professor shook his head sharply. 'No, no, my friend. Dudák would not feed on their bodies, he would absorb their life energy from them.'

'What does that mean? He sucks the life from them?'

'Again, no. Dudák does not kill, but the legend says he lives from death.'

'You say legend. So it's a story?'

'To some. To others, those who have studied, it is an ancient truth. One that most think too awful to speak of, especially since the creature has not been heard of in eight centuries.'

Nightingale lit another cigarette. It seemed he was in for a long night with the Professor. 'Please, tell me about it. As much as you know.'

'It is what I have been asked to do.' He paused to knock the ashes from his pipe and refill it. He settled further back into his chair and began to speak again. 'History holds many stories of the deaths and disappearances of a number of children at one time. Some you may have heard of. The Slaughter of the Firstborn in Ancient Egypt, Herod's Massacre of the Innocents, the Fever-plague of the Mayans, the Vanishing of the young in Nubia, the Children's Crusade...and of course, the story of the Rat-Catcher of Hameln.'

'But none of those stories are true,' said Nightingale.

'Are they not? The stories have persisted for centuries, and those of us who have studied Daemonology know of many other such tales. In the Market Church of Hameln, there was a stained-glass window, made in the 1300s to commemorate the disappearance of the town's children twenty years before. There is also a surviving manuscript from near the time, the Lueneburg manuscript, which stated that in the year of 1284, on the day of Saints John and Paul on June 26, 130 children born in Hameln were seduced and lost at the place of execution near the koppen by a piper, clothed in many colours.'

'June 26,' said Nightingale. 'That's in two day's time.'

'I had noticed, it strengthened my suspicions.'

'So what is this creature?'

'A good question. I suspect it is a demon from Hell. A loathsome creation from millennia ago, set loose on the Earth to wreak carnage and despair. What could be worse than preying on children?'

'Not much,' said Nightingale. 'But how can you be sure it exists?'

'So many legends tell of such a creature, which can bend children to its will, and feeds off their death energies. Those legends have to originate from somewhere.'

'And it's called Dudák?'

'It has had many names. In the east of Europe, amongst the Carpathian Mountains, it was known as Dudák. In India it was Muraleevaala, amongst the Mayans it was Quetalpoca, the Nubians knew it as Egaiouppi. Perhaps the simplest name was the one used in Germany, which gives us the modern legend. Pfeiffer, which means simply the Piper.'

'But this thing was last heard of eight centuries ago, in Germany. What might it be doing in Tennessee now?'

'What it has always done. Causing death and feeding from it.'

Nightingale scratched his head. 'This is a lot to take in. But where has it been for eight hundred years?'

'I suspect it has been trapped,' said the Professor. 'Legend says the children followed it into a cave, and the cave was then sealed. How, or by whom, is not known, but I suspect the creature was unable to escape.'

'But surely, a demon wouldn't be contained by a few rocks?'

'The creature needs to take human form to exist amongst us, it would be bound by most of the limitations of that form.'

'So how did it get out?' asked Nightingale.

'I have no idea. Some more powerful force must have unsealed the cavern, and may be using the creature for its own purposes here. Purposes which seem to include revenge on you, and your principal via the deaths of children close to you.'

Nightingale stubbed out what was left of his cigarette in a metal ashtray. 'Okay Professor, now two important things. How do I find it, and how do I stop it, or better yet, kill it?'

The Professor again looked past Nightingale, as if there were something behind him. With a grunt, he rubbed his right shoulder, then rolled both shoulders, as if to unloosen them from the grip of the arthritis he had mentioned earlier. 'To find the creature will be all but impossible in a city of this size. It will be using a human body, but it could be literally anyone, of any age or race. If what you say is true, and it is bent on revenge, it seems far more likely that Dudák will find you, and your friend, to finish its work in your presence.'

Nightingale shuddered. The idea of this monster tracking him down was not appealing. 'And to stop it, Professor? What do I need to do?'

'Again, very difficult. You could kill the human body, but Dudák might well be able to keep it functional despite great damage, by pure force of its will. Better to separate it from the host, by exorcising the creature, and then contain the demon, and kill it.'

'Kill it how?'

'To be quite frank, Mr Nightingale, I would have no idea. Usually a demon is vulnerable to its opposite element. Dudák is a creature of Air, so in theory burial in Earth might destroy it. In practice, nobody has ever survived an attempt to finish the creature.'

Nightingale nodded, and gave a wry smile. 'So, all I need to do is find this host body in a city of six hundred thousand people, exorcise the demon from within it, then bury the creature in Earth. Still, there's one good thing about it.'

The Professor's eyes opened wide. 'What is that?'

'I've got three whole days to do it in.'

The Professor nodded, but didn't seem too amused at Nightingale's attempt at humour. He looked at his watch, and rubbed his shoulder again. 'I fear it is getting late, my friend, and I have told you all I can. You have my telephone number if you think of anything further.'

Nightingale pushed back the chair and stood up. 'Thanks, Professor, you've been a great help, I think. At least I have some idea of what I might be dealing with.'

The Professor nodded. 'Again, forgive me for not getting up. My wife will show you out.' He took off his spectacles and polished them as Nightingale left the room.

CHAPTER 40

The Professor sat back in his leather chair and took a final puff on his old pipe before knocking it out into the copper bowl. The pain in his right shoulder flared up again, and he rubbed at it, though it was the skin that ached, rather than the joint. He pushed his chair back and slowly, painfully, levered himself to his feet. He walked to the far end of his study, turned the key in the lock of the French windows, pushed the right-hand one open, and walked outside into his garden. There was no moon, so the only illumination came from the desk lamp back in the study and by the time he had gone ten paces he was in almost complete darkness.

He looked up at the stars, naming the constellations to himself. He shivered and he sensed that he was no longer alone. He fought the urge to turn around, and kept on staring upwards. Finally the voice came from behind him, quiet, almost affectionate in its tone, yet completely authoritative.

'It seems you have done well, Wilhelm. You carried out the instructions you were given.'

The Professor nodded but didn't turn. He kept his eyes on the stars above. 'I hope I did as instructed. Most of what I told him was true, though some of it you told me personally, rather than it being the product of my knowledge and research, as I said to him. I think no living man, or woman, could have known some of it.'

'I know, but it was important that he should know everything, and you were the means to inform him. You think he accepted your little lies?'

'Why not? Many Germans came here before the war to escape persecution. He assumed I was Jewish. Why would he suspect I did not arrive until later? A fugitive from the Allies, rather than the Nazis?'

'Why indeed, but it was a necessary fiction. He would accept a learned Professor, with a hobby of research into ancient legends, but not the son of Himmler's coven master, and one of my most loyal followers. He is a trusting soul, and accepts too much at face value. He has always had problems in seeing beneath the surface.'

'Indeed so.'

'You have done well, as I knew you would.'

The Professor took a deep breath, as if summoning up the courage for what he needed to do. 'May I ask a question?'

There was no affection in the voice now, the tone was sharp, as it answered. 'You may.'

'It seems that many of those with knowledge of these matters have died recently. Am I to die this night?'

The voice spoke more calmly this time. 'No, Wilhelm, your life is not required from you tonight. You have served me well for many decades, as did your father before you. There is not long left to you, but you will die peacefully, and without pain. And then, of course, you will fulfil the pact you made all those years ago.'

'I know what will be required of me, and I will pay that price. My wife will never know? She still prays for my immortal soul.'

'She is wasting her efforts, but she will never know that. Farewell, Wilhelm, we shall not meet again in this world.'

There was no sound from behind him, but the Professor knew instantly that he was alone again. He turned, walked back to the French windows, through into the study, locking up behind him, then out of his study, and slowly, painfully, up the stairs to his bedroom. His joints ached with the effort, but the skin on his shoulder no longer burned.

CHAPTER 41

Nightingale was almost falling asleep as he drove back to the Peabody, but he made it safely after one short stop at a 24/7 store to replenish his supply of Marlboro. He handed his keys to the valet in the parking garage and made for the lobby. A room-service sandwich, a bottle of Corona and finally some sleep were all that occupied his thoughts.

He was destined to be disappointed.

As he walked across the lobby to get his key, a figure rose from a table over to his right and came towards him. For a moment Nightingale struggled to recognise the figure in black jeans, zipper jacket and aviator sunglasses, but then his memory clicked. 'Sergeant Parker. A little late for a social call, isn't it?' She looked very different in casual attire with her hair tied back.

'It's not really that, Nightingale. Why not have a beer with me? A nightcap?'

'I never understood why they call a late-night drink a nightcap. It's not as if you wear it on your head, is it?'

'Is that a yes, or a no?'

Nightingale grinned. 'It's a yes.'

The Peabody Lobby Bar was quiet at this time of night, and there were plenty of empty tables near the one that Parker led him to. A waiter arrived quickly. Parker's glass was still three-quarters full, and Nightingale took a quick glance at the menu, and flicked through pages of cocktails and wines until he reached the beer section. They had Corona, but when in Rome... 'I'll take a Wiseacre Tiny Bomb,' he said. 'I've heard good things.'

The waiter nodded and strode off. Parker looked across the table and raised her eyebrows. 'Three days here and you've gone native?'

'I met a guy this afternoon who seemed to think it was a good beer,' said Nightingale. 'I'm all for new experiences.'

The waiter clearly wasn't too busy, and came back with Nightingale's beer straight away. Parker raised her glass in salute, Nightingale followed suit, then took a sip. 'Not bad, ' he said. 'So what brings you here, Sergeant?'

'Make it Bonnie. Actually I lied, this isn't official police business. Yet.'

'The clothes were a clue. Off duty?'

'Suspended. You may have noticed that I shot dead a ten-year-old black girl this morning. There's a departmental investigation.'

'Is it worse because she was black?'

'Probably. There's some people believe that cops will take every chance they get to execute black people. Fortunately, I don't think there's going to be riots happening here in Memphis.'

'There were plenty of witnesses, you had no choice, you probably saved lives.'

'Probably. But there's no doubt that I took one and that's the issue right now. I killed a child, Jack. If I had to do it again I would, but that doesn't make it any easier.' She shrugged. 'There's plenty of CCTV and I'll be exonerated eventually but that doesn't make it any less of a tragedy.'

Parker had finished her beer, and held up the glass to the waiter for another Samuel Adams.

'I'm guessing it doesn't feel good,' said Nightingale.

'Not in any way at all,' said Parker. 'You were a cop, you ever shoot anyone?'

'No,' said Nightingale. 'It doesn't happen often in Britain. Shooting is a last resort. The way it works in the UK, if a cop shoots anyone they are immediately taken off active duty and treated as a murder suspect. It's up to them to prove that the shooting was justified, and if it isn't they can face criminal charges.'

'It's my first time,' said Parker, 'and, Christ, a kid. A little girl. You got kids?'

'Not me,' said Nightingale. 'You?'

'Two, son of twelve and a daughter of ten. The same age as Julia Smith. Shit, it could have been my daughter, and some cop shot her.'

Nightingale nodded, and wondered how many drinks Parker had downed while she'd been waiting. 'So, you going to be in trouble?' he asked.

'Doesn't look like it.' said Parker. 'The Mayor's met with the "Black Lives Matter" people, local community groups, pastors, that kind of thing. Like you said, there were plenty of witnesses, and the CCTV shows exactly what happened. Shows me shouting warnings when I didn't have to. And, which is an awful thing to say, it sort of helps that the two dead guys were black, and me too, takes the race element out of things. Maybe more black people would be dead if I hadn't fired.' She shrugged. 'Every silver lining has a cloud.'

'But that's not helping you?' said Nightingale.

'Not one little bit. Jesus, Jack, I killed a ten-year-old girl for Christ's sake.'

Nightingale nodded and frowned. For a moment, it had seemed as if Parker's words had awoken something in his own memory, something that should have been there, but, strangely, wasn't. He shook his head but the feeling was still there, a sense that he was missing something. He looked at the clock on the wall over Parker's shoulder. It was late and being a sympathetic ear wasn't moving things along. He needed to get the woman out of her self-pity. 'Yeah, I was there. And I'm sure the Memphis PD would put you in touch with counsellors and shrinks if you need help dealing with it. I'm neither of those, and I'm tired, so why are you wasting my time?'

Parker's fists clenched and her face flushed with anger. For a moment Nightingale thought he might have gone too far, but then the detective relaxed back into her seat, and a smile crept across her lips. 'I see what you did there,' she said, 'You've done this kind of thing before. I didn't come down here to whine, I want some answers, and I think you might have more than you've offered so far.'

'Why would you think that?'

Parker held up her left hand, and started to emphasise points by counting them off with her right index finger. 'Three reasons. First you came down here nosing around into something when it was at such an early stage it hadn't even registered with anyone as a thing. Second, you were right on the spot just when the last two kids on Kim Jarvis's list died. What are the chances of that?'

'Pretty high, I guess. And third?'

'Third, I've been talking to our computers about you, Mr Jack Nightingale.'

'I've got no record.'

'No you haven't. Not so much as a parking ticket or a littering fine, in any State. But you are all over the system like a virus, for anyone who cares to look a little deeper than criminal records.'

Nightingale didn't like the sound of that, and was beginning to need a cigarette, but it might be good to keep Parker talking, rather than suggest a trip outside. 'What do you mean by that?' he asked.

'Gotta love that accent. What I mean by that Jack Nightingale is that it's just ridiculous the number of times your name comes up, every time some weird shit goes down. You've been taken in for questioning in California, New York, Florida, Texas, Louisiana, Nevada and half a dozen Mid-Western States. In cases of unsolved murders, disappearances, baby-farming, supposed hauntings, bizarre phenomena and God knows what all else, up to and including alien invasions.'

Nightingale grinned and shook his head. 'I've never investigated little green men.'

'I think they're grey these days,' said Parker. 'Okay, maybe not alien invasions. But trouble sure does seem to follow you around. Or maybe you follow the trouble.'

'I told you, I work for people who take an interest in unusual and unsolved cases. They send me in, I nose around, ask questions, lift up a few rocks and see what's under them. It tends to bring me into contact with the cops, who want to know why I'm asking and what I've found out. Sometimes they forget to ask me politely.'

'I'll bet they do.'

'But as you said, I've never been charged with anything. I'm clean.'

'You say. But let's come back to this case.'

'I've told you everything I know.' said Nightingale, looking into his glass.

'My ass,' said Parker. 'I'll bet you haven't even come close to doing that. There's just no way that some English guy wanders into town, meets up with a local reporter, then finds himself at the scene of three violent deaths, including the very same reporter. Maybe it happens in the movies, but not in Memphis.'

'But you know full well I had no direct connection with any of those deaths. So what are you saying?'

'What am I saying? I'm saying that Kim Jarvis had a list in her purse of eight names. Six of them committed suicide in the last week, the seventh was found dead in the Crystal Grotto, the place where Jarvis killed herself an hour or so later, while you stood watching. The eighth name on that list walked down Beale Street this morning, opened fire on everyone in sight and made me shoot her. Now how did Kim Jarvis come to have that list, and how did she know Julia Smith was going to do what she did twelve hours after she died?'

'What's your guess?' said Nightingale.

'My guess is that Kim Jarvis had that list because you gave it to her. Now I want to know if that's true. If it is, I want to know where you got it from, and I want to know if there are any more names on your copy.'

Nightingale took a deep breath. 'Bonnie, what do you think about psychic phenomena?'

Parker gulped down the rest of her beer, set the glass carefully on the coaster and wiped her lips with the back of her hand. She got up from the table.

'I think I need a cigarette,' she said. 'You want to join me?' As the two of them passed the waiter, Parker gestured at the table and held up her cigarette packet. 'Outside for a smoke,' she said. 'Set us up with two more beers, please.'

They walked twenty yards or so from the main entrance and lit up. The night was warm and sticky, but Parker kept her jacket on. Nightingale held his under his left arm.

'You asked me a question, 'said Parker. 'About psychics.'

'Not quite,' said Nightingale. 'I asked about psychic phenomena.'

'Like what? Most cops get weirdos coming in all the time, telling us their spirit guide's shown them where the body's buried or something. Never known it work.'

'What about the Occult?'

'What, you mean Black Magic? Wizards and witches? You think there might be some ritual element behind this? Because of Jarvis's tattoos, maybe? What, Satanists or something? Surely you don't believe in that kind of crap?'

Nightingale inhaled deeply, exhaled and watched the smoke rise up, while he chose his words carefully. 'It's not a case of what I believe. It's what the people who might be behind this believe. It's their motivation, not mine.'

'What do you mean, "behind this"? How can anyone be arranging for kids to commit suicide?'

'You've heard of hypnotism?'

'Sure,' said Parker, 'but who'd get chance to hypnotise these kids? And besides, I read somewhere that you can't hypnotise someone into doing something they wouldn't normally do.'

Nightingale had cause to know different, but kept that to himself. 'Maybe not, but you could maybe put them in a situation where it wouldn't conflict. If you hypnotised someone into thinking a red signal was green, they'd walk into the road. If you told them vodka was Coke, they might drink a bottle, if you told them they were at a shooting range, in front of targets...'

'Okay,' said Parker, 'I get the picture, but it's way out there, Not that I have a better idea. But let's get back to you. Tell me about that list.'

Again, Nightingale paused. Parker wasn't likely to believe the story of a cursed list. On the other hand, the cop had clear evidence that Julia Smith had been identified as a victim twelve hours before her death. With so little time remaining, Nightingale needed to clutch at any straw. 'Okay. You were right. I had that list with me when I got to Memphis. It was sent to the guy I work for, last week.'

'I need his name.'

'Not yet, Bonnie. The children on that list are dying, in order. From top to bottom, one after the other. And the last name on the list was a member of his family.'

'So why didn't he call the cops?'

'And tell them what? That twelve people who were just names, and very common names, had been threatened? There was no geographical connection at the time, apart from the last name. It wasn't until the third or fourth suicide made the news that we made the connection that they were all in Tennessee, and he sent me here. I contacted the reporter who wrote the story about Timmy Williams, and the rest you know.'

'And you still didn't tell any of this to the police?'

'What was to tell? There was nothing suspicious about any of the deaths, you called them all suicides. At best, I had a list that predicted the future...it's not illegal, it couldn't be used in evidence of anything, unless you can prove that whoever made the list caused the death of the kids.'

'So what are you telling me? Either this list comes from a fortune teller who's seven for seven on their predictions, or someone sent it to your guy and is now putting a hex on children to go out and kill themselves?'

'I'm not saying either of those things. I don't know...but the list is accurate so far.'

Parker threw her cigarette butt to the sidewalk and stood on it. She took a notebook and pen from her jacket pocket. 'You said twelve names. Kim Jarvis's list had eight, so that's all you gave her?'

Nightingale nodded.

'I want the other five. Right now.'

'Okay. Kaitlyn Jones, Emma Miller, Carmen Garcia...'

Nightingale never even saw the punch coming. It was a textbook right hook, travelled at full speed with every ounce of body-weight behind it, exploded against his jaw with sickening force and knocked him flat on the sidewalk.

'Get up you bastard, get up, now!' Parker shouted.

Nightingale shook his head and tried to make sense of what was happening, through a mist of pain cantered around his jaw. Bonnie Parker was standing over him, red-faced and screaming threats and abuse while a crowd was starting to gather. Parker pulled out her badge and waved it around.

'Police officer, back off,' she shouted, but the crowd continued to gather. Sirens started to get closer, which caused a few people to disperse, and then Nightingale saw a patrolman approaching, gun in hand.

He seemed to recognise Parker, but kept his gun ready. 'Sergeant Parker? We have a situation here?'

'All under control, Jimmy,' shouted Parker, 'all under control.'

The patrolman didn't seem too convinced, nor did his partner who had now arrived. Parker's speech was a little slurred, and the uniformed officers must have been able to smell the beer on her breath.

'Uh...Sergeant, perhaps we ought to call this one in,' said the patrolman. 'What's this guy done?'

Nightingale painfully staggered to his feet, only to find the two patrolmen pointing their guns at him.

'Take it easy now sir,' said the older one. 'Please keep your hands where we can see them.'

Nightingale looked at Parker, wondering what the hell had just happened. He rubbed his jaw and winced. Bonnie Parker packed a decent punch, no question of that.

Parker shook her head at the patrolmen. 'Stand down officers. Mr Nightingale isn't under arrest or suspected of anything. We'd been having a few drinks and had a little misunderstanding.'

The patrolmen looked at each other, the older one nodded, and they holstered their guns. The older one turned to the crowd. 'Okay, people, move along now please, nothing to see here.'

Parker took the two patrolmen aside, while Nightingale leaned against the wall, still holding his damaged jaw and trying to clear his head. He could just about make out what Parker was saying. 'Look guys, you did a good job, I'm sorry for this. Could you just let this one slide for me? I don't know if you heard, but I had a hell of a day, maybe had one too many.'

'Sure, Sergeant. Maybe be an idea to head home though, can we organise a ride for you?'

'No thanks, I'll be fine, honest. I'll just go back inside, settle up, maybe get a black coffee and then call a cab. I really appreciate this.'

The younger patrolman seemed to remember Nightingale, and walked over to him. 'Are you okay sir? Do you require medical attention?'

Nightingale rubbed his jaw, worked it around a little and winced. He put his fingers inside his mouth and felt his teeth on the left-hand side. They all seemed to be there, with none of them loose.

'No thank you,' he said. 'No bones broken as far as I can tell. Probably have a hell of a bruise in the morning. My own fault.'

The two patrolmen headed back to their car. Nightingale turned and walked to the Peabody front entrance, then across the lobby and back to the table where his beer was waiting for him, a little warmer and a little flatter than he would have liked, but he took a mouthful and forced it down. Moments later, Parker returned, sat down, but ignored the beer in front of her. Nightingale gave her an unfriendly look, rubbed his aching jaw again, and put his beer on the table. He kept his eyes on Parker's hands.

'You going to tell me what the hell that was all about?' he said.
'Why did you hit me?'

The fury flared up on Parker's face again. 'You damn well know what it was all about, you bastard.'

'I damn well don't, so how about you explain it in short words, before I have you charged with assault.'

'Me charged? Yeah, that'll work, I ought to run you in now.'
'For what?

'Any number of things. Let's start with threatening my daughter.'
Nightingale frowned. 'What?'
'Like you didn't know? Emma Miller is my stepdaughter.'
'Oh shit,' said Nightingale. 'I swear I had no idea, how would I know? Your name is Parker.'

'Miller is her father's name, I use my own name for work. I should have just shot you where you stood.'

Nightingale raised his hands in what he hoped was a calming gesture. 'Easy, Bonnie. Like I said, I didn't know, how could I? I didn't send that list. All the names on it are pretty much the most common forenames and surnames in the USA. There must be dozens of Emma Millers in Tennessee.'

'You're not even convincing yourself, Nightingale. Someone has marked down an Emma Miller, her mom just happens to be involved in the case, and I'm meant to believe it's a coincidence? What would you believe, if she were your child?'

Nightingale looked down at the table, and spoke quietly. 'It's no coincidence, is what I'd believe. You can't afford to believe anything else.'

'Christ, I'd take you in right now if I could think of anything I could make stick, but that tight-ass lawyer of yours would have you out in minutes. As it stands, all I can prove is that you've been present at three suicides and warned me my daughter might be in danger. I couldn't even charge you with unlicensed fortune-telling, since you haven't asked for money.'

At any other time, it might have been a joke, but neither Parker nor Nightingale saw any humour in the situation. Parker was still very angry and very scared, while Nightingale was completely bemused, and possibly concussed.

Parker looked Nightingale full in the face. 'Tell me, mystery man. Gospel truth, whether you believe in the gospel or not. You didn't know I was related to Emma Miller?'

'I did not. I swear I did not. If I had done, I'd have mentioned it immediately, obviously.'

'And now you do, do you think she's genuinely in danger?'

He nodded slowly. 'I genuinely do.'

'Honest to God, you think there's a chance that someone, or something might induce her to harm herself in the next few days?'

Nightingale took a deep breath. 'Yes, Bonnie. I really think that could happen. I'm sorry.'

'And how exactly do I protect her?'

Again Nightingale paused, took another deep breath, and shrugged his shoulders. 'I genuinely wish I knew. Whatever is happening here, it's centered in Memphis. If I were you, I'd send her as far away as you possibly can, and keep her there until this is over. And no, I don't know how long that might be.'

Parker leaned in close to Nightingale. She dropped her voice to a whisper, but spoke very precisely. 'Mister, I still don't trust you an inch, I have no idea what any of this is about. But my kid's going on the first plane out of here tomorrow, and she'll be two thousand miles from here by night-time. And if anything, anything happens to her, I will personally find you and kill you, whatever they care to do to me afterwards.'

Nightingale nodded. 'If I had a kid, I'd feel the same way. Get her out of here, Bonnie. Do it now.'

CHAPTER 42

Nightingale lay on his bed in room 1215 and worked his aching jaw. He'd managed to eat two-thirds of a ham and mushroom omelette from the overnight room service menu, which he'd chosen purely on the basis that it would need less chewing than any of the other options. It seemed to go well with the two Ibuprofen tablets and one codeine that he'd taken to try to ease the pain. He'd managed to switch off for a few minutes while eating, but his mind started buzzing again almost immediately afterwards. Even at 1am there might be things he could do. His first duty was to report to Wainwright, maybe repeat the advice he'd given to Parker, and see if there were some system for removing Naomi Fisher from Memphis. Time zones didn't seem to matter to Wainwright, and Nightingale was pretty sure he wouldn't be sleeping any too soundly at the moment. He rang Wainwright's number and a minute and a half later the phone was still ringing, but nobody was answering. Nightingale put it down and stared blankly at the wall. In all the time he'd known Wainwright, the billionaire had never failed to take one of his calls, except for the very rare occasions when it had transferred straight to his assistant Valerie. No answer at all was completely unheard of, and very worrying.

He tried twice more in the next ten minutes, with the same lack of result. He tried to think of an explanation, but nothing occurred to him which could be anything but very bad news. Finally nature took over, his body succumbed to the inevitable, his eyes closed, and he fell asleep, fully clothed, on top of the bed cover.

CHAPTER 43

In fact, Wainwright was just a few blocks away, in one of the Holiday Inn's less luxurious rooms, booked and registered under a name that was not his own, paid for with a credit card that could never be traced back to him. He was lying on the queen-size bed, his mobile phone to his ear, his cigar burning in the ashtray on the nightstand. 'No, everything's fine, Valerie. I know it's not my usual style, but I don't want to attract attention here. And there's not much choice if I need a hotel with smoking rooms. I doubt anyone will be looking for me here. Did he call? Yeah, I know, I hate to leave him dangling, but this is getting too near and too personal, and he's run out of time. Any other calls on the personal line? Really? Same goes for her, she was almost bound to pick up vibes, but there's no way I can explain this to her and Matthew over the phone. No way that would make any sense. The teams checked in okay? Nothing to report? I'll go down there tomorrow, tell them what I can to convince them, and we'll move all three of them. The Cessna's all ready to go? I'll choose the flight-plan just before we take off, so nobody will know which way we're headed except air traffic control. We should have two clear days to spare. And the Gulfstream's ready to take off as well? Antigua. With any luck, if anyone has the means to follow us, that's where they'll head. Look, you may not be hearing from me for a few days now, and I won't be taking calls. Just need some time for all this to blow over. I don't think there's anything pressing at the moment. You can keep an eye on most things, and Leroy and Charles will handle the market stuff.'

He put down the phone and picked up his cigar. It seemed that everything was in place for tomorrow's operation. Shame about not being able to bring Nightingale up to speed, but family came first, and there was pretty much nobody that Wainwright planned to trust with their safety now, not even Jack Nightingale.

He finished the cigar, stubbed it out and put the air conditioning on full to clear the room. Then he lit two large candles, took out a photo of his niece, poured some herbs into a bowl, lit them too, and proceeded to chant some words in Greek, He took a large blue crystal from a centuries-old leather bag, and held it tightly in his palms, while he continued to chant, and visualised the blue of the crystal spreading out from his hands and forming an aura around Naomi Fisher. He concentrated as firmly as he could, ensuring in his mind's eye that the aura surrounded her completely. Finally, he quenched the herbs, replaced the crystal in its bag, snuffed out the candles, lay down on the bed and fell into a deep sleep.

The Spell of Protection was complete, and would hopefully keep her safe until morning, by which time, with any luck, his other arrangements for her would be complete.

Across the city, Naomi Fisher slept peacefully, unaware of her uncle's spell, but happy to be wearing her grandmother's gold crucifix round her neck.

The old religion and the new combined to try to keep the little girl safe, for the moment, from the evil that approached nearer with every passing hour.

CHAPTER 44

At 9am on Thursday morning, the National Civil Rights Museum on Mulberry Street was just opening its doors. Based around what had probably been Memphis's most infamous building, the Lorraine Motel, the Museum documented the progress of the Civil Rights movement in obtaining equality for all races in the United States, and commemorated the leader of the Civil Rights movement, Martin Luther King, who had been assassinated with a rifle bullet on a balcony of the motel on April 4, more than fifty years earlier.

That morning, there was nobody waiting to pay their sixteen dollars for admission, though the Museum did have four school groups from other parts of Tennessee scheduled to visit later in the day.

Their visits would be cancelled.

As the security guard unlocked the main entrance doors that morning, he noticed a small blonde girl, standing about a hundred feet up the street, dressed in a white t-shirt and blue jeans, holding a WalMart bag in one hand and a mobile phone in the other. The guard would say afterward that he thought it unusual that she should be standing there, seemingly just watching the museum, but making no attempt to come over once it opened. Especially on a day when she should have been in school. She hadn't seemed in any distress, so he'd figured it was no concern of his, and he went back inside.

If he'd stayed outside, he would have seen the young girl open the WalMart bag, toss in her mobile phone, take out the sixty-four ounce bottle of barbecue lighter fluid, and undo the child-resistant cap. She'd taken it from her father's garage, and it was only two-thirds full, but that would be plenty. She lifted the bottle above her head, and poured the liquid all over her hair, then down onto her t-shirt. Finally she brought it down to waist-level, and soaked her jeans. The pungent fumes stung her eyes and nose, but she didn't blink or cough. She put the empty bottle back into the bag, and took out from it one of her mother's disposable cigarette lighters.

She walked towards the museum.

She was just inside the door, when the security guard noticed the stench and fumes from the lighter fluid and started to walk over, but he was still ten feet away when she clicked the lighter and erupted into a ball of flames. The guard took one horrified look, and sprinted away, racing back in under thirty seconds with the fire blanket he'd pulled from the wall, frantically tearing it open. He held it in front of him, used it to push the girl to the ground and tried desperately to wrap her in it to smother the flames, all the time shouting for more help.

The paramedics arrived inside five minutes. Security guard Jefferson Wood was taken to hospital with multiple second-degree burns, and took weeks to recover.

Kaitlyn Isabella Jones, aged eleven, was pronounced dead at the scene. The coroner would later return a verdict of suicide.

Nobody paid any attention to Dudák who stood by the side wall of the museum and fed, eyes closed and smiling with pleasure.

CHAPTER 45

Nightingale woke at 9.30 and immediately regretted it. His jaw ached furiously, and he could feel the swelling with his fingers. A glance in the mirror showed a fine collection of colours, and a lump the size of an egg. He swallowed two more Ibuprofen tablets, then called for a room-service breakfast, since he had no way of knowing when he might next find time to eat.

The full Peabody breakfast arrived inside ten minutes, and Nightingale did it full justice, despite the aching jaw. He gave silent thanks for Wainwright's bottomless credit cards when he saw the price, boosted by delivery charge, service charge and the inevitable State sales tax.

He collected his car from the hotel garage, and headed to the Galilee Baptist Church parking lot, left the car there and walked the hundred yards or so to the Fisher home. He wasn't looking forward to this chat at all, but he'd come to the conclusion that the only way to keep Naomi safe was to persuade the Fishers to take the same advice he'd given to Bonnie Parker the previous night, and to get the little girl as far away from Memphis as possible. He was hoping at least one of her parents would be at home, but he hadn't wanted to call ahead to try to explain the reason for his visit.

A Mercedes GLS SUV stood parked on the opposite side of the road from the Fisher's house, and about fifty yards past it, Wainwright had mentioned getting some security in place, and Nightingale wondered if the dark-tinted windows concealed a few heavies, a watcher team to ensure no harm came to the girl or her family. The car was a little conspicuous, but then it would be hard to stay hidden and yet keep a close watch.

He arrived at the Fishers' front door, and pressed the bell, but immediately noticed that the door was ajar. He heard no signs of movement inside the house, and he felt the hairs on the back of his neck start to rise. Nightingale didn't like the feel of this at all. He pulled his jacket sleeve over his right hand, and pushed the door gently. There was still no sound from inside.

He slowly edged through the door and into the hallway. He trod carefully, making no sound, and then ducked his head into the open door of the dining room on the right. The table wasn't laid, everything seemed to be in the right place, and there was nobody there. Another few steps, and he looked into the sitting room on the left. Again, nobody was inside, everything seemed neat and tidy. The television was on, playing a Memphis news channel, with pictures of paramedics and police outside a low building that looked like a motel. There was no sound, and the mute logo showed on the top-right of the screen. Nightingale shuddered, hoping there wasn't a dead child involved.

He moved on down the corridor, to the foot of the stairs, then turned left. He looked up at the first floor and his eyes widened in horror.

Matthew Fisher was hanging from the top bannister post, a thin rope round his neck, his body swinging against the handrail, his head at an impossible angle, his face blue, and his swollen tongue protruding from between his teeth. Nightingale's hand reached for his cigarettes, almost in a reflex action, but he pushed them back down into his pocket. He had the feeling he wouldn't want to leave any evidence of his presence here. He forced his eyes downwards, and moved on to the kitchen, and then the study. Nobody in either of them, and nothing looked out of place to his casual glance. He had the feeling there'd be no time for a search, and he had no idea what he might be looking for.

He paused again then edged his way upstairs, testing each step before he put his weight on it, hoping for no loose, squeaky boards. His luck held, and as he neared the top he stared at the wall, to avoid looking into the dead eyes of Matthew Fisher.

He could hear a voice, coming from the room at the end of the corridor. The door stood half open, so he edged his way along, stood outside and listened. A man's voice. Quiet, and repetitive. 'I'm so sorry, honey, I'm so sorry. I never thought, I never thought, it's all my fault, I'm so sorry, so sorry...'

Nightingale tried to peer through the crack at the side of the door, but it was the wrong side, and he just saw the side wall. Inch by inch, he moved forward until he could see round the door.

Sarah Fisher lay on her bed, her head practically severed from her body by the huge gash across her throat. The bedspread, walls and floor ran red with the blood that had fountained everywhere. Sitting on the bed next to her, looking down at her, was a man in a dark jacket and jeans, both of them stained with the dead woman's blood. In his right hand, he held a large, black handled kitchen knife, which was also covered in blood. He kept on talking to the dead woman, apologising and begging her forgiveness.

Nightingale must have made some kind of noise, or the man sensed his presence somehow. He spun round, rising from the bed in one movement, like an uncoiling spring, his face a demented mask of murderous rage, his fist clenched around the knife.

It was Joshua Wainwright.

The fury vanished from Wainwright's face, he laid the knife down on the bed and straightened up again. 'You scared the life out of me,' he said. He took a step forwards, but Nightingale raised a warning finger.

'That's far enough, Joshua. Don't come any nearer to me. Now tell me what happened, and make it very quick.'

Wainwright didn't waste time arguing, nor did he move any closer. He took a deep breath and let it all come out, his voice sounding like a machine, and his eyes never leaving Nightingale's. 'Long story short, I decided to handle this my way, get them out. Came into Memphis incognito, took a taxi down here this morning, planning to get my guys across the road to help me move them, if I couldn't persuade them. I got two dead men across the road, I walked in on this. I'd say it all went down twenty minutes before I got here. Jack, Naomi's gone.'

'Any signs of a struggle in her room?'

'Not that I can see, but how much struggling could a ten-year old girl do against someone who could do all this?'

'She could be in school,' said Nightingale.

'I'll guess not.' said Wainwright.

The landline rang on the bedside table, Joshua picked up. 'Uh-huh,' he grunted into the phone.

Nightingale couldn't make out what the caller was saying, just Wainwright's replies.

'No...sorry...it's probably just a stomach virus...day or two...thanks for calling.' He hung up. 'Speak of the devil,' he said, without irony. 'That was the school. They wanted to know why Naomi didn't show up today.'

'That settles that,' said Nightingale, 'someone has got her. We need to leave, now.'

Wainwright shook his head. 'That's my sister, Jack. I can't leave her like this'

Nightingale hated to be brutal, but there was no choice. 'She's dead, Joshua. Nothing you can do for her. Whoever did this might be watching the house, seen us come in and be planning to call it in. If the Police find us here, all the lawyers you can buy won't get us out inside a month, and Naomi needs us. Wipe the knife off. Get yourself one of Matthew's overcoats to cover yourself, wait for me downstairs and then we're going to walk slowly and calmly to my car. Do it now.'

Wainwright was accustomed to giving orders, rather than taking them, but he didn't argue. He wiped the knife handle on a pillow-slip, He gave one last anguished look at his sister's body and headed out, down the stairs, picked an overcoat off the hat stand in the entrance hall and stood waiting.

Nightingale walked quickly into Naomi's bedroom. The bed was neatly made and everything seemed to be in its proper place. There was a gold crucifix and a copy of the New Testament on the nightstand. Nightingale picked them up and dropped them into his coat pocket.

He left the room, hurried downstairs and walked straight out the front door with Wainwright directly behind him. Neither of them stopped to shut the door. They walked up the street to the church parking lot, barely glancing at the Mercedes across the way.

'I touched nothing this visit,' said Nightingale, 'except the doorbell, and I wiped that. I'm guessing you touched almost everything.'

'Probably,' said Joshua.

'We had no time to clean up,' said Nightingale. 'The knife was the important thing. If it comes to it, you're family and can spin some story about visiting last night. But better hope it doesn't come to that.'

They reached the Escape, climbed in and Nightingale drove off, slowly and carefully, in no particular direction. He took turns at random. In the distance he could hear sirens, gradually getting closer. It could have been a coincidence, but Nightingale was glad not to be sticking around to find out.

CHAPTER 46

The woman in the wheelchair was up early again, the pain making a full night's sleep an almost impossible dream. She sat in front of her computer screen and played the recording of the early news from Memphis. The girl who'd set herself on fire at the Civil Rights Museum was the top item, with pictures of ambulances, police cars and a fire truck in front of the building. The cops weren't naming the girl yet, but the woman knew who she must be. Three more and the list would be complete, and her revenge finalised. Then she could give up the struggle, and die contented.

It was a shame that Nightingale was not in custody, and an even bigger shame that he had not been shot dead in Beale Street the previous morning. That had been her wish, but even under control, Julia Smith had not been experienced in handling a gun, and bullets had flown in every direction. Nightingale had been lucky, some others not.

Still, Nightingale was just a minion, and would be taken care of in due course. The main focus of her hatred was the other, and it seemed that he had been flushed out from hiding. She would richly enjoy seeing him lose everything he held dear.

She thought back bitterly to a time when it had been her who made great plans, gave orders and pulled strings. Now she was reduced to watching, while others moved the chessmen around the board. Some of the plan had been explained to her, and it had been promised that the man who had orchestrated her destruction would himself be brought down, and she would live long enough to see his death, and Nightingale's. But she had not been told why or how the other children had to die, or what was bringing about the deaths. The one she had made her pact with had promised her what she had asked for, but did not welcome questions.

The Memphis news channel was now bringing updates on a new, breaking story. Police had been called to a house near the Galilee Baptist Church, where reports were coming out of two people dead in what might be a domestic murder-suicide incident. Again, no names were being released yet.

The woman in the wheelchair forced her mouth into a smile of triumph, then she pressed the bell for her nurse.

She needed to be changed.

CHAPTER 47

Nightingale pulled into the parking lot of a small shopping plaza, found an empty space with no other cars within thirty yards and turned off the engine, 'Why have you stopped here?' asked Wainwright.

'We have to be somewhere,' said Nightingale. 'And this is as good a place as any. I'm pretty sure we weren't followed, and we can't be overheard.'

'We need to find Naomi, and fast.'

'Saying it won't make it happen. We're in a city of over half a million people spread over three hundred square miles. We won't be tracking her down. It's a job for the Memphis PD.'

'No. They'll never find her in time. Whoever's done this had it planned all along.'

'You're probably right. Plus the first thing they'd do is arrest us. Maybe I could think of another way to play this, but we're going to need a place to operate from. And not in Memphis.'

'You think we're going to leave town with all that's left of my family in their hands? Jack, I just lost my sister and her husband back there, I'm not about to turn tail and run. We need to get Naomi back, and then these bastards are going to pay.'

'No argument about that,' said Nightingale. 'And I know what you're going through, believe me I do. But we can't just react blindly, and we have nobody to react against. Neither of us can go back to those hotels, and I can't do anything there. We need to get out of town, and fight them with their own weapons. Help me, and trust me. I'm invested in this too. Sophie Underwood means a lot to me, and they may have her too.'

Wainwright stared out the windscreen. His eyes were red, and there was a twitching muscle in his cheek. He took a deep breath, the twitching stopped and he gave a sharp nod, He pulled out his mobile phone, and punched in a number.

'Tyrone? It's Joshua. Man, I need the house. Two hours. Maybe a week, not more. No, we'll take care of ourselves. Thanks, appreciate it.'

He put the phone away and turned to Nightingale. 'We're all set. Jack. Programme the GPS. We're headed for the home of country music, Nashville.'

He gave Nightingale the address and he tapped it into the SatNav, then followed the soothing voice east out of Memphis.

CHAPTER 48

Nightingale concentrated on the unfamiliar streets as his GPS guided him through east Memphis. Wainwright sat in silence, staring straight ahead through the windshield. Finally the SUV pulled onto the I-40 following the signs for Nashville, Nightingale set the cruise control at 65mph and relaxed a little. He looked across at Wainwright. 'You want to tell me about it?'

'You got a cigarette?' said Wainwright. 'Seem to have mislaid my humidor.'

Nightingale took a cigarette and handed his pack across. 'Hertz won't like it.' he said.

Wainwright suggested what Hertz could do about it.

'They might not like that either,' said Nightingale. Even he felt that his system of trying to 'lighten the moment' might not be working, but what was he supposed to say to a man who'd just found his sister butchered, and his niece missing?

Nightingale lit his own cigarette and handed the lighter across. Wainwright lit up and took a long drag, then went back to staring straight ahead. Nightingale said nothing. His training as a negotiator had stressed the importance of empathy, and also to know when not to push, when to keep quiet. Wainwright smoked in silence for a full two minutes before he spoke.

'Shit, these things don't last no time at all,' said Wainwright scornfully. 'A good cigar keeps me going over an hour.'

'There are more, if you need them. Tell me what happened, Joshua. Everything.'

'Down in Haiti, I pulled out some old voodoo stuff, Jack. Took a look into Naomi's future. Seemed like there was something pretty nasty on her tail, so I decided to come up here, pull her out, Sarah and Matthew too, Whether they liked it or not. Thought I had a few days to spare. Never thought whoever would move so soon.'

'I guess you plan for what they could do, rather than what they might do.'

'Would have been good advice yesterday. I told nobody I was coming, don't know why, I wasn't sure I could trust my own people. Just a snatch team I brought in from New York.'

'And you didn't think to tell me,' said Nightingale.

'Nope. Figured if you just kept nosing around here, whoever's behind this would have their attention fixed on you, and I could be in and out with them before they noticed. I figured wrong.'

'So I was a distraction? Or bait?'

'I had to do what I had to do,' said Wainwright. 'But I failed miserably. My sister's dead and my niece...' He left the sentence unfinished and massaged the bridge of his nose.

'Joshua, this isn't your fault,' said Nightingale, knowing, as he spoke, that his words were useless.

'No? If she was anyone else's sister she'd still be alive and her husband too. Slice it anyway you want to, Jack, she died because of me.'

Nightingale couldn't find an argument against that, and it was something Wainwright would need to live with. But there was no time to start the grieving process now, so he changed the subject. 'You talked about something nasty following her?'

'Yeah, saw it in an old crystal. Some kind of demon, following her, catching up to her, then kind of devouring her. Never saw anything like it before.'

'Maybe I can shed some light on that,' said Nightingale. 'I went to see a guy last night who knows what's going on.'

'That where you got your face messed up?'

'No, that was a girl.' He saw the look of astonishment on Wainwright's face. 'Don't ask. The guy was a Professor of German History, but I got the impression he knew an awful lot about our...about your world. He told me a different version of a very old story. Ever heard of the Pied Piper?'

'Sure,' said Wainwright, lighting another of Nightingale's cigarettes. 'The townsfolk offered him a purse of gold to catch all the rats, then reneged on the deal afterward.'

'Well, according to Professor Schiller, the Pied Piper is some sort of demon called Dudák that has been operating in different countries for thousands of years. He quoted a few instances he knew of, and probably there were lots more. But not for the last eight hundred years, because he'd walled himself into a cave in Germany. Or someone had walled him in.'

'But why does this Dudák steal kids?'

'Apparently this thing, whatever it is, can exercise a huge influence over children. Right up to making them kill themselves. And then it feeds off the death energies.'

'And you think that's what's loose in Memphis, and what's got Naomi?'

'I really don't know Joshua. The Prof seemed to attach some importance to June 26. It's the anniversary of the day the Piper stole the kids from Hamlin.'

'It's also Saturday,' said Wainwright. 'We have to find her before then. And we're heading in the wrong direction.'

'My guess is she's still safe till Saturday,' said Nightingale, 'and we won't be finding her by looking. We need specialist help, and I need a place to summon it.'

'But what if you're wrong, and this Dudák decides not to wait until Saturday?'

Nightingale gave him a rueful look. 'Well, then I guess that won't be good at all. If you have a better idea, I'll go with it.'

Wainwright opened the window, and threw his cigarette butt out. He sighed.

'I'm all out, Jack. My last idea didn't work out too well. We'll play it your way.'

CHAPTER 49

They arrived in Nashville after three and a half hours on the road. The two men had sat in silence after their brief conversation. Nightingale concentrated on the road, though it was an easy drive with the morning rush-hour long over. Once inside Nashville, Wainwright told Nightingale to ignore the SatNav and guided him in monosyllables, until he turned onto Northplace Drive, and up a short driveway on the left, where Nightingale parked in front of the front door, next to a white BMW M6. The front door of the house opened the moment he turned the engine off, and a tall black man in an immaculate lime-green suit came down the steps towards the car. Wainwright opened the passenger door and jumped down, gesturing at Nightingale to stay put. The man held out a set of keys to Wainwright. 'All set, man. Good to see you again.' He grinned, showing a gold tooth at the front of his mouth.

The two men hugged. Tyrone was a couple of inches taller than Wainwright and his skin a few shades lighter, but they could have been brothers.

'Appreciate it, Tyrone. Keys to the box in the same place?'

'Sure are. Lose them if you use them, man,'

Tyrone walked round to the driver's door of the BMW, got in, started it up and was gone in a flurry of screeching tyres and flying gravel.

'Come on out, Jack,' said Wainwright. 'Apologies for the lack of introductions, but the less Tyrone knows, the fewer questions he can ever answer.'

'Same goes for me, I suppose.'

Wainwright grinned. 'There is that.'

Nightingale stood and looked up at the house. 'Mansion' would have been a better description. It was a blend of Classical and American styles, and nobody could have called it subtle. Four giant two-storey high white columns supported a pediment over the front entrance. On either side, white walls, arched windows and grey triangular roof sections stretched out until they blended into a white-walled grey-roofed set of garages on the left, and finished in immaculately kept lawns and trees on the right. Behind the slate triangles, the grey roof rose high, punctuated by dormer windows that indicated a third storey. Nightingale let out a whistle. 'You know Tyrone through business or the other thing?'

'We go way back, let's go inside.'

Which seems to close down that conversation, thought Nightingale, as he took his bag from the back seat of the SUV, and walked up the steps of Tyrone's place. Wainwright had no luggage, and was still wearing Matthew Fisher's overcoat over his blood-stained clothes. Nightingale hoped he hadn't stained the seats, that might not be easy to explain to Hertz. Still, on a list of his current problems, it didn't rank too high. Wainwright could always buy them another car.

Nightingale put his bag just inside the front door and looked around. The entrance hall reached up to the full height of the house. At the far end stood a sweeping curved staircase which led up to balconies running round both sides of the hall, with doors leading off them. Downstairs, there were several more doors, and passages either side of the stairs leading off into the other wings of the house. Everything was painted a dazzling white, with bannisters, balcony rails and door panels picked out in gold. Wainwright pointed at the second door on the left.

'Make yourself at home in the main sitting room, while I shower and change, Jack. Be down right away.'

He hurried up the stairs, and Nightingale opened the door and walked into another room painted white. It was huge, with a black grand piano at one end, and French windows leading out onto the grounds at the other. In the middle were three large, black leather sofas and a selection of leather chairs, loosely arranged round a black marble coffee table. A giant black television hung on one wall, above shelves that housed an expensive hi-fi system. To one side of the shelves a black wood bar had been installed, with fully-equipped liquor shelves, and a black fridge.

He looked round the room again, trying to decide what was wrong with it, and it came to him. It looked as if it was a page from a furniture catalogue, and had been ordered in all at the same time. There wasn't a single personal item here, not a plant, a book, a magazine or an ornament. Nightingale wondered if it always looked this way, or if Tyrone had spend two hours frantically clearing up, in response to Wainwright's call. Not that he looked the type to do much in the way of domestic chores.

Nightingale walked to the French windows and found them unlocked. He opened one, stepped outside and lit a Marlboro. The grounds stretched a few hundred yards back, the immaculate lawn finally giving way to shrubbery and trees, with a high stone wall marking the end of the property. Over to the left he saw the pool and pool-house, with a paved walking and eating area next to it. If this really was Tyrone's house, the man certainly had money.

He finished his cigarette and went back inside. He walked across to the television, turned it on and flicked through channels until he found the Memphis News channel. The top story was the death of a young child at the Memphis Civil Rights Museum, after setting fire to herself. As yet she hadn't been identified. 'Kaitlyn Jones', whispered Nightingale to himself.

Further down the bulletin was news of the death of a local Memphis Herald reporter who had been killed while trying to cross a road in Memphis last night. He's been named as Peter Mulholland. Nightingale cursed out loud.

'Friend of yours?' asked Wainwright from behind him.

'Not really,' said Nightingale. 'I met him yesterday, he was a colleague of Kim Jarvis, the reporter who killed herself at the grotto. We went to talk to her house-mate, but didn't find out much. He looked like a guy who liked a drink, might have forgotten to look both ways.'

'Yeah, he might have,' said Wainwright. 'But did you ever notice how a lot of people who you meet seem to end up dead?'

'It had occurred to me,' said Nightingale.

'Come and sit down, Jack,' said Wainwright. 'I've just declared this whole house a smoking zone.'

Nightingale turned and went back into the room. Wainwright went behind the bar, opened a humidor and took out one of his favourite cigars. He had changed into a grey silk shirt, black jeans and a pair of black western boots. The shirt collar was open, showing a thick gold neck-chain, with a pentagram hanging from it, matching the gold Patek Philippe watch on his left wrist and the heavy gold chain on his right. He poured two large malt whiskies, gave one to Nightingale and then sat down on a sofa. 'This is a fucking mess, Jack,' he said. He gulped down some whisky. 'Is it possible that Matthew killed my sister?'

Nightingale paused, thinking of similar scenes he'd come upon in the last few years. 'I don't know, Joshua. Someone wanted the police to think he did. If he did, then it wasn't the Matthew that we knew, but the chances are there was someone else in that house. Naomi wouldn't have left by herself.'

'You mean they might have been controlled?'

'We've both known it done. I've seen you do it.'

'True enough. I can influence people, but I wouldn't know how to get a husband to kill the wife he loved. And they did love each other, Jack. I've always known that.'

'Tell me about the guys in the car,' said Nightingale, thinking a change of subject might be a good idea.

'I opened the driver's door and took one look, then I shut it again. It was a bloodbath, Jack. They'd been hacked to pieces, but inside the car. Who could have done that? How is it even possible?'

'I don't know, I'm sorry. You said they were good guys? Professionals?'

'The best, there's no way anyone could have snuck up on them, no way anyone could have done that without them putting up a fight. Nobody.'

'Maybe nobody human, at least. But maybe we're not dealing with humans here.'

Wainwright looked him full in the eyes. 'You know something, Jack. And you have some ideas. That's part of why we're here. Tell me.'

Nightingale lit another cigarette and gave Wainwright the full story of what he'd learned from the Professor, and then told him about his meeting with Bonnie Parker. Wainwright sat in silence until Nightingale had finished. 'I'd heard about demons who feed off fear and death, but never one who preyed on kids,' he said.

'So it's common?'

'Well, not common, but it happens. That kind of demon inhabiting a human body, whether alone or sharing it with the human is what explains people like Jeffrey Dahmer, Dennis Nilsen, Jack the Ripper, the Boston Strangler. Christman Genipperteinga, the Red Inn murderers in France...'

'All demons?'

'That's the explanation I've heard for them. There's meant to be a death energy they feed off, released when their victims die. But kids? New one on me. Though there may be others, I'm no expert. But look, Jack, do you trust this Professor guy?'

'I'm not sure I trust anybody these days, but he came with a good introduction, and what would he have to gain by making the whole thing up?'

'Beats me. But if it is this Dudák creature that's making the kids kill themselves and feeding off their death energies, that still leaves quite a few questions unanswered.'

'It does,' said Nightingale. 'For example, if Dudák has been in a blocked cavern in Germany for nearly eight hundred years, who, or what, released him?'

'Yeah, and why should he come out of there with a burning grudge against kids in Tennessee, and me in particular. I never heard of the thing, much less did it any harm.'

'Could one of the Apostles have released it and set it on you?' asked Nightingale.

'I doubt it, they didn't have that kind of power. And demons don't usually follow human orders. If one of the Apostles had gone to Germany, found the thing and released it, it would have probably killed them, rather than start listening to their list of grudges. The only one who could control a demon like Dudák, and use it to carry out this kind of thing, would be a much stronger demon. Maybe even a Prince of Hell.'

'Maybe even a Princess,' said Nightingale thoughtfully.

'Holy shit, you think Proserpine could be behind this?'

'I can only think of one way to find out for sure.'

'What's that?'

Nightingale shrugged. 'Ask her.'

'Are you insane?'

Nightingale smiled ruefully. 'It's been suggested before.'

'But why would she tell you anything, if she's behind all this?'

'Dunno, maybe I might have to offer her something she wants.'

'She wants your soul, Jack. You prepared to bargain with it?'

'Maybe there might be a second choice. Now look, Joshua, you either help me with this or you come up with a better idea.'

Wainwright was silent.

'I'll take that as a yes. Now, the first thing I'm going to need is a big empty room.'

Wainwright forced a smile. 'You haven't had the full tour yet, have you?' he said. 'Let's start with the basement.'

Wainwright led the way to the end of the entrance hall, along the left hand corridor, and down to a door on the right, which he opened with a key from his pocket. There was a light-switch just inside the door, and turning it on revealed a set of stone steps leading down. Nightingale followed him, but could see very little when they reached the bottom.

'Hang onto your hat,' said Wainwright, and pressed another switch.

Nightingale's jaw literally dropped, causing him to wince in pain. It was a vast space, which must have run under most of the house. Nightingale took a few steps inside, and then stopped to take it all in. It was a chapel. An underground chapel. There were lines of blood-red pews – enough to seat close to a hundred people - facing a wooden table which must have been thirty feet long, now mostly covered in a long red cloth. Two thrones, upholstered in red plush stood on the left and right hand sides of the table, with six-foot high blood-red inverted crosses hanging on the wall behind each one.

Between the thrones stood a figure carved from black wood which must have been nine feet high, its huge wings spreading out from its shoulders, the outsize phallus pointing at the room, the five-pointed star in the middle of the forehead, directly between the roots of the long curving horns which arched upwards towards the high ceiling.

'Baphomet,' said Nightingale quietly. 'The Goat of Mendes. The Devil incarnate.'

'Some might say that,' said Wainwright quietly.

The floor was mostly of grey flagstones, except for two large black squares directly before the statue, one of which was inlaid with a red five-pointed star and some other symbols Nightingale didn't recognise. The other bore a huge inlay of the head of Satan, also done in blood-red. The walls, and the vaulted ceiling, were painted in flat white, and bore no decorations.

'Joshua, what is this place?' said Nightingale. 'Who uses it, and what for?'

Wainwright moved his lips in a very small smile. 'Let's just say it's the basement of the house that Tyrone lives in, and leave it at that, shall we? Is it going to be big enough for your purposes?'

'Oh yes,' said Nightingale. 'Plenty big enough, and I'm sure she'll like it. I'm going to need a few things that I don't have with me.'

Wainwright nodded. 'I know. They should all be here except one, and I'll have that here in two hours. You plan to wait till nightfall?'

'It's meant to be best, but we can't afford to waste the time. According to the list, Naomi's due to die in three days time, but whoever made the list could change their rules any time they felt like it. Better to get started straight away.'

Another nod from Wainwright.

'Let's get on it. I'll show you where everything is.' He leaned towards Nightingale. 'Jack?'

'Yes?'

'You think you're going to need me here for this?'

Nightingale thought he could hear fear in Wainwright's voice, and understood. To a learned Satanist like him, the idea of raising one of Hell's most powerful Devils must have seemed almost suicidal, or worse. It was only Nightingale's almost complete ignorance of the danger involved that had ever allowed him to try it the first time.

'No, Joshua,' he said. 'This is a one-man job. I'd like you out of the house, please. There are some other things I think we'll be needing, so you could be organising those, maybe catching up on the news from Memphis. I'll give you a list, and you can take the Escape.'

'Don't think so,' said Wainwright. 'The Ferrari in the garage is more my style.'

'Probably is. But it might be a good idea to stay below the radar.'

Wainwright grinned. 'There is that. Let's go upstairs and you can give me that list.'

CHAPTER 50

It would probably have taken a professional cleaning team the better part of a day to have done a complete job on Tyrone's huge basement chapel. Jack Nightingale didn't have a day, and he had no wish to involve anyone else in his activities, so he settled for pushing some of the pews against the walls, leaving a space around twenty yards on each side, and spent an hour scrubbing the stone-flagged floor until he was satisfied that it was spotlessly clean. The first time he'd ever tried this, he'd been warned that any kind of impurity could lead to disaster, and he'd seen enough of the Occult world to know the danger of complacency, so he was meticulous about the cleaning.

When he was satisfied, he headed to the shower in what Joshua had called the 'Robing Room', where he scrubbed himself with coal tar soap, cleaned under his nails, fingers and toes, with a new plastic nail brush, shampooed his hair twice, then rinsed himself off for ten minutes. He dried himself on a new towel, then put on brand new black jeans and a black cotton shirt, both of which had come wrapped in plastic from the wardrobes upstairs. New and spotless grey trainers completed his outfit, and then he returned to the Satanic chapel.

As Wainwright had promised, everything he needed had been placed in a large cardboard box near the table. He took a piece of consecrated white chalk and drew a circle with it, around six feet in diameter on the stone floor. There were birch trees in the grounds, and one of them had provided the fresh branch he used to brush round the outline of the circle as an extra safety measure. With a fresh piece of chalk, he drew a pentagram, the ancient symbol of a five-pointed star, inside the circle, with two of the points facing north. Then came a triangle to enclose the circle, again with the apex facing north. At the three points of the triangle, he wrote MI, CH and AEL to spell out the name of the Archangel Michael.

The next item was the one thing that the house had been unable to provide, since it was essential that it was freshly blessed. Nightingale had no idea where Wainwright might have found a priest to do the job, but the flask of consecrated salt water had arrived well within the promised two hours. Nightingale took the bottle and sprinkled water around the circle, being careful not to leave any part of it untreated.

He took five large white candles and placed them at the points of the pentagram, then lit them all with his lighter, being sure to move clockwise round the circle. Then he took out plastic bags containing herbs, and a lead bowl. Again moving clockwise, he sprinkled the herbs over the flames, until the air was filled with pungent smoke that caught in his nose and irritated his lungs. The remainder of the herbs were placed in the lead crucible, which he put down in the centre of the circle. He took his lighter and set fire to them too.

This time the smoke was almost unbearable, and set Nightingale coughing furiously, but he choked it back down, and composed himself. He looked around his circle, checking that he had forgotten nothing, and that there were no gaps in any of the chalk lines. Any mistake could be fatal.

Or worse.

He took a deep breath, and began to recite the Latin incantation that he knew by heart, after using it more times than was probably healthy. He still didn't know what the words all meant, but he took care to pronounce each one carefully. Almost without thinking about it, his voice grew louder as he spoke, and was at full volume when he shouted the final three words, which were in a language which long pre-dated Latin.

'Bagahi laca bacabe.'

The fumes grew thicker, it felt as if the floor and ceiling were shaking, and, despite being indoors, there was a flash of lightning and a roll of thunder.

His eyes were streaming, and the fumes caught horribly at the back of his throat, but he concentrated on remaining motionless as he used what little breath he could muster to shout again the final three words of the summoning incantation.

'Bagahi laca bacabe.'

Again the room shook, there were two more flashes of blinding lightning, then the air in front of him shimmered. One moment there was nothing in the outer circle of the pentagram, the next the air flickered, time and space seemed to fold in on themselves, and then she was there, standing between the tip of the triangle and the edge of the circle, her face contorted with rage.

Proserpine, Princess of Hell.

The same jet-black hair and eyes as dark as pools of oil. The same leather coat over the short skirt, high studded boots and torn fishnet tights. The t-shirt had changed, this one was black and had a red inverted crucifix on it. The black and white sheepdog was by her side, as ever, and it stared hatefully at Nightingale, a threatening growl in its throat.

Proserpine's face was twisted in fury. 'Damn you to Hell, Jack Nightingale. I told you not to summon me. I come to make pacts, not for social chit-chat or any time you need a helping hand. You'll be sorry for this. I promised you I'd kill someone close to you for this. Do you think I make idle threats? Do you think I don't mean what I say?'

Many years ago, in another life, Jack Nightingale had been trained as a Police negotiator. His instructor had impressed one thing on the class on the very first day.

'Ladies and gentlemen, there are two rules in negotiating which are more important than anything else you'll learn here. Rule one, stay very calm. Rule two, if you can't stay very calm, make everyone else think you're very calm.'

It had been excellent advice, though Nightingale doubted that Detective Inspector McGee had ever meant it to be used when dealing with a raging Princess of Hell. He took a deep breath and gave Proserpine a serene smile. 'Of course I know you mean what you say. I'm sure you mean exactly what you say. Which is why I listen very carefully to everything you say, and everything you don't say.'

The fury disappeared from her face, and she frowned in confusion.

'What do you mean by that, Nightingale?'

'Just what I said. You swore that if I summoned you to Memphis, you'd kill someone I cared about. So I haven't. I've summoned you to Nashville instead.'

'You're playing with words.'

'No, I'm following your instructions, to the letter. I did exactly what you said. You can't blame me for that.'

She nodded slowly and she actually looked amused. She sniffed. 'Nashville, eh? I've done business here a few times over the years.' She smiled. 'You'd be surprised what some people will do for fame and fortune.'

Nightingale shrugged. 'Nothing really surprises me any more,' he said. 'But it seems people often don't prosper from your deals.'

She smiled slyly. 'Mostly they're not specific enough, and never read the small print.'

'It's true, the devil is in the detail,' said Nightingale.

She laughed and looked around the vast basement. 'I must say, Nightingale, your taste in decor has improved. Though I assume you didn't choose it. A girl could feel quite at home here.'

'More your style than mine. It was the best I could do at short notice.'

'So here I am in Nashville, not Memphis, and aren't you a clever boy. Should have been a lawyer, they'd call you Mr Loophole.'

'What's done is done. And I don't think I'm being clever at all. You were very precise, I think you wanted me to summon you. '

'I hate being summoned without a deal, you know that. Why would I want idle chit-chat? Here or anywhere?'

'Maybe you have things to tell me, things you can only tell me if I ask. And I think you must have had reasons of your own for not wanting to be summoned to Memphis. Someone you need to avoid there? Somebody you wouldn't want to know you were there?'

She laughed again, this time so loud that the walls shook. 'Ha, don't pretend you understand our world, Nightingale. There'd be as much chance of an...'

'Yeah, I know,' said Nightingale. 'As much chance of an earthworm understanding nuclear fission. Well, maybe this earthworm's on a learning curve.'

Her laughter seemed genuine this time. 'Oh, Nightingale, you do make me laugh. I shall miss you when this is over.'

'Maybe you won't need to. Maybe I'll still be around.'

'Maybe that's not the way it's written. Now, was there something you wanted, Nightingale? I'm a busy girl.'

'Time means nothing to you, you always say. So why the rush? But yes, there was something I wanted. Why did you get Professor Schiller to tell me everything I needed to know about Dudák?'

She gave him another sly smile. 'What makes you think I did? Isn't he one of your white-hat posse, maybe dear old Mrs Steadman put him on to you.'

Nightingale shook his head. 'No, she told me she couldn't help. So why would she call someone else to help me within hours? And if she had called him, why would he not say so? He was evasive about that, and said the lady 'wouldn't want to have her name mentioned'. And who do I know who hates having her name taken in vain?'

'We all have our little foibles,' she said. 'But why would I want to help you?'

'That's what puzzled me for a while. Especially since you seemed to be the only one who could have freed Dudák and be controlling him. You didn't seem to have any grudge against me lately, or Wainwright ever, so it occurred to me you might have made a pact with someone, someone who certainly did have a grudge against us, and you were working on their behalf.'

'Goodness me, the ideas you come up with, Nightingale. I don't discuss my deals with anyone, except the co-signatory. Or 'The Damned' as I like to call them.'

'I wasn't expecting you to. But it makes sense, this nasty little plan has got your fingerprints all over it.'

'I'm flattered you're such a fan of my work.'

'It just took me a while to figure out why you're using Dudák to do the nasty bits for you.'

'Dudák enjoys that sort of thing, and has talents for it. I can't do everything myself. Not that I'm admitting I've done anything at all. Things like Dudák are not too pleasant to have around. And there's more than one demon in Hell with the power to release it, control it and make pacts.'

'No, it won't wash. If someone wanted revenge on me and Wainwright and made a pact with you to do it in exchange for their soul, you could have done it in ten minutes. If Dudák's involved, it's because you want it that way, and you wanted me to know all about him.'

'And why exactly would I do all that, Sherlock?'

Nightingale smiled. Make them think you're calm. Time to play his one and only card. He took a long slow breath before answering. 'Because you want me to kill Dudák for you.'

She stared at him for a long time, her face a blank mask. Then she tilted her head on one side. 'Go on,' she said. 'Explain yourself.'

'Why bother? You know what your plans are. And as ever, I'm chief pawn.'

'Ha, always the ego, Nightingale. You're not even on the board. Why would I want Dudák destroyed? Assuming I have anything to do with all of this.'

'Beats me, maybe it's another one of those things that's not meant to be walking the Earth. You were pretty keen for me to stop Bimoleth from returning in San Francisco, and I don't think you shed any tears about the demons I killed in New York. In fact, I seem to remember you being pretty pissed about them escaping from Hell, and helping me get rid of them. Maybe there are laws about your kind killing other demons, and you need me to do your dirty work for you.'

'You do see things in such simple ways, Nightingale. Sometimes I envy you your blindness.'

'Well, I never envy you. So, am I right? Are you working on two things at once? Revenge on us, and using this Dudák thing as your puppet, so it can be destroyed?'

'Sorry, Nightingale, I've told you before, it's not 'phone a friend'. The workings of my kind are not to be shared with you. And why do you always imagine that you have my full attention at all times? There are eight billion souls currently on the planet, and then there are all the ones to come. What makes you so important?'

'You tell me, you seem to keep visiting me.'

'And what makes you think I don't visit billions of others? You're a speck of sand in the Sahara, Nightingale.'

'But you've said before that you want my soul.'

'Of course I do, it was pledged to me and I was cheated out of it. But there are billions of others. If yours is denied to me, I shan't sit up at night crying about it.'

She turned her soulless eyes on him, those dark pools of nothingness, and he couldn't imagine them ever shedding tears.

This wasn't getting Nightingale anywhere, and the strain of keeping a Princess of Hell imprisoned in the pentagram was beginning to tell. He could feel the sweat running down his brow, and he needed a cigarette badly.

'You're sweating, Nightingale,' she said. 'And you need a cigarette. You can't keep me here forever.'

Had she read his mind? Or was she just observing and guessing? Either way, what she said was true enough. 'I need to know where to find Wainwright's niece,' he said. 'She was taken from her home. After her parents were killed.'

'Why? What's she to you? Wainwright's been a fool, exceeded his job description and upset powerful people, and powerful entities. They want revenge. I should get out of the way, if I were you. He's not your problem.'

'I work for him.'

'My advice would be to find a new employer, and quickly. Your prospects of promotion aren't good. And a gold watch on retirement is looking very unlikely.'

'I don't abandon people,' said Nightingale.

She gave a sarcastic, sneering laugh. 'Aren't you the hero? Maybe you would revise that policy if you had even an inkling of what you're up against.'

'And this isn't just about Wainwright and his niece, that thing of yours has got Sophie Underwood in its sights.'

This time the laughter seemed genuine, and went on for what seemed like minutes. 'Did they try that on you? Someone does know your little weaknesses if they used her to bring you running. Dudák has no idea who Sophie Underwood is. She's probably in London now, who knows, pregnant by some dopey boyfriend. She's in no danger from Dudák and certainly not from me. Far too old for his tastes, and I can't harm her.'

'What do you mean?'

'Forgotten already? You pledged your soul to save her life. That's powerful protection, Nightingale, even against my kind. As for Dudák, it wouldn't be interested. It's children it craves, one whiff of puberty and the death-energies are different. No use. Now...if there's nothing else, say the words, I'm a busy girl, what's happening here will play itself out as its written. Maybe some of you will survive it, maybe not. Say the words.' There was a hardness to her voice now as if he had pushed her to her limit.

Nightingale had nothing left to ask, so he pronounced the words of dismissal. The air shimmered around her, time and space folded, and she and the dog were gone. Nightingale walked out of the pentagram to the altar at the front of the chapel, picked up his cigarettes, lit one, then sat on the nearest pew, shaking from head to foot.

CHAPTER 51

Nightingale finished his cigarette, held out his hands to check that they had indeed stopped shaking, then went back upstairs to the sitting room where he messaged Wainwright that the coast was clear. He sat smoking on one of the black sofas until he heard the noise of the SUV on the gravel outside the front door. Wainwright walked in, a straw shopping bag in each hand, obviously heavy. He put them down behind the bar, poured himself a Glenlivet, took a cigar from the humidor, then sat on the sofa opposite Nightingale. He lit his cigar then stared at Nightingale's face. 'You look like shit, Jack,' he said. 'How did it go?'

'It doesn't get any easier. There's such a darkness, such an emptiness about her...'

Wainwright held up a hand to cut him short. 'I don't want to know. In theory I know a lot more about the Occult than you, but there are things you've done that simply terrify me, and summoning Proserpine is just about top of the list. I've known people who tried to summon her kind, and they always ended up dead. Or worse.'

Nightingale shrugged. 'I know. You told me. Maybe it's ignorance that's protected me so far. Anyway, it's done.'

'You learn what you wanted?'

'I'm still not sure,' said Nightingale. 'She's hardly the helpful type when it comes to information. But there's more to this than simple revenge on you and me. A lot more. And it seems I might not even be a target here.'

'You mean it's all about me?' said Wainwright. He took a slug of whisky. 'It figures. I was the one who shoved my nose in places it had no right to be. You were just the hired help.'

'Thanks for that.'

'You know what I mean. Without me leaning on you, you'd never have got involved. Guess I overestimated my power, my abilities and my chances of staying in the background. But if it's not about you, how come that Sophie girl's on the list?'

'A bluff. She's too old and too well protected, apparently. But she's on the list because Proserpine, or someone, decided to make it about me too. I'm meant to be here. But Sophie is in no danger from Dudák. That's just about the only good news so far.''

Wainwright leaned forward on the sofa, knocked the ash off his cigar into the glass ashtray on the coffee table and looked up at Nightingale again. 'You know, Jack, if Sophie's just a lure to get you into this for some reason, you don't have to stay. I have the feeling this could turn even nastier, and it looks like it's cantered round me, and I brought it on myself. Couldn't blame you if you got in that car, and started putting lots of miles between you and this. Couldn't blame you at all.'

Nightingale lit a fresh cigarette, blew a smoke ring up at the ceiling and watched it widen and disperse. 'That's not going to happen, Joshua,' he said, 'If I'm here, it's for a reason that's bigger than I know. There are a lot of dead kids in Tennessee because of this Dudák thing, and it needs to be stopped.'

Wainwright gave a weak smile. 'I appreciate it, Jack. Thanks.' He raised his glass in salute. So what happens next?'

'First I've got to finish cleaning up downstairs.'

'And then?'

'I'm still thinking about that,' said Nightingale.

'The clock is ticking, Jack.'

'I know.'

'Tick, tock. Tick tock.'

Nightingale flashed him an annoyed look. 'Mate, I know what a fucking ticking clock sounds like.'

CHAPTER 52

Nightingale looked at his handiwork. There were no traces left of the pentagram, so Joshua or Tyrone or their associates could continue with their own rituals without interference. He shuddered a little as he wondered what actually happened down in the chapel. It was none of his business, but it reminded him how easy he found it to forget what Wainwright really was. The affable exterior was always so convincing but Satanists didn't get their power by being nice to people.

He glanced at his watch. There was still time to find Naomi, and Wainwright would help with that ritual. It came to him that he'd forgotten something, so he pulled out his mobile phone. There was no signal down in the chapel, so he headed back upstairs, remembering to turn the basement ventilation up to the highest setting to disperse the smell of burnt herbs and candles.

Once upstairs, he walked through the sitting room, out the French windows and onto the lawn, where he lit a cigarette, then started to scroll through the call register of his phone. He found the entry he was looking for, noticed with surprise that it had been only thirty-six hours ago that the first call came through, and pressed the green phone icon to return the call. It was answered almost immediately.

'Nightingale?' said Bonnie Parker. 'Where the Hell are you and where the Hell have you been? I've been calling you all day.'

'That would be the eighteen missed calls then,' said Nightingale. 'And I thought you didn't care.'

'Spare me the English humour,' said Parker. 'Answer the question. Where the Hell are you?'

'Out of town. What's the panic? I thought you were suspended.'

'I'm unsuspended. The place is going crazy, we had another one.'

'Another kid dead?'

'Don't you watch TV? Just like you called it last night, ten-year old girl called Kaitlyn Jones lit herself on fire in the entrance to the National Civil Liberties Museum. Another one, and another public place so everyone gets to hear about it. A guard saw her talking on her mobile phone outside, then she apparently poured lighter fuel over herself, walked inside and flicked a lighter. The guard was badly burnt, but he'll make it. The girl died at the scene.'

Nightingale sighed and closed his eyes. This was no fault of his, except that he hadn't been able to stop it. Parker kept talking. 'Now you named her last night, said she was on your mysterious list. It's time to stop pussy-footing around. I want you down at headquarters within the hour, and I want to know who you got that list from, and then I want to talk to them.'

'Sorry, Bonnie,' said Nightingale. 'Can't be done at the moment. I'm out of town. There are still some names on that list I need to try to save. Talking of which, where's Emma?'

'She's with her grandmother. Two thousand miles away. I just got through talking with her, she looks fine.'

A warning bell seemed to go off in Nightingale's head. 'You said she looks fine? You saw her?'

'Sure, video call. FaceTime. Welcome to the twenty-first century.'

'Shit.'

'What's your problem?'

'That might be how the children are contacted. Look, Bonnie, this is vital, Get on to the grandmother. Tell her no more video calls while the girl's there. And she needs to take away her mobile phone, tablet, laptop and anything else in the house that's capable of receiving a video call.'

'Are you nuts? Emma will get withdrawal symptoms without her phone.'

'She might get a lot worse than that if you let her use it. Just do it. And when you've done it, see if you can check Kaitlyn Jones's phone records, see where her last call came from. And the rest of the kids, check if they received a video call, a Skype call or FaceTime or WhatsApp or anything similar on their phones or computers, just before what happened happened.'

'You are nuts. That's eight sets of grieving parents I would need to upset all over again. Can't be done.'

'It needs to be done, Bonnie. I think I know what you'll find.'

Nightingale cut the connection and turned the phone off. Joshua had always assured him that the phone was completely untraceable by normal police methods, and Nightingale hoped he was right. The last thing he needed was a posse of police cruisers showing up at the Nashville house.

He went back inside to find Wainwright, and tracked him down to the kitchen by the smell of food. The freezer held a huge store of meals in plastic containers, which someone must have worked very hard to prepare, and Wainwright had just removed two from the big microwave oven that stood on the black granite worktop. The kitchen was another study in white, with just the black tops and handles providing a contrast. There was an island breakfast bar, with four stools grouped round it, and Wainwright carried the two containers to it and set them down.

'Guess we'll save on washing plates and take it straight from the plastic,' Wainwright said. 'What's it to be, chilli and rice, or tagliatelle alla carbonara?'

'I'll take the chilli,' said Nightingale, 'I was never much good at eating that long Italian stuff. Too messy. I doubt I'll taste much anyway, but we need to eat.'

'Guess we'll do without the wine.'

'Be better to avoid alcohol from now on.'

'Just when I needed it most,' said Wainwright, gripping his fork so hard that it started to bend.

CHAPTER 53

Dudák sat and watched the Memphis news channel on the widescreen television that hung on the wall. It was still showing the scenes from the Civil Rights Museum suicide that morning, with the victim identified as ten-year-old Kaitlyn Jones now that her parents had been informed. In one of the shots, Dudák was visible, but by then there were so many people milling around that nobody had taken any notice.

The journalists were now beginning to link the recent spate of child-suicides, particularly the ones that had happened in public places - the station, the Crystal Grove and now the Museum. Some diligent reporter had also added in the death of Timmy Williams, who had walked under a truck, especially since the reporter who'd written the story for the Herald had also committed suicide. Nobody, so far, was calling Julia Smith's shooting a suicide, though it was getting mentions as another unusual death of a child. The police were not currently commenting on the speculation.

Dudák listened with interest, then smiled contentedly. The feeding had been good here in the last few days, with the prospect of a few more yet to come. The police could do nothing, the only risk had come from the intended victims of the plan, but removing the Fisher girl early had negated any threat from them. The death of the parents was not Dudák's work, and there was no feeding to be had from it, but neither did it cause any regret or sympathy. It needed to be done, as part of the pledge.

Despite the high quality of the feeding, Dudák was not enjoying being controlled in this way, but it had been the price of freedom. Once this was over, the list was complete, and the task fulfilled, Dudák intended to move to another city, and resume feeding in a much less public way. In this modern world, communication was far too rapid for the old ways to continue. There would be no more Pied Piper mass disappearances.

Dudák muted the television and listened for any sound from the bedroom, but the Fisher girl slept peacefully. She had shown no fear when told to leave her parents' home and go with Dudák. The hypnotic influence over children was strong enough to overcome all resistance, when directed fully. No need for the old prop of the pipe these days. The passage of time meant little to Dudák, but the world had changed greatly in eight hundred years. Adapting had not proved difficult, especially with the knowledge and memories of the new shell to call on.

It was 10pm now, and there was nothing to be done for twelve hours. Dudák had eaten and imbibed water, since it was necessary to keep the shell in working order. It could be maintained by sheer force of will, as had happened during the centuries of imprisonment, but it was effort that distracted from other things. Dudák turned off the television, sat upright in the armchair, and stared straight ahead for the next twelve hours.

The child slept on, unaware of the horrors that had taken place around her, and those which awaited her. She would not wake until Dudák roused her and gave her the final instructions of her short life.

CHAPTER 54

Nightingale lit the two small blue candles that stood on either side of the solid crystal ball in the middle of the coffee table in the sitting room. He'd showered again, and was wearing a new white bathrobe that Wainwright had provided from a store in what he'd described as the 'Robing Room'.

Wainwright himself was sitting opposite, also freshly showered and robed.

They had decided to perform the ritual in the sitting room to keep the vibrations well away from the summoning.

'You sure you prefer me to do this?' asked Nightingale. 'You're more experienced.'

'Could be,' said Wainwright, 'but I haven't had chance to recharge my crystal since I flew back from Haiti, and besides, I'm too heavily invested in this. You'll need to concentrate fully, and my mind's too full of finding Naomi, and seeing her...'

'Probably right,' said Nightingale.

'You going to be okay with this, Jack? Two rituals inside a couple of hours is a hell of a strain.'

'Don't worry,' said Nightingale, 'after summoning Proserpine, this is just a walk in the park.'

Nightingale sprinkled herbs from a brass bowl into the flame of each candle, and they burned with blue smoke. He made a small pile of lemon twigs in the bowl. He put the two items he'd taken from Naomi's bedroom, the crucifix and the bible, on top of the pile, and added more twigs. The candles continued to burn steadily, and Nightingale nodded to Wainwright to turn off the room lights, so the only illumination now came from the twin flames. Nightingale spoke three sentences in a long-dead language. He had learned them by heart years ago in Mrs Steadman's shop. He had no idea what they might mean, but they had always worked for this ritual. Nightingale lit the lemon twigs with his lighter, watching as the flames burnt all round the book and crucifix, without seeming to harm them at all.

A small brown leather bag lay on the table, next to the crystal ball. It was centuries old, wrinkled and faded in places, but the leather still felt soft and supple as Nightingale picked it up, untied its lace, then took out a pink crystal, the size of a pigeon's egg, which he held by the chain attached to the gold mounting at one end. He lowered it gently, until it was hanging just six inches above the flames. The pink crystal began to glow, as if there were a strong light inside it, almost as if it were a living thing. Nightingale spoke again in the same ancient language. 'Asmla oscsub ascihc odsidrept Naomi Fisher. Asmla oscsub ascsihc odsidrept Naomi Fisher. Asmla oscsub ascsihc odsidrept Naomi Fisher.'

The crystal started to swing round slowly, then moved backwards and forwards regularly, from the south-west to the north-east

'Asmla oscsub ascihc odsidrept Naomi Fisher. Asmla oscsub ascsihc odsidrept Naomi Fisher. Asmla oscsub ascsihc odsidrept Naomi Fisher '

This time the clear crystal ball on the table clouded over with a pink mist and Nightingale repeated the incantation for the final time.

'Asmla oscsub ascihc odsidrept Naomi Fisher. Asmla oscsub ascsihc odsidrept Naomi Fisher. Asmla oscsub ascsihc odsidrept Naomi Fisher '

The Spell Of Propinquity was complete, and the two men watched intently as the spell forged a link between the items and their missing owner. The mist in the crystal began to clear, and a city came into view.

'Memphis,' breathed Wainwright, recognising it immediately.

Nightingale said nothing, just concentrated on keeping the swinging crystal centered over the burning twigs and Naomi's possessions.

The image in the crystal ball began to focus in now, as if someone were reducing the scale of a map. The two men saw a street, and a patch of grass, though the image was still blurred.

'Closer,' whispered Wainwright, 'come on. What the hell...'

The image of the street was gone, In its place was an indescribable face, Inhuman, with almost no recognisable features, apart from the huge mouth, and saliva-drenched fangs, which roared malevolence and defiance at them. A sheet of black lightning shot from the crystal ball to the centre of the pink crystal, and Nightingale yelled and dropped it as the chain in his hand turned red-hot, and felt like an electrical charge had coursed through it. The table was suddenly shrouded in choking black smoke.

'The window, Joshua,' shouted Nightingale. 'Now!'

Holding a hand over his mouth and nose, Wainwright ran to open the French windows, turned the air-conditioning on, and set the fan to maximum extraction. The smoke began to dissipate, and both men could breath freely again.

Nightingale surveyed the damage. The crystal ball had cracked into hundreds of small shards that lay scattered all over the coffee table and the white carpet. His crystal was a burnt and carbonated black husk, the chain had snapped apart where it joined the melted setting. The candles had been reduced to stumps of wax and the lemon twigs to ashes. The bible and the crucifix seemed to have survived undamaged.

Wainwright ran his hand through his hair, and wiped sweat from his brow with the sleeve of his ash-stained robe.

'What the hell just happened, Jack?'

'I have no idea. At a guess, I would say that someone, or something, doesn't seem to want us to find Naomi.'

CHAPTER 55

Wainwright had been nearly frantic with worry and had wanted to drive straight back to Memphis, but Nightingale managed to dissuade him by pointing out that they would have no hope of finding the child if they left. 'I sort of get the feeling that if Dudák has her, he's not going to want to have anything happen while she's hidden away,' Nightingale had argued. 'The whole idea of this plan is to cause you as much anguish as possible, so however this is meant to end, we'll be around for it.'

'That's really not much consolation, Jack,' Wainwright had said. 'For a start it's pure guesswork, for another thing, there's no way I'm gonna sit on my ass here for another two days on the chance they're gonna send for me to watch my niece die.'

'I said that's what their idea is, I didn't say we'd be going along with it. But we're only human and we need to get our strength up, we need to eat, drink and sleep.'

'Bullshit. You think I can sleep at a time like this?'

'Neither of us will be any use to Naomi if we don't. You know you can will yourself to sleep, so do it. And maybe sleep will bring a few answers.'

'What do you mean by that?' asked Wainwright.

'With a little luck, I'll tell you in the morning.'

'I wish I could believe that, Jack. But yeah, you're right, we need to recharge our batteries. Take any bedroom you like, they're all ready.'

By now, Nightingale had pretty much come to the conclusion that the house didn't belong to Tyrone at all, but had probably been purchased through one of Wainwright's many shell companies. He wondered how many more places Wainwright owned around the world, and how many of them were so clearly set up for the rituals of the Left-Hand Path.

The bedroom he chose was about twice the size of his last hotel room, with a massive bathroom complete with a roll-top bath with feet in the shape of a lion's claws. The king-size bed had grey linen and a black and grey striped counterpane. The fitted wardrobes contained, on one side, a selection of robes covered in polythene and hanging from the rail, and half a dozen sets of pyjamas, still in their plastic bags. The other side held shirts, socks, underwear, jeans, sweaters, suits and jackets. All looking brand new, and in various sizes.

Against the wall opposite the bathroom door was a fridge, Nightingale opened it and saw that it was well stocked, though there was no Corona. Alcohol wasn't a great idea under the circumstances but he figured he'd need something to ease him into sleep. He helped himself to a miniature of Glenfiddich and a glass from the tray on top of the fridge. He put his drink down on the nightstand to the right of the bed, then undressed as far as his boxers and slipped between the covers. He lit a final cigarette, sipped the whisky and tried to clear his mind. His body needed sleep, and it was important that he put all his current stress aside. He felt his eyelids growing heavy, so immediately stubbed out the cigarette, finished the drink with a gulp, and lay back on the pillow. He closed his eyes, visualised the colour light blue, and tried to relax every muscle.

Sleep came quickly, but it seemed only a few minutes later when his eyes opened as if of their own accord. His whole body felt as if it were being tugged towards the ceiling. He recognised the sensation, relaxed and allowed himself to float freely upwards, beyond the house, much more easily and quickly than last time, until he found himself again walking through a light morning mist, over damp grass, towards a familiar figure in black, sitting on a park bench, knitting some long shapeless red garment. This time, most of her silver hair was hidden under a black, woollen cap, and her black dress stretched to her ankles, leaving just the pointed toes of her black boots visible. He sat on the end of her bench, and stared into the greenest eyes he had ever seen. 'Mrs Steadman, and this time it really is you.'

She smiled reassuringly and nodded. 'Of course it is, Mr Nightingale. Look at me with your inner eye, disregard the outward appearance, and you will always know.'

He nodded. 'I do know. I don't know if it's my inner eye, but there's no mistake now. I don't know how I was fooled last time.'

'Oh dear, I have often warned you not to judge by appearances, you know. They can be so deceptive.'

'Someone else told me that, quite recently. I think it's something I need to work on.'

'You do.'

'This time was much easier, because you called me here.'

'Yes, at your inexperienced level, it can be dangerous to come here alone, your dreams and memories can be used against you.'

'They were, and I nearly got lost. But why have you called me here? You said you couldn't help.'

She bowed her head, as if ashamed. 'I know, and I feel rather bad about that. I thought I couldn't help, yet now I find I must help. And yet there is so little that I can do. Oh dear.'

'I don't understand,' he said.

'Let me try to explain.' She put down her knitting, put her hands in her lap, and looked him full in the face. 'It seemed at first that this whole unpleasant episode was being directed against you in revenge for your interference in someone's affairs. Rather like when the Order Of The Nine Angles wanted revenge on you. Not something which I could be involved in, as it might be thought to be redressing The Balance, and I have no authority in such matters. But now I have learned, from a quite remarkable source that I cannot share with you, that there is far more to it than that. There are forces at work here that must be stopped. As you know, I can only act if the order of things is threatened from outside, and now it seems that it is.'

Nightingale had no idea who Mrs Steadman's 'remarkable source' might be, He had always assumed that she knew pretty much everything, but he kept quiet, as she went on.

'What is happening is rather more complex than just that horrible Dudák creature using its power to have children kill themselves, and feed off them.'

'So you know about Dudák then?'

'Yes, I recognised what was happening. I have encountered it before.'

Nightingale frowned. That was surely not possible, if Dudák had been trapped in a cave in Hamlin for eight hundred years. Mrs Steadman couldn't be more than seventy. Could she? Conversations with her always seemed to raise more questions than they answered.

'But, as I say, there is far more to it than just Dudák's foul habits, and a desire for revenge. Far more and far worse, and you must stop it.'

'But you're not telling me what it is.'

She clenched her tiny fists on her knitting needles. 'That's the worst thing about it. I cannot explain to you what is happening. It is not permitted. But you must stop it.'

Nightingale opened his hands and spread the palms. 'I'm lost, Mrs Steadman. How can I stop whatever it is, if I don't know what or how?'

She pressed her lips together, and closed her eyes. Whether she was just thinking, or communicating with someone, Nightingale couldn't tell. Eventually her bright green eyes flew open, and were staring at him again. 'You must find Dudák and destroy it,' she said.

'How?'

'You have killed demons in human form before. Destroy the host.'

'But I can't find it. My crystal was shattered when I tried.'

'The pink one?'

Nightingale nodded.

'Oh dear. I wonder how that could have happened...unless...yes, yes, of course. A shame, that crystal was perfectly in tune with you. It will be a long time before you find another as good. But you can find Dudák by simpler means. Look within yourself, and you will already know where to find it.'

Nightingale paused and thought. 'I think I may know who, but where is harder. The last time, I was given a sign.'

'Oh, of course,' said Mrs Steadman, her green eyes flashing. 'How stupid of me to forget. Hold out your hand.'

Nightingale did as he was told, Mrs Steadman turned his left hand palm downwards and picked up one of her knitting needles. She drew it across the back of his hand, and where it touched, the flesh opened into cuts that oozed blood. It was the shape of a pan pipe. 'Dudák's sigil,' she said. 'As you get close, it will burn.'

Nightingale winced.

'It hurts?' asked Mrs Steadman.

'A bit,' he said. Actually it hurt a lot. A hell of a lot.

'The pain will intensify the closer you get to your quarry,' she said. 'I'm sorry about that, but you may well find that it is the least of your worries. But there is more.'

'Destroying Dudák isn't enough for me to have to worry about?'

'It would be, but it is not the most important thing at all. It is absolutely vital that you save the girl, Naomi Fisher. At all costs, literally at all costs, she must not be allowed to kill herself on June 26. The consequences are unthinkable.'

'But you're not allowed to tell me what they are?'

She bowed her head, but said nothing.

'You're not making this easy for me, Mrs Steadman,' said Nightingale.

'I am sorry,' she said. 'But I have done all I can. Good luck, Mr Nightingale. And do be careful,'

She waved her hand at him, and Nightingale watched as the mist round his feet rose up to hide her from view, then covered everything, so he couldn't see at all. Then, slowly, a blinding light burnt the mist away and shone straight into his eyes.

He woke up, the morning sun streaming through the opened curtains. He lifted his left arm and stared at the back of his left hand. The flesh was still singed and the sigil was red now and raised and it hurt like Hell.

CHAPTER 56

Bonnie Parker sighed in frustration. There were over a hundred people named Ann Davies in the greater Memphis area, and Bonnie Parker had no hope at all of tracing them, much less trying to get a list of all the ones aged around ten inside a day. Tracing adults was usually a simple matter because they had bank accounts and driving licences and social security numbers, but children were more often than not invisible online, at least in official databases. She had tried social media and again there were dozens of possibilities. Even if she had been able to track down every one of them, what was Parker meant to do? Take them all into protective custody on the say-so of some English ex-cop who claimed to have a mysterious list of potential suicide victims? An Englishman who had now conveniently disappeared from his hotel, after his hire car had been spotted by a witness near the scene of a horrific murder-suicide. The Commissioner and the Mayor would have her badge inside ten minutes and her pension in twenty. They didn't have anywhere near enough men available to detail one to watch every kid called Ann Davies. And what would they be watching for anyway? There were so many ways someone could kill themselves, in or out of the home, and how could a patrolman be expected to stop them.

She stood outside headquarters at 9am smoking her seventh cigarette of the morning, trying to make sense of what was happening. She had still been a little drunk when she'd packed her daughter's bag and shipped her off to Emma's grandmother's in Las Vegas. Maybe she was acting like a fool. But then if her daughter had wound up dead, and she'd done nothing, how could she ever have lived with it? The mysterious list had called it right on Kaitlyn Jones and Julia Smith. So what was happening here? Were the police missing something, had all the suicides been murders, and was this Nightingale character just working through a list of victims?

She shook her head and muttered 'Nah, can't be,' much to the surprise of a mail-carrier walking past her.

No, she knew exactly how Julia Smith had died, and there were solid witnesses for lots of the other suicides. So could there be anything in this idea of someone hypnotising kids into killing themselves. But how? And why? At the moment, they're wasn't even a case here, nobody had put her in charge of investigating a bunch of highly public suicides of Junior School kids, or even suggested how they could be connected.

Parker threw her cigarette butt on the sidewalk and walked back inside, fervently wishing two things. First, that Nightingale would show up, so she could force him to tell her what the hell was going on, and second that the day would pass without a kid called Ann Davies killing herself.

CHAPTER 57

It turned out that neither of Bonnie Parker's wishes was to be granted. Nightingale had his own reasons for not showing up in Memphis at the moment, and Ann Davies was already on her way to her death.

The class of children had been taken in a hired bus down to Riverside Drive for their outing. They all had backpacks with sandwiches and wore baseball caps in their school colours for ease of identification by the two teachers who counted them all off the bus. There were twenty-two children, and the tall, grey-haired man and the shorter, younger, pretty blonde woman lined them up in twos to walk to the landing stage.

The Island Queen stood waiting for its passengers to board for the ninety-minute sight-seeing tour of a very small part of the Mississippi river and a look at Memphis from the water. A hundred feet long, its three decks and superstructure were painted gleaming white, in contrast to the two high black funnels which rose at either side of the wheelhouse, and the huge red paddle wheel at the rear. It looked as if it might have steamed straight from the pages of a Mark Twain novel, but was in fact less than forty years old and diesel powered. The excited group of children didn't care too much about its history, a day out of class and a trip on the river had got them all buzzing.

The passengers walked up the gangplank, the teachers making sure that they counted all twenty-two hats onto the ship, then taking a last glance at the landing-stage to make doubly sure that nobody had been left behind. The passengers spread themselves around the three decks. The boat was nowhere near full, so there was no need to jockey for vantage points. The children split up into smaller groups, with the two teachers having told them where they could be found in case of the emergency they hoped would never occur. The older man had done this trip a dozen times with classes, but it was the first time for his young companion. Neither of them were worried, there was nowhere for the kids to go, and nothing more dangerous than the high-fat potato chips they'd probably all brought with them for lunch.

The boat whistle blew, the big paddle wheel started to turn, and the Island Queen eased its way out into the murky waters of the USA's second-longest river. The two teachers settled down with a cup of coffee each, to enjoy a peaceful hour and a half.

The peace barely lasted ninety seconds.

The screaming started at the stern of the vessel, before it had travelled more that two hundred yards from the shore. Instantly terrified, the two teachers ran towards the stern, and then up onto the top deck, where the children's screams were loudest. As they reached the stern, they were met by a group of girls, each still obediently wearing their school caps. The screaming was awful, but the male teacher took command, shouted for quiet, the screaming stopped, then the girls started talking at once.

'Mr Dillon, it's Ann...'

'Ann, she just jumped up on the rail...'

'She jumped in, Mr Dillon...'

'We couldn't stop her...'

'Look...'

The teacher looked over the stern rail of the riverboat, to where the great wheel spun round, chewing up the distance along the river, but now chewing up something it was never meant to. Pieces of clothing followed in its trail, and, as the paddles rose from the water, they brought with them the broken remains of the girl who had been impaled on them when she jumped.

Dillon vomited over the side of the ship and into the water, his hands gripping the rail in horror. Around him was chaos, as the panic spread, the boat's crew became aware of what had happened, and the captain gave the order to stop all engines. All far too late.

Unnoticed in the crowd that thronged to the stern of the boat, Dudák stood, eyes closed, against the rail and feasted on the child's death agonies. Very soon now the task would be complete, and Dudák would be free to leave this city and feed elsewhere.

CHAPTER 58

'So the plan is that we just cruise around Memphis until the scar on the back of your hand starts to sting?' said Wainwright.

'See now, that might take rather a long time,' said Nightingale, 'time we don't really have.' They were sitting on kitchen stools drinking coffee that Wainwright had prepared.

'No shit. If you ask me we've waited way too long out here, when we could have been in Memphis looking for Naomi.'

'Time spent in reconnaissance is seldom wasted.'

'Says who?' asked Wainwright.

'Sun Tsu. Or Field Marshal Rommel. Or Han Solo. I forget now.'

Wainwright frowned and stared at him. 'Tell me, Jack, of all the people you ever met, any of them ever laugh at your jokes?'

Nightingale lit a cigarette, while he considered the point. 'Not many,' he said. 'I'm just trying to lighten the moment.'

'Time and a place, Jack. This is neither. So what is the plan?'

'Something Mrs Steadman said to me last night. That if I looked within myself, I could find Dudák.'

'What does that mean?'

'It means I've been trying to piece together a lot of the things that have happened, and how they could have been made to happen. And I think Mrs Steadman is right, I can find Dudák. But I can't afford to be wrong, so I need to talk to a few people and confirm a few things first.'

'Anything I can do? I have a lot of contacts.'

'I'm guessing not in the Memphis Department of Education.'

Wainwright shook his head. 'Probably not.'

'Well, I need to find some people who do. But I guess there are some things you can be getting on with.'

'Like what?'

'Like maybe you could open that mysterious metal box you talked about with Tyrone, and we'll see if I guessed right about what's in there.'

Wainwright grinned. 'Maybe you did. Come on.'

Wainwright led the way upstairs to the bedroom he'd been using, and opened the bathroom door. Next to the full length mirror was a shaver socket. Wainwright pressed the voltage selector switch on it, there was a click, and the mirror shot open an inch or two on concealed hinges. Wainwright pulled it fully open, to reveal a metal locker. He took a key from the pocket of his jeans and opened it.

'Wow,' said Nightingale. There were three shelves in the locker, with three or four guns on each. Nightingale saw Colt and Remington revolvers, Glock semi-automatics, an Uzi, Berettas and, standing upright at the side, two AK-47s. At the bottom were boxes of ammunition. 'Planning to start a war?'

'Tyrone likes to be prepared for all eventualities. Choose your weapon. None of them traceable, none of them ever been fired.'

'I'll take a Glock and a dozen shells.'

Wainwright took out two Glock pistols, a box of shells and holsters that could be clipped to their belts.

'Anything else we gonna need?' asked Wainwright.

'More gas for the car, a priest, and an awful lot of good luck,' said Nightingale. 'Same as always.'

'Gas and the priest I can organise,' said Wainwright. 'What you need him for?'

Nightingale told him.

CHAPTER 59

Bonnie Parker was watching the local Memphis News Channel on her laptop. It was a live feed from the riverside, where the Island Queen had been towed back to the landing stage, and the entire area cordoned off by white Police cruisers. There was also an ambulance and a water rescue unit, and the whole place was awash with people, as the cops tried to marshal the passengers ashore so they could take witness statements, at the same time trying to deal with shocked children, confused and angry adults and the Press, who had turned out in force.

The two Homicide Detectives at the scene had pretty quickly decided they weren't going to be needed. Parker was talking to one of them now via radio, Detective Mary O'Brien. 'Looks open and shut, Sarge,' she said. 'Any number of witnesses, mostly kids admittedly, but they all say the little girl just ran at the rail and vaulted straight over.'

'The rail's pretty low then?' said Parker.

'Not at all. Standard size, meant to prevent adults accidentally falling over. Kid would have had to put in a pretty good effort to vault it, but they all say she did. She vaulted straight down onto the rear paddle wheel. A pretty ghastly mess, apparently. Not sure they found all the pieces.'

Parker shuddered. 'Any ID on the kid yet?'

Parker kept her voice casual, but her knuckles were white as she gripped the handset. She knew what she was going to hear, but was still terrified of it.

'The teachers have all named her as Ann Davies, aged ten. It'll be a while before they can get forensic confirmation, but she's the only child not accounted for so there's no doubt.'

'My God,' said Parker, more to the ceiling than the radio. A cold chill ran down her spine.

'Yeah, ten, it's a bad one, sure enough. Uniforms tried to contact the parents, but there was nobody home. They could be on their way down here though, lots of parents saw the news and have come down to collect kids.'

'You talked to the teachers?'

'Yeah, older guy who's been at the school forever, and a young woman who's pretty new. They were on the lower deck having coffee when it happened.'

'Aren't they meant to supervise the kids?'

'There are always school trips on the boat, Sarge. It's supposedly a safe environment.'

'Until today.'

'Yeah, but what's safe if someone decides to kill themselves? That's what it looks like, no question. The kid just took her own life.'

'So what about this kid, she a loner? Being bullied?'

'The teachers say not. She was very popular, she had lots of friends. Nobody has any idea why she did it. We'll talk to the parents, obviously. But you know as well as I do, in cases like this the parents usually have no clue as to what their kids are thinking.'

'You're right, it doesn't look like there's anything there for Homicide on the face of it. You might as well head on back to the station..'

Parker put the radio down, sat back in her chair and cursed Jack Nightingale with every ounce of venom she could muster.

CHAPTER 60

If Jack Nightingale's ears were burning he was too busy to notice as he cruised east along the I-40. Wainwright had lit one of his huge cigars as they left Tyrone's place, and it looked like it would last him all the way to Memphis. Nightingale was still trying to figure the best way to approach Wainwright's recent bereavement. On the one hand, he needed information, on the other, he had a certain liking for Wainwright, and had no wish to make things worse. In the end, he decided to stay away from it. 'No more word on Abaddon, if she's still alive?' he asked.

'Not a peep,' said Wainwright. 'She was never treated in any official US health facility, she never left the country by scheduled flight, boat or car. Could be she was dead in that chapel and one of her minions took the body away.'

'You believe that?'

'I'm not sure. I sometimes get a feeling when powerful adepts are carrying out important rituals, but nothing with her since the 'Frisco thing. Of course, maybe I don't have enough power.'

'Power's a pretty important thing in your world, isn't it, Joshua?'

'Maybe it's everything, here on Earth, Jack. The power to shape life by your will.'

'So you're always looking to increase your power?'

Wainwright inhaled deeply on his cigar, then gave a smile. 'Me, Jack? I'm just a guy who collects books, and got lucky.'

Nightingale nodded. 'So Abaddon would have had more power than you?'

'Hard to say,' said Wainwright. 'You never got round to reading Aleister Crowley's diary before you made a present of it to me, did you?'

'I'm not much of a reader,' said Nightingale.

'Shame. He detailed the various levels of Occult power, and there's a whole lot of them. With the top three, the whole idea is to gain an understanding of the way the Universe works, and to use the power of your will to shape it as you wish.'

'And you think Abaddon might have got to one of those three levels?'

'Almost certainly,' said Wainwright. 'Probably she got to Magister Templi to even consider raising a demon like Bimoleth. You told me she could hold people motionless, with the power of will alone?'

Nightingale shuddered, as he remembered his final encounter with Abaddon in the chapel of the San Francisco mansion. 'Yes,' he said. 'We were damned lucky.'

'Or the forces of light smiled on you. Anyway, she'd have had to reach a pretty high level to do that.'

'And how do people reach that kind of level?'

Wainwright shrugged. 'Years of dedication. Study. Sacrifices to Lucifer.'

Nightingale looked across at him. 'You mean human sacrifices?'

'Well, you saw that in San Francisco. And there are higher grades, where the price of admission is even steeper.'

'Steeper than murder?'

'Oh yes, and even that's not enough. You want to reach Magus or Ipsissimus and you need to have that power bestowed on you. Maybe that's why Abaddon was trying to raise Bimoleth, she thought he might bestow that higher power on her.'

'In exchange for what?'

Wainwright laughed. 'I wouldn't know, and if I did, I couldn't tell you. Adepts who reach those levels are never permitted to speak of it. But, apparently, they achieve power that is incomprehensible to anyone else. Practically limitless on Earth.'

'Doesn't sound good,' said Nightingale.

Wainwright laughed again but there was a harshness to the sound. 'Guess there's no need to worry yourself about it. There's talk that Crowley may have reached that level, and drove himself mad doing it. Probably nobody since. You ask me, there's not a Magus walking this Earth right now. Much less an Ipsissimus.'

Nightingale nodded. 'And how far along the trail have you gotten, Joshua? As far as Abaddon?'

Wainwright grinned slyly. 'It's like Fight Club, Jack. The first rule is that you don't talk about it.'

'I hear you,' said Nightingale. It was obvious Wainwright was bringing a curtain down on that subject. 'You sure you'll be able to find a priest in Memphis?' he asked.

'Already arranged,' said Wainwright. 'I've got contacts pretty much everywhere these days, a quick call gets most things done.'

'You never struck me as the type to associate with the clergy.'

'Ain't. But if I need something done I can always find someone. Not all priests are shining examples of piety, Jack. Plenty of them would offer Ted Bundy absolution if there was a couple of hundred dollars in it for them. Consecrating a few bullets will be no problem.'

'Good, said Nightingale. 'From what I've seen of demons, they laugh at ordinary weapons, and we need to take Dudák down before the twenty-sixth, one way or another.'

'You still think you can find Dudák?'

'I think I've got a pretty good idea, I'll know more after an interview, and maybe a phone call or two. I can't afford to be wrong.'

'So maybe your magic bullets are gonna work fine on Dudák, but have you thought about what we're going to do about whoever's behind him?'

'What do you mean?'

Wainwright looked across at Nightingale, and his face was worried. 'From what I hear, this Dudák is a nasty piece of work, but he's still minor league. He's not a Prince, an Earl, a Marquis of Hell, he's got no real clout, he can't be making pacts and bestowing power. Seems he couldn't even get himself out of a cave for eight hundred years, he had to wait for someone more powerful to show up and free him. And make use of him.'

'It had occurred to me,' said Nightingale. 'It's hard to believe Dudák decided to move all the way to Tennessee, send you that list, track down your niece, kill your sister and brother-in-law all by itself. But could Abaddon do all that?'

'I doubt it,' said Wainwright, 'She had power, for sure, as head of a coven, and she was a very strong adept, but most of that was destroyed when her coven broke up. And freeing a trapped Demon is major-league power, much less actually obliging it to do your bidding. I think we're looking at someone much further up the scale.'

'I thought it might be Proserpine, but I didn't get the feeling she's behind it,' said Nightingale. 'But she knows all about it though.'

'Got any other guesses?'

'Well, Lucifuge Rofocale was behind that mess in New York, and he has a pretty big grudge against me,' said Nightingale. 'This might be his doing.'

'We'd best hope not. He's a Prince of Hell, ain't going to be stopped by sprinkling Holy Water on a few shells.'

'No,' said Nightingale. 'If it is him, or someone like him, that's where my plan sort of runs out.'

'Anyways,' said Wainwright, 'one step at a time, I guess.'

'Yes,' said Nightingale. 'And step one is Elise Wendover.'

'Who's she?'

'The mother of Charmaine, the girl who killed herself in the grotto. I've some questions for her.'

CHAPTER 61

Kim Jarvis had claimed to have found Charmaine Wendover by calling all the Wendovers in the book and asking for the girl, but Nightingale had his doubts about that now. His search had been much easier, since there was only one Elise Wendover listed in the Memphis directory. He slowed the SUV to a halt opposite her apartment building. It was four stories high, built as three sides of a rectangle, with a well-kept green area in the middle and a few benches dotted around it. The bricks of the walls were chocolate brown up to halfway between the second and third floors, where they changed to white. The roofs were all grey slate, and the whole building looked to be relatively modern and kept in good repair.

'Nice place, I guess' said Wainwright. 'Do you think the cops are going to like you talking to her?'

'It's not against the law to knock on somebody's door and ask to talk to them,' said Nightingale. 'And the cops aren't investigating a crime here. They've probably forgotten she exists. It's not a great time to call, but then we can't afford to wait. You going to take the car to go see your tame priest?'

'I'll call a cab,' said Wainwright. 'I always prefer to have someone else do the driving.'

Nightingale nodded, and he headed across the street, while Wainwright took a blue sports bag out of the back of the car, slammed the tailgate and pulled out his phone.

The building didn't appear to run to a doorman, and Nightingale was considering his options for getting inside when a tall black man in blue overalls, carrying a toolbox, opened the main door. Nightingale held it for him, and the man grunted an acknowledgment. He said nothing more, seeming either to accept him as a resident or, more likely, not in the least bit interested who he was, so Nightingale walked in.

The Wendover apartment had been listed as 315, so Nightingale only had two flights of stairs to climb. He opened the stairwell door on the third floor, walked along to 315 and rang the bell. He heard the shuffling of feet, and the door opened on a security chain. He could make out a pair of reddened eyes and some long mousy hair, and then the woman spoke. 'Who are you? What do you want? I'm not seeing any more reporters.'

'I promise you I'm not a reporter,' said Nightingale.

The woman's nose wrinkled in puzzlement. 'You Australian?'

'English. My name's Jack Nightingale. Mrs Wendover, I was the one who found your daughter. In the grotto. Can I talk to you?'

The door was immediately closed in his face. Nightingale thought for a moment that he'd have to try a different approach, but then he heard the security chain being taken off, and the woman opened the door again.

'Come in,' she said. 'The place is a mess, and so am I, I'm afraid, but I need to talk to you, too.'

Nightingale took a look around, and decided she was probably right on both counts about the mess. It was an upscale apartment that had been let go. The sitting room had a good view of the lawn outside, but the windows were dirty, and the curtains needed cleaning. The sofa and chairs looked grubby, with food and wine stains everywhere, and shoes lay on the floor where they'd been kicked off. Empty wine bottles lay in a basket to the side of the sofa, and there was a pizza box and a half-empty bottle of Californian Chablis on the coffee table. The woman straightened a cushion on one of the armchairs and waved him into it. Nightingale noticed there seemed to be no television, though there was a wooden unit across the room where one might have been. An open laptop stood next to the wine bottle.

Elise Wendover looked like a woman whose life had fallen apart. She was wearing a robe and slippers at 1.30 in the afternoon, her hair badly needed washing and a cut, her face was bloated with flushed cheeks and chin, and her eyes were red from crying. She looked as if she'd put on quite a few pounds recently, and her eye-liner and lipstick were badly smudged. She smelled of stale sweat and fresh wine. She slumped onto the sofa opposite him and Nightingale felt even more guilty for being there.

'Mrs Wendover, I'm really sorry to call here at such a bad time for you...'

She waved his apology away with her left hand, while the other lifted up the wine bottle. 'Forget about it,' she said, 'I got the feeling there are never gonna be any good times again. You want a drink?'

Nightingale really didn't, but anything which might establish common ground was probably a good idea. 'Thank you,' he said.

She looked around for a glass and didn't see one. 'You want to get yourself a glass?' she said, 'First cupboard on the left.'

She waved her hand at the door behind her, which was obviously the kitchen, and Nightingale got to his feet. The kitchen was a worse mess, with dirty crockery piled in the sink, food remnants on the worktops, and splashes of liquid on the floor. Nightingale found a glass, held it up to the light and rinsed it out before taking it back into the sitting room. He set it on the coffee table, and Elise Wendover splashed some wine into it. She raised her own glass, as he took his.

'Well, cheers to you, Mr Nightingale, though I guess I have nothing left to cheer.'

'Cheers. Call me Jack,' said Nightingale, raising his glass to her in return and taking a sip of the wine. He wasn't much of a wine drinker but he nodded approval, and forced down another sip, before setting the glass back on the coffee table. He looked across the table at her, and noticed fresh tears in her eyes.

She pointed at a photo on the mantelpiece, showing an attractive young blonde woman, raising a champagne glass at the photographer, clearly in some restaurant. 'You wouldn't recognise me now, would you? Would you believe that was taken eighteen months ago?'

Nightingale couldn't think of a good answer to that so he stayed silent.

'Yeah, just a couple months before I found out my husband was banging some slut he met off Tinder. Very kindly she called me up to tell me. And to tell me she was pregnant. He never came home again, not even for his clothes. Saved me shooting him.'

'You have a gun here?' asked Nightingale.

'Nah, just talk,' she said. 'But I'd have loved to. Bastard deserved it.'

'He's not helping you financially?'

'Haven't heard a word from him since. It's like he cut me and Charlie out of his life like we never meant anything to him. He cancelled his cellphone so I can't even call him. Turned out he was six months behind with the house repayments, the bank repossessed it, and all I could find was this place, which I'm getting a deal on from a friend. I owe her three months rent as it is, so I don't know how much longer she'll be staying a friend.'

Nightingale nodded, but said nothing. He had no solutions to offer, nothing at all except a listening ear, so he let her talk.

'All seemed to happen at once, I was working as a secretary for a construction company which went under, and all I've been able to find since is waitressing. Doesn't pay much, and they tend to want their girls younger and prettier. And soberer. And now this. Jesus, what did I ever do to deserve this?'

'Nothing at all,' said Nightingale. 'Just sometimes life doesn't give us what we deserve. Things just happen.'

She nodded, and now the tears were really flowing. He wondered about moving to the sofa and putting an arm round her, but that kind of thing was easily misinterpreted these days, so he stayed put.

'Shit happens, eh?' she said, and sniffed. 'Well you can say that again. But what happened to me, maybe I can deal with, but I killed my daughter, Jack. I killed Charlie.'

'No, you didn't, said Nightingale. 'You'd never have done that.'

'But I did, I just made things too hard for her to cope with. You know, she was only ten, but since Hank gave up on us, she'd been the adult round here. She used to make me dress to walk her to school, she'd do the washing up, clean the place, and she'd always be asking me to eat better, drink less, wash my hair. And in the end, it got too much for her, she couldn't cope with having a child for a mother, and she killed herself. It was my fault.'

Nightingale shook his head again. 'No, this isn't on you. You've been through hard times, but this is something different. Have you heard about other kids recently who've killed themselves? Same age as Charlie, in public places?'

She waved at the empty TV unit. 'I don't hear about much these days, sold the television. I guess the computer will be next. You telling me there've been other kids like Charlie, just up and killed themselves?'

'It's been happening a lot, all in the last few days. One boy walked in front of a truck, another threw himself under a train, there was another child who hanged herself at home. All Charlie's age. And all with no warning and for no reason that anyone could find.'

She looked at him as if struggling to understand what he was telling her. 'So what are you saying? They were killed or something?'

'No,' said Nightingale. 'They killed themselves. But I think someone else, or something else, made them do it.'

She poured the last two inches of wine into her glass, not offering to share since Nightingale had barely touched his. 'I don't see what you're saying, how can someone make a kid kill themselves?'

'I don't really know,' said Nightingale. 'But Charlie never talked about hurting herself, did she?'

Elise Wendover shook her head emphatically. 'Absolutely not, most of the time she was incredibly positive, kept telling me not to get too down, telling me we'd get through all this. The only time I ever saw her sad was when she was talking about how her father had just abandoned her. She...we...never so much as heard a word from him after that slut phoned. Not a damned word.'

'Did you try to trace him?'

'How? Police aren't interested in a guy who just goes away, I didn't have money for lawyers or detectives. Anyhow, in all that time, Charlie never once talked about hurting herself. Tell you the truth, couple times I talked about it and she was horrified. Kept telling me we had to be strong, we were all that each other had. You want some more wine? I got another bottle.'

Nightingale shook his head. 'I'm good,' he said, then watched as she levered herself up from the sofa and walked unsteadily to the kitchen. He heard the sound of the fridge opening, then the cork being drawn, and she tottered back in, set a full bottle down next to the empty one, then sat down again.

'Last one for today. I keep thinking if I stay drunk, all this won't have happened, not unless I sober up. You ever try that?'

The words weren't that coherent, but Nightingale got the sense of them. 'Once,' he said. 'In another life.'

'How'd it work out for you?'

He forced a smile. 'Not too well.' He took another sip of wine, just to keep her company, then tried to get back to the point. 'So Charlie wasn't unhappy, she didn't have any problems at school?'

Again the over-emphatic shake of the head. Elise Wendover was getting pretty drunk now. 'No, she was happy at school, lots of friends. She liked her teachers, though she missed Mrs Dominguez. She's had a baby, so they had a few substitutes in, Charlie said they were okay, but Mrs Dominguez was really special. She was looking forward to her coming back to school.' She dabbed at her eyes with a tissue.

'Did she see her friends outside school?'

'Not so much lately. Maybe she was a little ashamed of me and this place. Maybe the other moms didn't want their kids hanging round a drunk.'

'Did she talk to them on the phone much?'

She hung her head. 'No. She wasn't a great one for the phone.'

The woman's eyes were beginning to glaze over, and he thought she might not stay coherent for too much longer. He'd probably got all he could from her, but his human sympathy wouldn't let him leave it at that. 'You shouldn't be alone now,' he said. 'Is there anyone you can call?'

She shook her head. 'That's what the police said. Nah. My parents hated Hank, haven't heard from them since they didn't come to the wedding. Looks like they had it right.'

'Why not try calling them? Maybe time to build some bridges? They might want to help.'

'I'll think about it,' she said, 'been a long time, but maybe you're right. Maybe not.'

Nightingale stood up to go, but she stayed seated, and put her head in her hands. 'Mister. Jack. Why were you there?'

'Where?'

'The grotto. Where it.... happened.'

Where her daughter killed herself with alcohol and tablets, is what she meant. Nightingale couldn't imagine how the woman felt, knowing that her daughter had taken her own life. Suicide was a terrible thing on every level, but it was always worse for those that were left behind.

'I got a call from a reporter,' he said. 'She'd been looking into other kids and suicides. I don't know how she knew Charlie was...where she was, but she called me there.'

'The reporter woman shot herself, they said. Why?'

'I don't know that either,' said Nightingale.

'Seems you don't know much, but then neither do I. Just know my little girl's gone, and she never hurt anyone in her life. And I'm here without her.'

Her eyes closed, and her head slumped to one side. Nightingale walked over to the sofa, turned her onto her side, and put a pillow under her head, then turned to leave. Her voice came again from behind him.

'Hey, Mister. I saw her in the morgue, but you saw her there in that Crystal Grotto. Tell me, how did she look when you saw her?'

Nightingale took a deep breath and didn't look back. 'She looked ...peaceful,' he lied.

'Peaceful. God, I hope so.'

He looked round again now, but her eyes were closed, and she was breathing rhythmically. He walked out of the sitting room, but stopped in front of the table in the hallway and took out his wallet, There were a half-dozen hundreds, plus a couple of fifties, and everything else was small stuff. He left the large bills on the table, then let himself out.

So many people with problems, they were like stray dogs. You couldn't take care of them all, but every now and again, you did what little you could.

CHAPTER 62

Nightingale lit a much-needed cigarette and walked back to his car. He leaned against the hood to smoke, pulled out his mobile phone and un-muted the ringing tone. No messages, so he called Wainwright. 'I'm done here, Joshua,' he said.

'You get what you wanted?'

'Maybe. Be nice to make sure, we'll only get one chance at this. The mother's in a hell of a state. Drunk, broke, blames herself.'

'Understandable, but what's happening isn't the parents' fault.'

'Might be a nice thing if I could find a way of explaining that to them that didn't sound like a fairy story. How you doing with the priest?'

'I found him at home and he was happy to do what you wanted, especially after a generous donation to the Church Restoration Fund. Might get spent on gin, but that's not my affair. He's gone into his church now to do the whatever to them. I'm not big on churches, so I'm waiting outside. He said it would be better if I joined in the ritual, but I took a pass on that. Can't see anyone being fooled by me mouthing Christian stuff. He's got the deputy priest to help him instead. Cost me another hundred.'

'I think they call them curates,' said Nightingale.

'Call them snowdrops for all I care. Be ready soon, where do I meet you?'

Nightingale mentally ran through the short list of bars he knew in Memphis. 'How about Huey's Burger on South Second Street. We can meet and eat.'

'Okay, though I don't think I'll be too hungry.'

'Long day, best to refuel when you can, not when you want to.'

'I guess. See you there.'

'Good. And Joshua, you remembered to ask the priest to load the guns? It's important nobody else touched the shells once they're consecrated.'

'He's not happy about loading the guns,' said Wainwright. 'I guess I can understand his logic. But I've got a solution, don't worry. See you.'

Nightingale stood on his cigarette butt and got into the car. He hadn't been proud of bothering Elise Wendover, who had enough to contend with, but the visit had at least served to strengthen a theory that had been growing inside him for a day or so now. He needed more confirmation, and he thought he knew where he might get it, provided his boyish charm was working today.

Nightingale drove to Huey's Burger and left the car in a parking lot. There was no sign of Wainwright, so he sat at the bar to wait. His heart said beer, but his head won, and he ordered a tomato juice, after a little debate with the young bartender about the correct pronunciation. The giant television behind the bar was showing a group of police cruisers standing in front of a landing-stage by the river, with a large old-fashioned white boat in the background. Nightingale looked at the bartender and pointed to the screen. 'What's happening?'

The bartender moved a little further up the bar towards him. He was young, maybe yet another college student working to pay his tuition. He had short dark hair, still a few teenage acne spots on his chin. 'How awful is that?' said the bartender, gesturing at the television. 'Bunch of kids on a school trip on the Island Queen, that paddle-steamer there. Seems like one of them fell off, straight onto the wheel.' He shuddered. 'Can you imagine that? Must have chopped her into a dozen pieces.'

Nightingale froze, and the hairs on the back of his neck stood up. Another one, he thought.

'Did they identify the kid who died?' asked Nightingale.

'Does the name matter?' asked the bartender. 'Dead's dead.' The bartender moved away to serve another customer, and Nightingale kept staring at the screen. There was a group of children in uniform baseball caps, being lined up and counted by two adults, presumably their teachers. Nightingale stared long and hard at them, then pulled out his mobile phone and punched in Bonnie Parker's number.

'Bonnie? Jack Nightingale.'

Sergeant Parker was not happy. Not by a long way, and she yelled into his phone. 'Where are you, you bastard? And how come your mobile phone can't be traced?'

'It's magic, Bonnie. I'm in a bar, looking at a news report from the river. Do you know the name of the kid who died?'

'You bet your pasty English ass I do, you bastard. Get yourself in here, right now.'

'Can't do that, Bonnie. But please tell me the name.'

'You know it damned well. Though how you know it, I have no idea.'

'Ann Davies?'

'In one. Now you tell me what this is all about, or I swear to God I'll have an APB put out on you to have you shot on sight.'

'I doubt that, Bonnie. Now I need you to do something for me. 'Can you get me a list of substitute teachers in the State and the schools they have been to?'

'Why?'

'Just a hunch.'

'I'll need more than a hunch to get something like that done,' she said. 'It'll take hours and hours of work. My boss is going to want to know why. So no, I can't do that. Not without a solid reason and you don't seem to be giving me that.'

'Okay, then how about this? I want you to call your daughter and ask her if she's had any substitute teachers in the last few months.'

'There are always substitute teachers,' said the detective. 'The schools couldn't function without them.'

'So ask her for the names.'

'Not a chance. Since I cut off her phone and internet, her grandmother says she won't speak to me. Anyway, why the sudden interest in substitutes?'

'Because these kids are being reached somehow and it occurred to me it might be happening in the schools. Substitute teachers are always moving around, so…'

'That's a hell of a leap, Nightingale.'

'It's all I've got. But I did speak to the mother of Charmaine Wendover and her daughter had substitutes.'

'I'm sure every kid in the State has,' said the detective. 'Okay, I'll try to talk to Emma, but I can't promise anything.'

She ended the call. On a sudden hunch, Nightingale Googled the number of Saint Richard's academy and called it. A female voice answered, who, he assumed, would be the secretary.

'Hello there,' said Nightingale in his best American accent. 'Jack Jones here. Wanted to leave a message for one of your staff.'

'Certainly Mr Jones, which member of staff?'

Nightingale gave her the name. As he did so, Wainwright walked in and joined him at the bar, putting his blue sports bag down by his side. Nightingale gestured with one hand for him to wait.

'Oh…right…I see,' said Nightingale into his phone. 'Yes…three weeks? Shame, my daughter was very impressed. Sorry to bother you.'

Wainwright raised an eyebrow in a silent question as Nightingale ended the call and put his phone away. 'Just a theory,' said Nightingale. 'But one that is rapidly turning into a fact.'

'Care to share?'

'Very soon, just waiting on another call. Let's eat.'

Wainwright ordered a coffee from the young barman, and they headed over to one of the vacant tables, taking menus with them. Nightingale set the remains of his tomato juice down on the red and white checked table-cloth, but had barely had time to open it when the waitress arrived.

'Well, hello again,' she said to Nightingale.

'Hello again…Diane,' he said, hoping she hadn't noticed the pause while he looked at her name badge again. 'You work long hours.'

'Different shift today. You want to try the Heart Healthy Mahi-Mahi Plate again?'

'Sure,' he said, 'and another tomato juice.'

'Gosh, I just love your accent, Australian, right?'

'Right,' said Nightingale. He was often mistaken for an Australian and sometimes it was just easier to go with it rather then getting into a discussion about accents.

'And what about your friend, then? I don't think he needs to watch his weight.'

Wainwright grinned at the compliment. 'I'll take the Special Hueyburger and fries, and I should have a coffee coming,' he said.

She nodded, ticked off the orders on her pad and headed back to the kitchen.

'Girl's got a good eye,' said Wainwright, still smiling.

'Not so sure,' said Nightingale. 'I mean, do I look out of shape to you?'

Wainwright looked at him, as if he were appraising cattle. 'Well, maybe you could stand a little sun, maybe spend some time in a gym. Tone up some, gain a little muscle.'

'You may have noticed I don't get too much spare time for that kind of thing. And how come people over here keep calling me middle-aged? I'm not even forty.'

'When you reckon "middle-aged" starts?'

'I don't know,' said Nightingale. 'Maybe fifty, fifty-five.'

'Makes sense,' said Wainwright. 'Provided you're planning to live to be a hundred and ten.'

'Okay, when this is over, maybe I'll need to find time to get myself back into better shape.'

Wainwright lost his smile. 'When this is over, you better hope we're around to be in any shape at all.'

CHAPTER 63

Bonnie Parker's shift was over for the day and she walked out of police headquarters, got into her car and lit another of the cigarettes she was meant to have given up months ago. She cursed Jack Nightingale for his damned predictions, his list of names, his disappearing acts and for starting her smoking again. She pounded the steering wheel and let loose another volley of abuse while she tried to fight back the tears in her eyes. Ann Davies was dead, she'd known the child's name in advance and there had been nothing she could do to save her. The fact that the child's death was clearly suicide, and therefore couldn't possibly be Parker's fault, made no difference to her feelings of guilt.

And now maybe there was one more child lined up for death, and she couldn't do a damned thing about that either. Her ears were still burning from the discussion she'd tried to have with her Lieutenant. She'd thought long and hard about how to approach it, and finally decided to go with the 'psychic tip-off' routine. Which had got her precisely nowhere. Lieutenant Donaghue was a Homicide veteran who'd seen every kind of murder in his twenty-year service, but never a serial killer who persuaded kids to kill themselves and who let some mystery man know in advance who they might be.

'Look, Bonnie,' he'd said. 'There isn't even a Homicide case here. These kids killed themselves, there's no doubt about that. For most of them, there are witnesses who'll swear there was nobody near them.

One or two, there were parents around, but no suggestion they were harmed.'

'Come on, Mike, we've had half a dozen suicides of Junior School kids in a week. That just never happens, someone's making it happen.'

'So how?'

'I dunno. Maybe they were hypnotised, or something?'

'By who? They don't go to the same schools, have the same friends, the same doctor or even live in the same part of town. There are simpler answers.'

'Like what?'

'Copy cats. Maybe one or two are just the normal run-of-the-mill suicides, and then someone reads about the kid who walked under the beer truck, and sees the coverage he got. Or the one who threw himself in front of the train. All over the TV, and maybe they think they'll get themselves some notice, be on TV too, if they do something public.'

'But that doesn't make much sense, Mike.'

'They were suicidal, Bonnie. They're not obliged to make sense.'

'But what about the guy who gave me Ann Davies's name? The day before she died.'

'So who is he? Bring him in and he can talk to us.'

'I don't know where to find him.'

'Well that's no great help, is it? Think of the sensible explanations first. Maybe she told this guy she was planning to kill herself, maybe she discussed her plan on some social media thing. Maybe it was his way of tipping us off, trying to save her.'

'Well, it didn't work too well, did it?'

'Look, Bonnie, you're a good cop...'

'Oh, come on, Mike, not that old soft-soap.'

'Bonnie, I mean it. But you've had a hell of a few days, getting shot at on Beale Street, ending up with three deaths, that kid. You're seeing connections where they don't exist. Go home, get some rest. I know these suicides are hell, but we're going to find they're all copy-cats. There's no case for us here.'

Parker had bit back the urge to tell Donahue about Carmen Garcia. There was no way the Lieutenant was going to order a city-wide operation to notify every parent of a Carmen Garcia that their daughter might be about to kill herself, based on a tip from an English guy that Parker couldn't even produce. She tried one last time.

'But Mike, can I at least have a couple uniforms, do some questioning of parents, background checking, maybe see if these kids had something in common, something that triggered them off.'

'Not a chance. You know we don't have the manpower to deal with the cases we have, never mind inventing new ones. Look, Bonnie, I know how you feel, you got a kid around that age, but there's nothing to this, just a statistical freak...what do they call it, a 'cluster'?'

'I guess.'

'Now, you got anything else?'

Parker did have one other thing. The fact that Nightingale suspected that a substitute teacher might be involved. But that was just a hunch and her boss wasn't a big believer in hunches.

'No, I got nothing, Mike,' she'd said.

'Alright, get out of here, go home, have a few beers and forget about this job.'

And that had been the end of that. As Parker sat in her car, she thought that drinking a few beers might be good advice.

Until and unless some little girl called Carmen Garcia was reported dead.

She said a silent prayer for her own daughter, and pulled out of the police parking lot.

CHAPTER 64

The woman in the wheelchair pressed the lever forward, and the chair moved from the bed towards the desk under the window. She clicked the left-hand button on the specially-made large mouse, and the screen sprang into life, tuned as ever to the Memphis News Channel. When she had made her pact, she had been told that events in Tennessee would concern her, and she had waited months to find out what this might mean. Seeing the report of Nightingale being found in the Crystal Grotto had alerted her to the fact that it had all begun, but she was still unsure of what 'it all' might be.

But then, it was not her place to question the workings of the High Placed Ones among The Fallen.

She had connected the last few public suicides with the death of the girl in the grotto, and then worked backwards through online copies of the Tennessee newspapers to connect up a few less public deaths. It was puzzling to her, since there seemed no reason why the one to whom she had pledged herself would be causing such things to happen. Child murder was more the preserve of human followers, such as the Order Of The Nine Angles, whose rituals called for the sacrifice of innocent virgin children to their master.

Though her memory kept nibbling at the edge of an old story, a legend of a creature that might live off the deaths of children, but not slaughter them. Every time she strained to remember, the memory skated away, receding like the water of Tantalus. Or was it Sisyphus? These days she seemed to forget so many things. Still, it would not be much longer, surely. The doctors had done all they could, and were reluctant to offer any prognosis at all now.

Her power was almost nothing compared to what it had been, Wainwright and his cats-paw had seen to that, but she could still sense the workings of a powerful adept, and knew now that Wainwright had joined his underling in Memphis. She knew that her own time was dwindling now, but she took consolation in knowing that her bitterest enemies would die before her.

After all, a promise was a promise, and a pact was a pact. It was an immutable law.

It was as she was reading about the girl jumping from the deck of the Ocean Queen that she first noticed the pain in her neck, and she moved her shoulders and head to lessen the stiffness, but it only seemed to make things worse. The pain spread rapidly from her neck to her forehead, and then seemed to take over her whole skull, as if she had been kicked by a horse. She cried out in agony, and reached for the call button mounted to the wheelchair, but her hands slipped over it as her head fell forward and she lost consciousness.

The cerebral aneurysm which had been slowly growing in her head had ruptured some time earlier, causing a sub-arachnoid haemorrhage and the blood flowing into her brain had finally resulted in a devastating stroke. Immediate neurosurgery might have been able to help her, but lunch had been an hour ago, and nobody came to her room until 7pm, by which time it was far too late.

CHAPTER 65

The Memphis 6 Downtown Motel was not the kind of place that anyone would ever expect to find billionaire Joshua Wainwright. It was far more typical of the kind of accommodation Jack Nightingale had been used to since his arrival in the USA. It was at least clean, but the furnishings were pretty spartan. A round table and two armless chairs with thin orange cushions, a very basic brown MDF desk, with an upright chair, also with orange cushions, a melamine drawer unit with a small television on top and two double beds, with counterpanes in an eye-scorching light blue abstract pattern. The bathroom seemed to contain all the necessary fittings, including the all important bathtub, but was about a quarter the size of the one in Nightingale's abandoned Peabody suite.

'It ain't much, but it's home,' said Wainwright. 'And at least it means the cops don't see some black guy handing guns and shells to a white dude in a parking lot.'

'There is that,' said Nightingale. 'Let's do it.'

Wainwright opened the sports bag, took out the two holstered Glocks and the box of shells.

'His Reverence was not happy with the idea of loading the guns for us,' said Wainwright. 'You ask me, he didn't know one end of a gun from the other and was scared he'd shoot himself. So I got some gloves in Walgreens.'

'Gloves are always a good idea,' said Nightingale and pulled on the pair of latex gloves Wainwright handed him. He opened the box of shells and put sixteen into each magazine. The clip held seventeen but Nightingale always left one out to ease the strain on the spring. He handed one of the guns to Wainwright.

'You sure this is gonna work?' asked Wainwright.

'It did last time, in New York.'

'Good to know,' said Wainwright. 'And you sure we have the right address?'

'Sure as I can be. There are only so many places you can take a little girl and keep her safe from prying eyes. Cops have no reason to call round, there's literally nothing to connect Naomi to Dudák.'

'You told Parker.'

'She's nowhere near convinced I'm not insane, and she has nothing to get a warrant for. Probable cause is big here, and I've heard nothing on the radio or TV that suggests the cops even know Naomi is gone.'

Wainwright reached into the bottom of the sports bag, and brought out a slim manila file, He put it on the desk and opened it.

'The List,' said Nightingale.

'Sure is,' said Wainwright. 'Only four names left on it now, Emma Miller, Carmen Garcia, my niece and Sophie Underwood.'

'I told you, Proserpine says Sophie's a bluff. Just put in to make sure I got involved, maybe stop me thinking straight. She must be fourteen now, way out of Dudák's age range, and thousands of miles away. I hope Emma Miller's safe.'

'How can you know that?' asked Wainwright.

'Because Bonnie Parker is her mother, and she sent her to...well, I don't know where, but she said it was a thousand miles from Memphis.'

'You told her? You told the police?'

'I had no idea it was her daughter when I gave her the names on the list. Once I knew, I had no choice but to tell her to send the kid away. Joshua, I've had to watch helplessly while a bunch of ten-year olds crossed themselves off that damned list. How do you think I feel about that? Innocent kids dying. If there was one chance in a hundred of saving one of them, I had to take it.'

Wainwright nodded. 'I guess so. But I sure do hope we're gonna be saving two of them. That thing has my niece, and we have to get her back.'

'We'll do it, Joshua. I know where Dudák is, and that's where Naomi will be. She's safe until Saturday. Seems like that's an important day to Dudák and she won't be harmed till then. I'm still pretty sure that Proserpine wants Dudák exorcised and destroyed, but it'll be easier to kill the host, and the thing will be forced to return to Hell.'

'You hope,' said Wainwright. 'You better be right.'

Nightingale nodded. He agreed with Wainwright, but he couldn't keep his thoughts off an unknown little ten-year-old girl somewhere in Tennessee, who shared the name of Carmen Garcia with lots of other little girls, and whom he could do nothing at all to save.

CHAPTER 66

There were dozens of children named Carmen Garcia in Memphis sleeping peacefully that night. Only one of them had turned off her iPad, sneaked out of bed, picked up the bag she'd prepared earlier, slipped out of her apartment, down the stairs and quietly out the main entrance to where Dudák was waiting in the car. Carmen smiled as she saw Dudák, opened the passenger door, slipped onto the seat and buckled the seat belt. She could barely see over the dashboard, but Tennessee State laws declared that she was old enough not to need a booster seat, and Dudák was not planning to drive her very far. It was probably unwise to appear with the child in public at all, but the chance of recognition was minute, and Dudák would be in another shell soon enough.

The car drove out to the west of the city, and stopped in the parking lot of the shopping and dining complex across the street from Memphis's most famous monument. It was long past dark now, and traffic was very light. Security at the gate would be tight, but nobody was going to try to break in, and it would all be over before the guards would have chance to react. Dudák smiled at the girl, who returned the smile. Control was complete.

The two figures left the car, walked to the end of the parking lot and crossed the street, where they separated, Dudák turning to the left, walking fifty yards and then stopping and leaning against the wall.

The child marched off to her right, until she came to the famous musical-patterned gates, where she dropped her bag, unzipped it, took out her mother's carving knife and plunged it into her heart with all the strength her lithe little body possessed. She fell back dying onto the gates before the guards had chance to move.

Dudák leaned back against the wall, eyes rolled up, the red flush spreading up the neck, as the child's death energy coursed from its body and was absorbed into the creature.

Dudák walked to the entrance of the nearby hotel, where there were three taxis in a row waiting, and got into the first one. It was a fifty-dollar fare from Graceland back to where Naomi Fisher still slept, but money was of no consequence, and it was pointless to risk using the car and being seen.

In fact it was four days before anyone bothered to do anything about the abandoned car, and by then the whole thing was long over.

CHAPTER 67

Wainwright looked at his watch. 'Getting to be around that time,' he said. 'You want to go first?

Nightingale nodded, stubbed out his latest cigarette and went into the bathroom, taking with him the two carrier bags they'd filled at the Broom Closet, which advertised itself as a 'Metaphysical Shoppe' and had pretty much everything they needed, apart from an item or two that Joshua's tame priest had supplied, for a further contribution to the 'Church Restoration Fund', no doubt.

Nightingale stripped off his clothes. He showered first, then cleaned his finger and toenails with a new nailbrush. He washed his hair in pure lemon juice. He dried himself with a clean towel, then placed a church candle at each corner of the room and lit them, then sprinkled half the large bag of herbs into the empty bath.

He got into the bath on top of the herbs and lay down. He said six sentences in Latin, then turned on the hot tap. He added just enough cold water to make it bearable, and lay flat as the water covered him up to his shoulders, his chest, his chin and finally over his face. As soon as the water covered his nose and mouth, he folded his arms in the sign of Osiris slain, then opened them and held up his hands in the sign of Osiris risen.

He sat bolt upright in the bath and made the obeisance of Set, a series of complex hand gestures he'd spent a long time learning several months before.

He pulled out the plug and let the water drain away completely, before getting out of the bath and letting himself drip dry over the next fifteen minutes. Finally he rubbed a laurel branch over his entire body, then sealed the nine orifices of his body with holy water, placed a blessed communion wafer on his tongue, and spoke two more sentences in Latin. He examined himself in the mirror then dressed in new Levis and a brand new polo shirt and the new Hush Puppies and raincoat he'd brought with him from Brownsville. The Ritual of Purification was complete.

He opened the bathroom door, and nodded at Wainwright.

'Your turn,' he said. 'You remember it all?'

Wainwright held up a piece of paper, covered in neat handwriting. 'Got it all written down, Jack,' he said. 'I must say this is a new one on me, where did you hear about it?'

'An old lady in Salem,' said Nightingale. 'I have no idea how effective it is, but she told me that, when heading into great danger, it's important to be cleansed, inside and out. I'm guessing that Dudák and whoever might be controlling it, come into that category.'

Wainwright shrugged. 'Can't hurt, I guess. See you in thirty.'

It was actually only twenty-five minutes later when Wainwright emerged from the bathroom, wearing new jeans, a pale blue silk shirt, shiny new cowboy boots and a black zip-up jacket. 'Even polished the watch and jewellery,' he said, with a grin.

'You'll be fine,' said Nightingale. 'Gold doesn't hold impurities.'

He nodded. 'Gun time.'

The two men strapped on the holsters, which held the Glocks in the middle of their waistbands, hidden by their coats. Nightingale piled the used supplies back into the bags, picked up his own holdall, took a last look around the room and followed Wainwright out to the parking lot.

They threw the bags into the back seat, then Nightingale started the engine and they drove off back towards Dudák's place. A mile down the road, Nightingale suddenly yelled out, and grimaced in pain.

'What?' said Wainwright.

Nightingale shook his left hand vigorously and cursed.

'The sigil on my hand just burned red hot,' he said. 'Dudák must have been within yards of us.'

'Maybe we passed it on the street or something. Do you want to turn around? We could go back?'

'No, it could be anywhere by now,' said Nightingale. 'Let's stick to plan A.'

They drove on in silence for another twenty minutes, then Nightingale pulled up on the right in a quiet residential street.

'That's the one,' he said. 'A hundred yards up on the left. No lights on, and my hand is hardly tingling.'

'So do you think Dudák's not at home?'

Nightingale nodded. 'Exactly.'

'And what about Naomi?'

'We'll soon find out.'

CHAPTER 68

Nightingale broke a window at the rear of the house, gingerly pulled away the remaining shards of glass and climbed inside. He stood in the kitchen, listening intently. There was enough light coming in to allow him to look around. When he was satisfied that the house was silent, he helped Wainwright in through the window.

'I didn't realise that house-breaking was a skill of yours,' said Wainwright as he stood in the middle of the kitchen.

'I attended enough burglaries when I was a cop,' said Nightingale. 'Though there isn't much skill involved, to be honest.' Nightingale's hand only tingled, so wherever Dudák might be, the house was safe enough, for the moment. He whispered to Wainwright. 'Dudák's not here, but this is the place for sure. I'll stay down here, why not check upstairs, see if you can find Naomi, or any sign that she's been here.'

Wainwright nodded, switched on the flashlight on his mobile phone, then took the gun out his jacket pocket and held it in his right hand.

Wainwright started to mount the stairs silently while Nightingale edged his way carefully into the sitting room and darted the beam of his phone around. As expected, the place was empty. He sat on a sofa, facing the door.

After a couple of minutes he heard a creak of a stair, and hoped it was Wainwright coming back down. He relaxed when he heard Wainwright's voice from the doorway. 'It's me, Jack. She's up there, thank God. Looks to be unharmed, but she's fast asleep, and I can't wake her.'

'Drugs or hypnosis, I guess,' said Nightingale. 'More likely the second one. Dudák seems to make a speciality of having kids under his power. I guess we can deal with bringing her round once Dudák's out of the way.' He yelped and blew on the back of his left hand, which felt as if it was on fire.'

'What is it?'

'The sigil on my hand, just starting to throb. Dudák must be getting nearer.' Nightingale started to grimace as the pain in his hand increased, until it seemed that the flesh would catch fire. He stood up and joined Wainwright in the hall. They heard the sound of a key in the lock, and heard it turn. Nightingale took out his gun and held it rock-steady, with a two-handed grip despite the pain, pointed at the front door. The door slowly opened and a figure stood there.

Wainwright also had his Glock ready and aimed as they strained to see in the darkness.

Then they heard the sound of a gun being cocked a few feet behind them. A deep gravelly voice spoke, loudly and authoritatively. 'Alright guys, you can both take your fingers off the triggers and point the guns at the floor, right now.'

'What the fuck?' said Wainwright.

He and Nightingale turned to see Tyrone standing behind them with a large pump-action shotgun in his hands. He had changed his suit since the last time they'd seen him and was now dressed in pale blue with bright yellow shoes.

'I won't ask again,' said Tyrone. 'It's not part of my plan for you to die here, but plans can change. Do it now.'

Tyrone didn't sound like he was bluffing, and Nightingale had no cards to call with, so he eased the pressure on the trigger, then pointed it at the ground. Wainwright did the same. 'What's this about, Tyrone?' Wainwright asked.

'You'll find out soon enough, Joshua,' said Tyrone. He looked over at the doorway. 'Dudák, it's safe to come in now.'

Dudák walked through the doorway, switched on the hall light, took off the woollen cap she was wearing and shook her long blonde hair free.

'Good evening, Mr Nightingale. Nice to see you again.'

'Hello, Carol,' said Nightingale. 'Or do you prefer Dudák?'

'As you wish,' said Carol Goldman, in a voice which carried a slight trace of a German accent now. 'I have learned quickly to answer to Carol in the last months, but I have borne so many names, and one is as good as another.'

'Will somebody tell me what's going on?' asked Wainwright. He looked across at Nightingale. 'Who is she?'

'Her name's Carol Goldman. She's the shell that Dudák has been using.'

'Ain't you the clever one,' said Tyrone. 'So sharp you're gonna end up cutting yourself.'

'Tyrone here has his own agenda,' said Nightingale. 'I'm guessing he's done a deal with someone. And that someone has linked him up with Dudák, who is using the shell of Carol Goodman. She's a supply teacher which gives her easy access to children across the State.'

'That's why you were so interested in supply teachers?' said Wainwright.

Nightingale nodded. 'And as Kim Jarvis's housemate, she was able to influence her to get her to kill herself in front of me.'

'Stop the chit-chat and drop the guns, gentlemen,' said Tyrone, gesturing with his shotgun.

They did as they were told. The Glocks clattered on the floor. Nightingale looked over at Dudák.

'Congratulations on identifying me, Jack Nightingale,' said Dudák.

'It wasn't difficult,' said Nightingale. 'Someone who had access to kids all over Tennessee, who they'd trust enough to let get close enough to establish control over them. Who better than a substitute teacher? And you could put them under your influence weeks or even months before, and then trigger them via social media. Or the phone.'

'And Tyrone here is local,' said Wainwright. 'He'd have all the intel needed to select the victims.'

'Well done, geniuses,' said Tyrone. 'This plan's been a long time cooking, hope you'll enjoy the final course.'

Tyrone stepped forward and slammed the stock of his shotgun against the back of Wainwright's head. Wainwright slumped to the ground. Nightingale turned and raised his hands to protect himself but Tyrone was too quick for him. The stock hit Nightingale just above the right temple and he went down like a pole-axed steer.

CHAPTER 69

Nightingale woke up with a splitting headache, but he consoled himself with the thought that at least he'd woken up. Either Tyrone or Dudák could easily have killed him and left his body to be discovered maybe weeks later. The consolation evaporated once he started thinking about the possible reasons why they hadn't done that. None of them seemed appealing. His current situation was nothing to get excited about either. His wrists and ankles appeared to be tightly bound with duct tape, and there was more of it over his mouth. A bag of some rough material had been pulled over his head. He could breathe, just about, but he couldn't see anything. He figured he had been placed face down across the back seat of a car or a truck.

He listened as carefully as he could, but all he could hear was the sound of the engine. Then he heard voices.

'Five minutes more,' said Tyrone. 'Then some preparation to make and we can rest up till midnight. Then we can make the sacrifice and you feed for the last time in that shell.'

'I have grown to like it rather,' said the woman, 'it is young and strong, disarming to the little ones. They instinctively trust it, and it makes controlling them that much easier. I think the new one will not be so appealing.'

'Maybe not, but you can't keep that one, it will be too easily recognised and connected with events here.'

'I guess so.'

'There's no guess. You need a new shell. You can use Nightingale until a more suitable shell becomes available.'

'It will be easy enough to find one. There is much to be said for inhabiting a female. They are considered so much less threatening.'

'Never judge a book by its cover,' said Tyrone, and he laughed savagely.

Nightingale felt the car slow down, then make a sharp turn to the right, and he guessed they had arrived. He had no idea how long he had been out, but had a pretty good idea where they would be ending up. The house in Nashville was the perfect venue for whatever Tyrone had planned.

He heard gravel under the wheels, and a moment or two later the car stopped. The doors were opened, and Nightingale was dragged out onto the gravel by his feet. He heard the front door open, then he was lifted over Dudák's shoulder, up the steps and dropped in a pile in the hallway, still face down.

He heard Dudák return a minute or so later and drop something heavy on the floor next to him. Wainwright, presumably.

Dudák left again, and as he returned Nightingale heard the car start up again and crunch over the gravel, presumably to the garage. Footsteps on the gravel, and the front door shutting again told him he'd been right.

He heard Tyrone's voice in his ear. 'Listen to me, Nightingale, and listen good. It's kinda awkward carrying you down stairs, so I'm gonna cut the tape on your ankles, and you're gonna walk down to the basement with us. I still have the gun, but you'll know how fast Dudák can move, and you'll have a broken neck before you go two paces if you try anything. So be careful. Not that you're going to be living much longer anyways, but I guess it's always better to die later than sooner.'

Nightingale felt a knife cut the tape round his ankles, and he was roughly pulled to his feet. He collapsed again straight away, and would have cried out in pain, if not for the gag, as the blood flowed back into his feet.

The bag was pulled roughly from Nightingale's head and he blinked his eyes as they became accustomed to the light.

Wainwright was lying on the floor, his wrists and ankles bound with duct tape and a hessian sack over his head. For a few seconds

Nightingale feared that the Texan was dead but then his chest moved. He was breathing. Tyrone prodded Nightingale in the back with the gun, guiding him down the hallway in the direction of the basement. They went down the stairs and Tyrone shoved Nightingale into a side-room he hadn't seen before. It was small and furnished only with a long wooden bench and a metal bucket. The walls and ceiling were plain white, and the floor just bare wood. There was a small window high up on one wall, with some steel bars cemented into the frame. The door was solid oak, and a couple of inches thick.

Tyrone kept the shotgun pointed at Nightingale's chest. 'Sit down,' he said and Nightingale dropped down onto the bench.

Tyrone backed out of the room and locked the door. A few minutes later Nightingale heard footsteps and the rattle of the door being unlocked again. It opened and Wainwright stepped into the room. The sack had been taken from his head to reveal the duct tape gag and his hands were still bound. Tyrone prodded him in the back and Wainwright staggered into the room.

Wainwright recovered his balance and turned to face Tyrone. He said something but the tape muffled the words. Tyrone laughed. 'I'd take off the gag,' he said. 'But you know, fuck you.' He slammed the door shut and locked it.

Nightingale shuffled along the bench to give Wainwright room to sit. Wainwright dropped down next to him and grunted. The two men looked at each other. Nightingale could see anger and frustration in Wainwright's eyes, but no fear. He hoped that he looked as resilient, but he doubted it. Nightingale was afraid. Very afraid.

Wainwright began to contort his face, gritting his teeth and moving his jaw from side to side. At first Nightingale thought he was having a fit, but then realised he was trying to loosen the duct tape around his mouth. Nightingale followed his example and concentrated on trying to move the tape. The exaggerated facial expressions were accompanied by a lot of grunting and at one point Nightingale started to chuckle, despite the pain in his jaw from where Parker had cold-cocked him. Wainwright also began to laugh and despite their predicament the two men were soon trembling from laughter, the sound muffled by the tape.

It took almost ten minutes for Wainwright to get the tape off his mouth and Nightingale followed suit a short while later. The two men sat on the bench breathing heavily from their exertions.

'Well this is another fine mess you've gotten me into,' said Nightingale eventually.

'That British sense of humour never flags, does it?' said Wainwright.

'Just trying to lighten the moment,' said Nightingale. 'What the hell is going on, Joshua? Tyrone's your guy, right?'

'I thought he was,' said Wainwright. 'But it looks as if he's branching out on his own.'

'He's a Satanist, right?'

'He was on the fringes, I thought, but it looks as if he's been making progress without my knowing. Fuck it, how did I miss this?'

'You think Tyrone summoned Dudák?'

'If you'd asked me that before today I'd have laughed, but now I'm not so sure.'

'So the sorcerer's apprentice is now the master? That's not good news, Joshua.'

'You're telling me.' Wainwright grunted. 'If we get out of this, I'll make him suffer, he'll wish he had never been born.'

'Yeah, well the "if" worries me. I'd be happier if you'd say "when we get out of this", to be honest.'

Wainwright laughed. 'You got any ideas?'

'The cavalry would be nice.'

'Yeah, well without our cellphones I don't see any way we can be calling for help, do you?'

Nightingale flashed him a tight smile. 'Actually, I do.'

CHAPTER 70

Nightingale lay down on the wooden bench and tried to relax. Wainwright was sitting on the floor, his back to the door. Nightingale took long, slow breaths and closed his eyes. He filled his mind with thoughts of Alice Steadman, and willed himself to sleep. Almost an hour passed before he managed to get himself into a trance-like state, but then he felt himself rising from the bench, moving upwards towards the ceiling, and then out above the mansion, until he was walking across grass and surrounded by mist. He kept the thoughts of Mrs Steadman firmly in his mind, and started to look for her. She had warned him about visiting the Astral Plane on his own, but he didn't see that he had any choice. She was his only hope.

The mist cleared, and he saw a figure moving towards him, getting much closer with every second. It was too large to be Mrs Steadman, but he couldn't make it out yet. Closer still it came, and now he could see it clearly, its scaly limbs changing colour and number as it ran, the facial features blurred and indistinct as the head grew and shrunk, the huge mouth opening and closing, revealing the giant, spittle drenched-fangs.

The creature roared and leaped at him, and Nightingale screamed, and was immediately awake again on the hard bench in the cell.

Wainwright was standing at his side, looking down on him. 'What happened?' he asked.

Nightingale was covered in sweat, gasping for breath. He sat up and shuddered. Somehow Tyrone set something foul and dangerous to guard any approach to the Astral from the house.

'We're screwed,' he said. 'We can't get help that way.'

'We'll think of something,' said Wainwright, sitting down on the bench.

'I hope so,' said Nightingale. 'But at the moment, I'm out of ideas.' He looked around the tiny windowless room. 'What is this place?' he asked.

Wainwright smiled ruefully. 'You won't like it,' he said.

'Just tell me.'

'It's the sacrifice cell.'

Nightingale leaned back and groaned. 'Terrific.'

'I told you that you wouldn't like it.'

CHAPTER 71

The Memphis PD police cruisers had responded within minutes to the call from the security guards at Graceland, but there was nothing they could do for Carmen Garcia. The damage to her heart had been immediate and catastrophic. Two Homicide detectives attended as a matter of routine, but the witness statements from the guards were convincing, and they recognised at once that there was nothing for them here. It was a suicide, plain and simple. The child was carrying no ID, and it was not until the following morning, when Mrs Garcia went to wake her daughter and found her missing, that the police were able to begin the process of identifying the dead child. By then, the story of yet another public child suicide had been all over the news channels for hours.

Bonnie Parker had been asleep at home when the story broke, so didn't catch up with it until she turned on the television to go with her morning coffee. Her husband had pulled an early shift at the firehouse, and wouldn't be home till mid-afternoon, and her son was on his way to school. She watched the news bulletin with growing horror, as the reporters stood outside Graceland detailing the events. They had no name to announce, but Bonnie Parker was in no doubt. 'Carmen Garcia,' she muttered to himself. 'Carmen Garcia, for sure.'

She picked her mobile phone up from the coffee table and punched in Nightingale's number. She let it ring for a good minute before she gave up.

'You bastard,' she yelled at the phone. 'What the hell is all this about? My God, you better be right about Emma, I just hope she's far enough away from all this. Anything happens to her, I will track you down and kill you, I swear it.'

CHAPTER 72

It was almost midnight when the door opened. Nightingale and Wainwright hadn't been given any food or water and they were both dog-tired. Tyrone was holding his shotgun and Dudák was standing behind him. They were both wearing hooded black robes with thick black cords tied around the waist.

'It's time,' said Tyrone. Nightingale was going to make a crack about stating the bleeding obvious but he knew that any attempt at humour would be futile so he just glared at Tyrone and stood up.

Tyrone noticed the bits of chewed duct tape on the floor and he nodded. 'Well aren't you the clever ones?' he said. 'It doesn't matter, the chapel is sound-proofed.'

Tyrone stepped to the side and motioned with his shotgun. Nightingale and Wainwright walked out and headed into the chapel.

'Sit,' said Tyrone, pointing at the front row of red leather-upholstered pews.

As they moved to the row, they saw Naomi asleep on the floor.

Wainwright gasped her name and took a step towards her, but Tyrone prodded him in the back with the shotgun. 'I said sit. So sit!'

Wainwright did as he was told. 'You don't have to do this, Tyrone,' he said.

'You don't know what I have to do or don't have to do,' snarled Tyrone.

'Whatever you hope to achieve by doing this, I can do it for you without you having to kill my niece.'

Tyrone shook his head. 'She has to die. That's the deal.'

'What deal?' asked Wainwright. 'What have you done?'

'Nothing you haven't done,' sneered Tyrone. 'I'm just following your path.'

'You should have come to me. I would have helped you.'

Tyrone shook his head. 'I was your servant, nothing more. A hired hand. You kept the real power to yourself.' He grinned triumphantly. 'And look where all your scheming has got you.' He handed the shotgun to Dudák. 'If either of them moves, shoot them.'

As Dudák kept the gun trained on the two men, Tyrone went about his preparations. He placed a small dark wood altar in front of the table at the top end, directly in front of the statue of the Goat of Mendes. He covered it with a blood-red cloth, which had designs embroidered on it in gold, which Nightingale could not make out clearly from where he sat, but he guessed they might represent the sigil of whichever demon Tyrone was in thrall to. He placed a golden inverted crucifix on top of the cloth, and four black candles in black wood holders, one at each corner.

'Tyrone, please,' said Wainwright. 'Don't do this.'

Tyrone turned and grinned savagely. 'Your niece is a blood sacrifice to my master, in exchange for the power I've been promised. She'll offer herself up to him freely, that's the whole point. Dudák will feed on the death energy, and my master will take her soul as a willing sacrifice. It's a win-win. Except for your niece, of course.'

'Why my niece? Was that your idea? Why would you do this to me after everything I've done for you?'

'You've done nothing for me, Wainwright. You used me. Now it's payback time.'

'Is that why you're using Naomi?' asked Nightingale. 'You wanted to hurt Joshua?'

'I was told that she has to be the final sacrifice,' said Tyrone.

'By who?' asked Nightingale.

'By whom,' corrected Dudák.

'Bloody hell, once a teacher always a teacher, even when you're possessed by a demon from Hell,' said Nightingale. He turned to look at Tyrone. 'Who told you to sacrifice Joshua's niece?'

'I was told, that's all that matters.' He turned back to the altar and poured some herbs from a crystal bottle into a golden bowl, which he then placed in front of the crucifix.

'What were you promised, Tyrone?' asked Nightingale. As he spoke he was working on the duct tape that bound his wrists, but he was making little impression on his bonds.

Tyrone stopped what he was doing and turned to face Nightingale. 'Once this final sacrifice is made, my pact is fulfilled and I'm going to attain the rank of an Ipsissimus of the left-hand path, that's more power than anyone ever dreamed of. Then I'm going to take your life from you, and Dudák is going to use your body for a new shell, while your soul wanders homeless.'

'And what about me?' asked Wainwright.

Tyrone shrugged. 'You're to be allowed to live.'

'Why?' asked Nightingale.

Wainwright turned to glare at him. 'Why? What is wrong with you?'

'I'm trying to find out what's going on, Joshua. Because it makes no sense to let you live, not after this.'

'He is to suffer, for the rest of his life,' said Tyrone. 'He will live knowing what happened to his sister and his niece and that he was the cause of their suffering and death.'

'So it wasn't your idea? You were told what to do as part of your deal?'

'Enough with your questions,' said Tyrone, turning away. 'I have work to do.' He placed a foot-long, golden knife with an intricately carved handle in front of the bowl of herbs.

'You're being used, Tyrone, can't you see that?' said Nightingale.

Tyrone kept his back turned and sprinkled a red liquid from a vial onto the herbs.

'Whoever you did your deal with isn't interested in you. This is all about getting back at Joshua. He stopped Abaddon from bringing Bimoleth back to the world and her power and her coven were destroyed. Then Wainwright had me stop Lucifuge Rofocale and his demons in New York. So it's one of those two pulling your strings, I'm sure. And Abaddon isn't in a position to do anything to grant you Satanic powers. That leaves Lucifuge Rofocale. You can't trust him, Tyrone, Lucifuge Rofocale is a devious bastard.'

Tyrone turned around. 'I have a deal, a deal that cannot be broken.'

'You can trust him about as far as you can throw him,' said Nightingale. 'Actually, that's not a good analogy, him being a dwarf and all.'

'We don't call little people dwarves,' said Dudák. 'It's offensive.'

'I'm starting to realise why I hated school so much,' said Nightingale. 'Your body has been taken over by a demon and all you can do is correct my grammar and slam me for not being politically correct.'

Dudák snarled and pointed the shotgun at Nightingale's face.

'Very smart,' said Nightingale. 'Blowing the head off the body you're planning to move into. Can't you keep your minion in line, Tyrone?'

'I'm not his minion,' said Dudák.

'Yes, you are,' said Nightingale. 'You both are. You're being used. You're pawns in some game that you don't even understand.'

'Ignore him,' said Tyrone. 'He thinks that by talking he can change the outcome.'

'That's what people do, Tyrone,' said Nightingale. 'They talk. They communicate. They negotiate.'

'I'm getting tired of the speeches, Nightingale. You'll never understand. This isn't about good or evil, it's about power, about bending the world to my will. Anyways, I guess you're not going to shut up, are you? I need to concentrate now, so looks like we're going to have to gag you again after all.'

He walked over to Nightingale carrying a roll of duct tape, and re-applied the gag.

'There now, you hush up and enjoy the show. My master particularly wanted you to have a ringside seat. He knows all about how you hate to see pretty little girls suffer. He doesn't like you very much at all. But then I'm sure you know that.'

Tyrone took a long black taper from a box on the table and lit it with a wooden match. He lit each candle in turn, then set light to the herbs in the golden bowl. Grey smoke rose up towards the ceiling. He nodded at Dudák.

'Time for you to wake the child, Dudák, and send her to her sacrifice. Time for you to feed.'

The pretty young blonde woman that held the millennia-old demon inside her body nodded and handed the shotgun to Tyrone.

She walked over to the child, bent down and picked her up as if she had no weight at all.

Nightingale strained at the duct-tape over his mouth, trying to force out some words to beg them to stop. Dudák never even glanced at him, just bent down and whispered in the child's ear. 'Naomi. It is time to wake now. You must give yourself as a willing sacrifice to your master. Wake now. Wake now.'

The child's eyelids flickered and opened. Dudák put the girl down and helped her to stand. Naomi stared at the altar, seemingly oblivious to Nightingale and her uncle sitting in the pews.

Dudák took the girl's hand and they walked together to the altar. They stood there, hand in hand, a blank gaze on Naomi's face, a serene smile across the woman's lips. She spoke to the child again.

'Are you ready, Naomi? Will you sacrifice yourself willingly?'

'Of course, Miss Goldman,' said the child, in a flat entranced tone.

Tyrone used his left hand to pick up a handful of herbs and threw them into the golden bowl. The flame flared up strongly, and a plume of purple smoke rose to the chapel's vaulted ceiling.

Tyrone kept the shotgun aimed at Nightingale and Wainwright as he spoke to Naomi, no emotion showing on his face. 'Do you give this sacrifice willingly?' he said.

The child looked blankly past him. 'I do,' she said.

'Then give it.'

He picked up the knife with his left hand and gave it to her.

'No!' shouted Wainwright. 'Please, no!'

Nightingale was frantic with his vain effort to break the tape that was binding his wrists, veins standing out on his reddened face, his eyes protruding, sweat pouring down his forehead.

Naomi held the knife in her right hand, the blade pointing towards her throat.

'Take me,' grunted Nightingale against the duct tape gag, 'Take my soul. Take me instead.'

'Nooooo!' wailed Wainwright, as Naomi pushed the blade into her throat and up into her skull.

And then it was over.

CHAPTER 73

Naomi Fisher's body lay at the foot of the altar, her blood still running from the huge gash in her throat.

Dudák was leaning against the wall, eyes rolled back in its head, a flush of blood creeping up the neck as it fed on the death energies of the child. An occasional groan of satisfaction came from between the red-painted lips.

Tyrone gave the shotgun to Dudák and knelt in front of the altar, a red aura dancing around his body as he trembled and groaned either in pain or pleasure. Nightingale couldn't see his face, which was turned towards the altar.

Wainwright had slumped in the pew, a look of desperation etched into his face.

A figure floated from the mouth of the huge Goat of Mendes on the altar. It was wrapped in grey smoke, and virtually transparent, but it was recognisable as a dwarf, about three and a half feet tall, the disproportionately large head covered in curly black hair, the eyes blood-red. It was dressed in a red hunting jacket, with gold trim and buttons, black jodhpurs and shiny black riding boots.

Nightingale had seen Lucifuge Rofocale before, but his form had always been far more solid. This time the malevolent manikin seemed almost a wraith, as it drifted from the goat to where Tyrone knelt, his whole body shaking. The dwarf turned his face towards Nightingale, twisted his features into a leer of pure malevolence, and then started to envelop Tyrone's body, dissolving as it did so. For an instant Tyrone was wreathed in crimson and black fumes, then the mist seemed to enter completely into him, and he gave a roar of triumph.

'It is done,' he shouted in a voice that shook the walls. 'It is done. My master's pledge has been kept. Oh, oh...I understand. I understand so much now. Such beauty. It is all so clear, so clear. And such power. Such will.'

Tyrone staggered to his feet. He still had his back to the pews. The ceremonial knife had fallen from Naomi's hands and lay on the floor. It was closer to Wainwright and Nightingale glared at him, then at the knife. Wainwright followed his look and shuffled along the pew. He bent low as he reached the knife, grabbed it and hurried over to Nightingale.

Nightingale held out his hands and rubbed the duct tape against the knife. The razor-sharp blade made short work of the tape. Nightingale grabbed the knife and turned towards Dudák.

Dudák had been staring at the altar but sensed Nightingale's attack and turned, swinging up the shotgun. Nightingale hit the barrel away with his left hand and thrust the knife into the woman's chest, praying that whatever magic it had been infused with would work against the demon inside her.

Dudák roared in pain and Nightingale thrust the knife in again. And again. Kill the host and destroy the demon, Mrs Steadman had said. But did the one lead to the other? The thought kept running through his mind as he stabbed and stabbed, blood spattering over his hands as he thrust the knife deep into the woman.

Dudák staggered back, blood pouring onto the chapel floor. The shotgun slipped from her fingers. Nightingale left the knife in Dudák's chest and grabbed for the shotgun.

He took a step back, aimed, and fired. The blast hit Dudák square in the chest and she fell back, arms flailing. She hit the floor and lay still, blood pooling around her.

Nightingale turned to see Tyrone advancing towards him. Nightingale pumped in a second shell and pulled the trigger. As he did, Tyrone raised his hands, his lips curled back in a savage snarl. The shot exploded from the end of the barrel but then seemed to move in slow motion for just a couple of feet and then fell to the ground, tinkling like rain on the flagstones.

Tyrone laughed in triumph. 'You have no idea of the power I have!' he shouted.

Wainwright roared and charged towards Tyrone, his bound hands in the air. Tyrone waved his left hand and Wainwright flew backwards through the chapel and slammed into the far wall. Nightingale was sure that Tyrone hadn't connected with Wainwright, he had used some sort of supernatural force to land the blow.

Wainwright slid to the floor, stunned, and Tyrone turned his attention to Nightingale.

'You said Lucifuge Rofocale would lie, that he wouldn't keep up his end of the bargain, but look at what he has done for me!' shouted Tyrone.

He waved his hands again and Nightingale felt himself being lifted off the floor. Another wave of Tyrone's hands and Nightingale was thrown against the wall. His legs kicked out in vain and he felt something fasten around his throat.

'I could snap your neck like a twig,' he said. 'But we need your body.'

He looked over at Dudák. 'Come,' he said. 'The vessel is ready to be filled.'

Dudák rose up from the floor, swinging upright as if being pulled on an invisible rope. There were no wounds on her body, no stains on the robe, though the chapel floor was still glistening with wet blood. She grinned at Nightingale. 'It is time,' she said. She took a step towards Nightingale. Then another.

The grip around Nightingale's neck tightened and his eyes began to bulge. He clawed at whatever it was that was around his neck but his fingers found nothing.

'It's no use struggling,' said Tyrone. 'In a moment you'll be dead, Dudák will inhabit your body, and your soul will stay in limbo forever. My master wishes it. Let it be so.'

He clenched both his hands, and Nightingale felt an indescribable pain rising from the pit of his stomach, as if his very essence were being sucked out of him. He cried out in agony, but the noise was drowned by a peal of thunder from the rear of the chapel. A flash of lightning shot across the altar, a soft voice said, 'Enough,' and the pain inside Nightingale subsided. The pressure went from around his neck and he fell to the floor, gasping for breath.

'You're looking uncomfortable there, Nightingale,' said Proserpine as she walked down the aisle towards the giant statue of the Goat Of Mendes. 'I did warn you about trusting the wrong people.'

Her coal-black eyes gazed at him briefly, and he found he could sit up and get to his feet. She kept walking, the long black leather coat billowing around her slender frame, the black and white collie trotting faithfully after her.

Tyrone had turned at the sound of her voice, and started to speak but she stopped him with a wave of her leather-gloved right hand.

'We haven't met, and Nightingale seems a little too upset to manage introductions. I have many names, but you may perhaps have heard of me as Proserpine. Princess of Hell, to give myself the full title. I won't say "at your service", since you're at mine.'

Tyrone was shaking, blinking in terror, but he made an effort to compose himself. 'Mistress Proserpine, I d-d-do n-n-not understand what b-b-brings you here,' he stammered. 'I serve another. M-m-y m-m-master is Lucifuge Rofocale.'

She smiled. Nightingale knew her well enough to know that there was no good humour in that smile.

'Don't you just. Lucifuge Rofocale is your master, and you have served him well. And now, after all these blood sacrifices, he has kept the pact he made with you. You have all the knowledge and earthly power a man could desire, and he has granted you the power of an Ipsissimus, the supreme position of an adept of the left-hand path. Congratulations.'

Tyrone bowed his head in acknowledgment, and his smile showed his returning confidence. 'Thank you, Mistress Proserpine. It's true. I feel the power burn within me, after years of study and work, after eliminating any rivals, I stand alone in power. And I understand all there is to be understood by a man.' His stammer had gone as his confidence had returned.

'You do, indeed,' said Proserpine, a sly smile spreading across her deathly pale face. 'You have achieved more power than any human could dream of. You got what you wanted. What you asked for. Well done, you.'

Tyrone seemed to remember to whom he was speaking, and his smile changed to a puzzled look. 'But why are you here, Mistress Proserpine? I have no pact with you, and no quarrel either.'

Proserpine smiled. 'Quarrel? That is a strange word to use. I do not quarrel, Tyrone. I take souls, I wreak havoc, I make the legions in Hell bow down before me. That's what I do.'

'I did not wish to offend you, Mistress Proserpine,' said Tyrone, his newly-found confidence rapidly evaporating.

'Your very existence offends me,' she said. 'But I am about to remedy that. Your pact with Lucifuge Rofocale is fulfilled. You wield supreme power, as promised. And I have come to take it from you. Together with your life.'

Tyrone gaped at her, seeming not to comprehend the words he had just heard.

'B-b-but...b-b-but...I was promised. A p-p-pact was signed. I g-g-gave my soul for this.'

'And the pact was kept. Nothing was said about how long you might enjoy your power, and you humans have such limited lifespan. And no pact ever promises immortality.'

'But what is it to you? Why are you interfering?'

She frowned. 'So many questions from a dead man. I too make pacts, Tyrone, and I made one with Margaret Romanos a while back. The woman who called herself Abaddon and tried to possess herself of Bimoleth. She promised me her soul, I promised to take from Wainwright everything he loved and I have held up that end of the bargain.' She turned to Nightingale. 'And she wanted to live long enough to see you die, Nightingale. And I agreed to that. And, as you know, I am a woman of my word.'

Tyrone was on his knees now, grovelling before her, his face lifted up in supplication. 'But M-M-Mistress...no...you c-c-can't...'

Again she frowned.

'Can't, Tyrone? Can't? That's really not a word you want to be using to a Princess of Hell. I can't say it's been a pleasure, I haven't much liked what I've seen of you. Time for Lucifuge Rofocale to collect on his deal. Time for your soul to be in Hell. Goodbye.'

Tyrone held up his hand and stared at her. 'No,' he shouted. 'I forbid it. I am an Ipsissimus and I forbid it.'

Proserpine threw back her head and shrieked with laughter, and Tyrone's hand was gone from his wrist. He stared at the bloody stump uncomprehendingly, too shocked to scream in pain. Blood spurted across the stone floor.

Tyrone glanced desperately to his left. 'Dudák,' he shouted, 'help me!'

Dudák stared back at him, her face a blank mask.

'No one is going to help you,' said Proserpine. 'It is time to pay the piper. Absolutely no pun intended.'

The dog growled and Tyrone stared at it in horror. The small black and white collie was moving forward, growing and changing shape with every step. It doubled in size, then doubled again, the black and white fur shimmered and became scales, its head seemed to split, and now it had three heads, waving on long necks. Each head had a huge, gaping mouth, dripping with hot saliva. The creature opened its mouths to bark furiously, and Tyrone saw the yellowed fangs, and forked tongues, the last thing he would ever see, as the creature leaped at him.

Nightingale buried his head in his hands, shutting out the sight, but not the appalling noise of the blended screams and barking. Proserpine gazed at the mess with no sign of interest. One of the three heads had what looked like part of a leg in its mouth.

'That's enough, boy,' she said. 'Put it down now, we don't want you getting an upset stomach. All done now, Nightingale.'

Nightingale opened his eyes, and tried to avoid looking at the remains of Tyrone, which was difficult as they were scattered all over the chapel. The collie dog was once again by Proserpine's side, licking her hand devotedly.

'Pity you couldn't have turned up sooner,' said Nightingale.

'And why, pray tell?'

'Naomi would still be alive.'

'Weren't you listening? She had to die. Wainwright had to be punished.' She looked over at Wainwright who was sitting with his back against the wall, his knees up against his chest. 'You understand, don't you, Joshua?'

Wainwright nodded but there was only blankness in his eyes.

She looked back at Nightingale. 'See, he understands. Margaret Romanos promised me her soul, and I am making Wainwright suffer in torment. Naomi had to die. That was the deal.'

'Why didn't you tell me this before?'

'I couldn't possibly have intervened while Lucifuge Rofocale's pact was still incomplete. Neither could your beloved Mrs Steadman. We can't interfere in a pact freely made. I rather think Mrs Steadman expected you to ride to the rescue and save the little girl in the nick of time, but that was never going to happen.'

'How do you know what she said to me?'

'You think I can't move as freely on the Astral Plane as I can here, or in the chasms of Hell? I go where I want to go, Nightingale. There are no secrets from me.'

Nightingale closed his eyes, and shook his head. He opened them again and gazed into the deep pools of nothingness that were her eyes. The eyes were meant to be the windows of the soul, but no light shone through hers.

'Chin up, Nightingale,' she said, 'you can't win them all. It's not like in the movies. Out here in the real world, the bad guys generally win.'

'What shall I do, Mistress?' It was Dudák, who had been standing motionless since the dog had ripped Tyrone apart.

'Oh, just go to Hell, Dudák.' She didn't bother to turn, just waved her hand dismissively. A green spark flew across the room, there was a sharp crack as Dudák left the realms of Earth, and the lifeless body of Carol Goldman lay on the ground, finally at peace.

The dog licked Proserpine's hand and growled softly. She scratched the black ears and smiled down at the animal.

'And what happens to me?' asked Nightingale. 'I have to die as part of the deal you did for the soul of Margaret Romanos?'

'Allegedly,' she said. The sly smile was back on her face.

'At least you won't have my soul,' he said.

'There is that,' she said.

Nightingale braced himself for whatever was to come.

'You don't want a cigarette?' she asked.

Nightingale had forgotten his Marlboro and lighter were still in his pocket. He took them out and lit one, drawing the soothing smoke deep into his lungs. The condemned man's last cigarette, he realised. He tried to blow a smoke ring up at the ceiling and failed miserably.

He took a deep breath and forced a smile. 'Might as well get it over with,' he said.

She shook her head, an amused smile on her face. 'You can be so melodramatic at times,' she said. 'I'll miss that.'

She blew him a kiss, then time and space seemed to fold in on itself, there was an ear-splitting crack and a flash of light and she and the dog were gone.

Nightingale stared at the spot where she had been in astonishment. Why was he still alive? Hadn't that been the deal Romanos had done with Proserpine?

'What just happened?' said Wainwright, his voice trembling.

Nightingale took another drag on his cigarette and blew smoke down at the floor. 'Joshua, I have no bloody idea.'

CHAPTER 74

Margaret Romanos lay in bed, the machines breathing for her, tubes running in and out of her veins, monitors attached to other machines by her bedside. The doctors had told her that the previous damage had worsened, but the main problem had been the stroke, which had effectively cut off her all bodily functions below the neck and robbed her of the power of speech. They weren't sure if she could hear or understand. She couldn't even tell them to turn the machines off and let her die, and there was nobody to take that kind of decision for her. Nobody that dared come near her any longer. Tears ran from her eyes, as she thought once again of all she had lost. Once she had been Abaddon, and had as much power as anyone in America, now she lay helpless, waiting to die.

She blinked the tears way, but there still seemed to be a blur in the air. Time and space seemed to fold in on itself, and then Proserpine was there, leaning over Margaret's bed, the dark soulless eyes boring into hers, the pale almost bloodless face devoid of any expression. 'Just a social call, Margaret, No need to get up.' The scarlet lips twisted into a cruel smile. 'Not looking good, Margaret, How are the mighty fallen, eh? Still, they can do wonders these days. Probably not for you though.'

Another tear crept down the cheek from the left eye.

'Never mind, eh? No use crying over spilled milk. Or blood. Anyway, I'm the bearer of good news. Our little deal. You invested your soul wisely. As promised, Wainwright lost the people that he loves and will blame himself until the day he dies.'

The woman in the bed smiled and closed her eyes, as if in satisfaction. Then a noise came from her mouth, a pained and wordless grunt, which Proserpine understood perfectly.

'Nightingale? Well, there may be a delay there, I could have uses for him. But a deal's a deal.'

Again came the noise from Margaret Romanos's mouth. And she opened her eyes.

'Yes, I know. The deal is that you would live to dance on Nightingale's grave. Though obviously you won't be doing any dancing, will you? You wanted to live to see his death. And you will, Margaret. You will. Let's see now, Nightingale's coming up to forty, smokes a lot and gets very little exercise, so I doubt you'll have to wait more than thirty-five years.'

There was panic in Margaret's eyes, and she grunted again.

'Well, maybe not so long as that, he does lead a dangerous life.'

Again the anguished grunt.

'No, I don't envy you the wait, not at all. But nothing I can do about that. A deal's a deal. You should have read the small print.'

Time folded in on itself again, and Proserpine was gone, leaving nothing but her mocking laugh ringing in Margaret Romanos's ears.

CHAPTER 75

Bonnie Parker sat on the bar stool in the lounge of the Luxor Hotel and took another sip of her beer. Las Vegas had always been one of her favourite cities, she enjoyed the glitz and fake glamour, though she was no gambler, so deciding to spend a few days with the in-laws while collecting Emma had been a no-brainer. The girl was out clothes shopping with her grandmother now, the two hundred dollars she'd been given just about chasing away her righteous indignation at being denied the internet for a whole, ghastly week.

Parker felt someone settle onto the stool next to her, but didn't look across.

'Corona for me, please,' said the voice by her side, and Parker raised her bottle to offer a toast to the mirror behind the bar. 'Nightingale,' she said. 'Why am I not surprised?'

'Detective Parker,' said Nightingale. 'Always a pleasure.'

'What brings you to Vegas, Jack?'

'Catching up with old friends. Is Emma okay?'

'Fine, and out of danger according to your call.'

'You can believe that.'

'Guess I can, there have been no more kids killed themselves since last week. It's over?'

'It's over.'

'And what exactly was 'it'?'

'You wouldn't believe me if I tried to explain. Not sure I believe it. But it's over, and it won't be happening again.'

'Good to know. Not that it was ever my case. No homicide involvement. No crime at all in fact. Anyway, I have my hands full when I get back.'

'Really?'

'Yeah, nasty one near St Luke's Church. Man and wife. Looked like a murder-suicide, but the forensics ain't right, so we're looking for a murderer. Seems he may have abducted a kid from the house too.'

Nightingale nodded.

'Sounds like a bad one.'

'You were in the job, you know there are no good murders, but we'll find the bastard.'

'Good luck with that.'

Parker took another swallow of beer.

'So, are you done in Tennessee?'

'Seems that way,' said Nightingale.

'Can't say I'm sorry, Nightingale. You're a bird of ill-omen.'

'You been waiting to use that line?'

'Maybe,' said Parker. 'Cop humour. Where to next?'

'Dunno. I'm keeping an open mind.'

'Waiting for the next assignment?'

'Something like that.' He drained his bottle and slid off his stool. 'Time to go,' he said. 'You know Bonnie, I'm really glad nothing happened to Emma. More than you could know.'

'Wait a minute, Nightingale,' said Parker. 'How did you know I was in Vegas?'

'Didn't you tell me?'

'I'm pretty sure I didn't. But even if I did, how did you manage to find me in a city this size?'

Nightingale smiled and winked at her. 'Would you believe it was magic?' He walked away before she could think of a witty retort and she settled for raising the bottle in a silent salute.

'Actually, I probably would,' she said.

Printed in Great Britain
by Amazon